LP   Thompson, James. 14
THOMPSON Helsinki white

8/12   30.99

PLZ 2/13
PLZ 10/15

HELSINKI WHITE

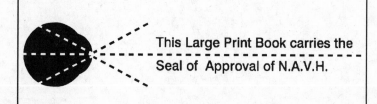

This Large Print Book carries the
Seal of Approval of N.A.V.H.

HELSINKI WHITE

JAMES THOMPSON

THORNDIKE PRESS
A part of Gale, Cengage Learning

GALE
CENGAGE Learning®

Detroit • New York • San Francisco • New Haven, Conn • Waterville, Maine • London

GALE
CENGAGE Learning·

Copyright © 2012 by James Thompson.
An Inspector Vaara Novel.
Thorndike Press, a part of Gale, Cengage Learning.

Thorndike Press® Large Print Thriller.
The text of this Large Print edition is unabridged.
Other aspects of the book may vary from the original edition.
Set in 16 pt. Plantin.

LIBRARY OF CONGRESS CATALOGING-IN-PUBLICATION DATA

Thompson, James.
    Helsinki white / by James Thompson.
      pages ; cm. — (Thorndike Press large print thriller)
      ISBN 978-1-4104-5017-3 (hardcover) — ISBN 1-4104-5017-1 (hardcover)
    1. Police—Finland—Fiction. 2. Homicide investigation—Fiction.
    3. Helsinki (Finland)—Fiction. 4. Large type books. I. Title.
    PS3620.H675H45 2012b
    813'.6—dc23
                                                     2012014518

Published in 2012 by arrangement with G.P. Putnam's Sons, a member of Penguin Group (USA), Inc.

Printed in the United States of America
1 2 3 4 5 6 7 16 15 14 13 12

For my son, Christopher.

And, as always, for Annukka.

With special thanks to neurologist
Dr. Jukka Turkka, specialist in
post-trauma neurological recovery and
cognition, without whom this book
would not have been possible.

PROLOGUE

It's May second, a sunny Sunday, a chilly spring evening. I walk around downtown, check out the main drags. The outdoor bars are packed, everyone drunk and happy. Yesterday was Vappu — May Day, the heaviest drinking holiday of the year — and most of these people have been drunk non-stop, morning to night, since they got off from work on Friday. Morning drinking delays hangovers. Eventually, the price has to be paid, but they can be sick at work tomorrow, on the company dime.

Raucous laughter emanates from everywhere. I stop under the clock in front of the main doors of Stockmann Department Store, the biggest and best in the city. I sometimes shop here because they almost always have what I want, and specialize in quality merchandise, even though the prices they charge for convenience and quality are highway robbery.

The clock is a traditional meeting place, central to everything downtown. It's become a habit. People just say, "Meet you under the clock," and nothing more need be discussed. Lovers especially are drawn to the spot. I'm waiting on Jyri Ivalo, the national chief of police. We're far from being lovers. I would describe our relationship as mutual enmity combined with respect. I trust him implicitly, however, because he fears me. The clock says five minutes of four. I'm right on time.

I'm a policeman and hold the rank of inspector. Because of the dime novel versions of some high-profile investigations as related by the media, my name, Kari Vaara, is synonymous with hero cop. Jyri is my boss. Ours is an unusual arrangement. There is no customary chain of command. I work directly under him with no intermediary authorities. The work I do is covert.

In a safe-deposit box, I have a video of him engaged in a fetishistic sex act involving a dildo up his ass a short time before a woman was murdered, at the murder scene, with the victim. Even though it was key evidence in the Filippov murder, I suppressed the video, which is both humiliating, and if you can manage to forget the horrific way his sexual partner was maimed and killed just after the filming, hilarious as well. The video would destroy his life.

A Romanian beggar prostrates herself on the sidewalk. Knees tucked under her. Head to ground, face hidden. Withered brown hands outstretched in an unspoken plea, a rosary interlaced between her fingers. A tough way to earn a living.

When Romania joined the European Union, and citizens from other member nations gained the right to come into the country and stay for ninety days without a visa, some resourceful Romanian entrepreneurs got the brilliant idea of hiring the most wretched souls they could find, bus them to other countries, and organize begging into a lucrative business venture.

The good citizens of Helsinki were outraged. The beggars were eyesores. The Gypsies set up a makeshift camp, and as winter drew near, city officials feared they would freeze to death and bought them plane tickets back to Romania. The good citizens of Helsinki were outraged because they had to pay the airfare. The weather is improving, the Roma are drifting back. The good citizens of Helsinki are outraged once again. Something must be done.

Like the rest of the Nordic countries, Finland is going through an ugly extreme right-wing phase with strong anti-foreigner sentiments. I used to think Finns hate in silence. No longer. After my brain surgery, I wasn't allowed to drive for a month and often relied on public transportation. One day, I took the tram. Two elderly women, one on a walker, asked the driver, a black immigrant, a question about where to get off to reach their destination. He answered in accented but understandable Finnish. The two grannies sat in front of me and spoke in loud voices, to make certain he could hear, and discussed how fucking niggers ought to learn to speak the goddamned language.

The grannies garnered guffaws. This sparked wit and inspired a teenager to tell a joke. "What do you get when you cross a nigger and a Gypsy? A thief who's too lazy to steal." Hee-haws all round. The driver had the right to kick them all out of the tram, but he didn't respond. He was used to it.

A gang of pretty young girls surrounds me, laughing, licking ice cream cones, swaying to and fro to the rhythm of a boom box blaring techno. The girls ignore the Rom beggar, shimmy around her, lick their ice cream. Despite the cool temperature, they're dressed pre-summer hopeful, exposing a bit of flesh. I decide the adage is true: sunlight makes breasts grow. They check me out with sidelong glances. It's because of the cane I carry. It's made of ash and cudgel thick. The handle is a massive, solid gold lion's head, weighs about eight ounces. One eye is a ruby, the other an emerald. The mouth is wide open, and I hold it with my left index finger curled behind its razor-sharp sparkling steel fangs.

The light changes. I take a last glance at the girls before moving. Looking down the street, I remember that I once shot and killed a man only a stone's throw from here. The sidewalks were crowded, like today, but it was summer, warm and sunny. There was a time when the thought would have depressed me. Now I couldn't care less.

I see Jyri coming toward me, on the other side of the street, at the junction of Mannerheimintie and Aleksanterinkatu. I walk to the corner and wait for the crosswalk light to change. I have the Rolling Stones song "Gimme Shelter" stuck in my head. The Stones and techno syncopate, reverberate and annoy.

Sulo, or Sweetness, as my lovely American wife has dubbed my new young protégé, would say, they bop, bebop, rebop some more. Sweetness admires and emulates me.

One of the forms Sweetness's veneration had taken for me is renunciation of his former obsession with death metal for a love of jazz.

Jyri's smooth way of moving reflects confidence. His suit is impeccable and coif perfect. I don't know him well, but believe him to be a complete narcissist. Egocentric, sybaritic, amoral, at one with himself, and untroubled by his all-inclusive lack of empathy for others. Whatever he is, it works for him. His career is marked by one achievement after another. We meet on the traffic island in the middle of the four-lane street, don't waste time with greetings or handshakes.

He gives me a large manila envelope containing dossiers of criminals and their planned activities. I pass the national chief of police two envelopes filled with cash, a hundred and fifty thousand euros in hundred-euro bills, the skim for Jyri and other politicos from yesterday's heist. It was a Vappu to be remembered. We trade the envelopes.

"Would you and that American wife of yours be interested in an evening out with me and some of my friends and colleagues?" he asks.

The concept fascinates me. I can't imagine

socializing with Jyri and his cronies.

"The evening is on me. An excellent jazz band is playing, and some people would like to meet you."

So he's run his mouth, and our black op is now an unknown shade of gray. "It's not much time to arrange a babysitter, and I'll have to ask Kate."

"Call now and ask her. Promise her that I'll arrange a dependable babysitter."

I move a couple of steps and turn away from him for privacy. Kate has a terrible hangover and I expect a firm no. I extend the invitation and mention that she'll meet people that might be valuable contacts in her work as general manager at Hotel Kämp.

She takes me aback, agrees without protest. "Sure," she said, "sounds great. Thank him for me and tell him I'll look forward to it." She pauses. "Can I bring Aino along?" Her assistant restaurant manager, new best friend, and object of my desire.

Kate was puking this morning. Enthusiasm? We ring off.

I turn back to Jyri. "We'd love to. OK if she brings a friend? She's good-looking," I add, because I know pussy-crazed Jyri would crawl through hell soaked in gasoline for the chance to even glimpse a beautiful woman.

He smiles, as if truly pleased. "Of course. Great. Invite your team as well, and tell them they're welcome to bring dates if they like. The babysitter will be at your place at eight thirty." He turns on his heel and his brisk walk, probably due to the hundred and fifty K in his hands, says he's on cloud nine.

The purpose of the dossiers is to provide info for me and my black-ops crew to target criminals, so we can rip off their money, drugs and guns.

I can remember, almost word for word, the conversation Jyri and I had during the Filippov investigation, when he talked me into heading up a black-ops unit while begging me to suppress evidence against him.

"I'll give you anything you want," he said, "just make this go away."

"That's a problem for you," I said. "I don't want anything."

He leaned toward me. "I've been thinking of putting together a black-ops unit. Anti-organized crime. The mandate is to go after criminals by whatever means necessary, to use their own methods against them. No holds barred."

"We already have such a group. Our secret police. They're called SUPO."

"There's a problem with SUPO," he said. "They don't work for me."

"So you want to be some kind of Finnish J. Edgar Hoover?"

"Yes."

I laughed in his face. "No."

"You think I don't know you, but I do," he said. "You suffer from a pathetic need to protect the innocent. You think you're some kind of a Good Samaritan in a white hat, but you're not. You're a rubber-hose cop, a thug and a killer, as you've demonstrated. You'll do anything to get what you view as justice. Let me give you an example of how badly we need this kind of unit. Only seven cops in Helsinki investigate human trafficking full-time. Here in Finland and the surrounding countries, thousands of gangsters orchestrate the buying and selling of young girls, and hundreds or thousands of those girls pass through this nation every year, most on their way to their destination countries. With our limited law enforcement resources, we can't possibly make even a dent in the human slavery industry. Picture all those victims and how many of their bright shiny faces you could save from abject misery, abuse and terror, from being raped time and time again."

He sensed my interest.

"Milo" — referring to my partner — "knows black-bag work," he said. "He's a genius with great computer skills, and he's also a killer. He could be your first team-member acquisition. Then you can staff it with whoever you want."

Milo learned black-bag work because he's a voyeur. He B&Es homes just to go through people's things. He's a violent nutcase with an IQ of a hundred seventy-two.

"I'm not killing anybody," I said.

"I'll leave that to your discretion."

"Milo is a loose cannon and a liability."

"Milo is a nervous puppy. He needs a firm hand to guide him. Yours."

"It would take a hell of a lot of money," I said. "Computers. Vehicles. Surveillance gear."

"In two weeks, Swedish and Finnish Gypsies are going to make a drug deal for Ecstasy. A hundred and sixty thousand euros will trade hands. You can intercept it and use the money for the beginning of a slush fund. I'll get you more money for equipment later."

"No."

Frustration gripped him, resonated in his voice. "I told you I know you, and I do. You hate your job. You're frustrated because you can't make a difference. You're a failure. To your dead sister." He brings up the high death toll from a previous investigation: "To Sufia Elmi and her family. To your former sergeant Valtteri and his family. To your dead ex-wife — and in your personal life — to your dead miscarried twins and, as such, to your wife. To that pathetic school shooter Milo capped. You're a failure to yourself. You've failed everyone you've touched. You'll take this job to make up for it. I'm offering you everything you ever wanted."

"Why me?" I asked.

"Because of your aforementioned annoying incorruptibility. You don't want anything. You're a maniac, but you're a rock. I can trust you to run this unit without going rogue on me."

"I'll think about it."

"No one ever finds out anything about my involvement in this case," he said. "I'll organize everything, get you the manpower. Fix this for me," he said, "and run my black-ops unit."

I bought into Jyri's specious diatribe like the naïve fool that I am. I've helped no one, but hurt several people, and there are more to come. I've succeeded only in alienating my wife, the person I remember being dearest to me.

There's a great myth believed by nearly

17

everyone that Finland is corruption-free. Police and politicians are scripture pure, dedicated to the good of the nation beyond all things. Foreigners even write about it in travel guides for tourists. The best thing going for our black-ops unit is that no one would believe such a thing could exist, or that corruption could be so widespread at such high levels of government.

I run a heist gang. I'm a police inspector, shakedown artist, strong-arm specialist and enforcer. Three months ago, I was an honest cop. I'm not sure I care how or why, but I reflect on how I could have undergone such a drastic change in such a short time. Jyri wanted me to recruit some other tough cops, but I refused. More than four people is too many in on a secret. The group is just me, Milo, and Sweetness. Milo is a sick puppy, but he's grown on me over time because of his enthusiasm. Sweetness is a baby-faced behemoth, whom I hired out of sympathy, because of his size and capacity to commit violent acts without enjoying them, and to piss Jyri off. Which it does. Jyri refers to him as "the oaf." Sweetness often seems a simpleton, but he's far from it.

To quote Sweetness: "Life just is. Ain't no reason for nothing."

1

A little over three months before my meeting with Jyri, Kate gave birth to our first child, a girl, on January twenty-fourth.

It was an easy birth, as childbirths go, no more difficult than squirting a watermelon seed out from between her fingers, only sixteen hours from her first contraction to me cradling our child in my arms. When I first held her, I felt a wealth of emotions I didn't know existed, and I wouldn't have believed it possible, but I loved Kate tenfold more for the gift she had given me.

She was an easy baby. Didn't cry much. Often slept through the night. She wasn't officially named until her christening, but we chose to call her Anu. A simple and pretty name, pronounceable by Finns and foreigners alike, important in a bi-cultural marriage.

Our bi-cultural marriage changed me. When I met Kate, like many Finnish men, I was unable to utter the words "I love you." I've heard women complain more than a few times that their husbands don't tell them they love them. The typical answer: "I told you I loved you when I married you. If anything changes, I'll let you know." But she told me often, with sincerity and without shame. I learned to return the sentiment. At first, it was awkward for me. Before long though, I learned to say it first, it felt natural, even good, and I couldn't understand why it had ever been difficult.

I had been suffering severe migraines for the better part of a year. I thought they were the result of stress related to Kate's pregnancy — she had miscarried twins the previous December, and I was scared that it would happen again — but Kate insisted I had tests run. My brother, Jari, is a neurologist. I went to him and he sent me for an MRI. The day we brought Anu home from the hospital, it fell upon him to tell me that I had a brain tumor.

Kate and I had always had a great relationship, were best friends as well as husband and wife, but there was a sticking point that stood between us. My failure to tell her about my past or current events in my life, especially if they're unpleasant. She isn't as bad as, say, characters on American television shows who throw hissy fits upon finding out that their spouse had a one-night stand twenty years ago and five years before the couple even met, and believe the lives of their spouses, even their deepest and most private thoughts and emotions, must be open books. But a couple times, Kate has found out things about me that shocked her, and she'd like me to open up, at least a little, so she can know and understand me better. It's hard for me, just not my nature. Kate said she viewed my failure to tell her about events relevant to our life together as a form of lying. And it disturbed her that I kept much of my past under lock and key.

I saw her point, and promised to try to learn to be more open. But she was a new mother, radiant, full of joy. I debated on how long to let her be happy before telling her I might die. I decided on two days. I probably would have put it off longer, but the biopsy to determine the nature of the tumor was scheduled in two days, on the twenty-eighth. It would have been hard to fabricate an explanation of why part of my hair was shaved off and I had a stitched-up surgical incision, and I figured she needed at least a day to get used to the idea.

I sat with Kate on the couch, asked her to prepare herself, and took her hand. "The

21

results from the MRI came back," I said, "and I have a brain tumor."

Her face fell and tears glistened in the corners of her eyes. She tried to speak and faltered. When she managed it, her voice cracked. "How bad?"

I explained the situation as best I understood it, as Jari had explained it to me, and told her that I would have a biopsy the day after tomorrow and it would give us the answer to that question.

I said the best case scenario was that I had a meningioma, a tumor that originates in the meninges, the thin membranes that cover the brain and spinal cord. If so, it could be removed by a craniotomy and, with luck, I might suffer no permanent consequences at all and be back home in three days, maybe even be back to work in a couple weeks. I would require no chemo or radiation therapy, no nothing. It could, however, possibly cause problems with my speech or balance, weakness, even paralysis. Physical therapy could hopefully remedy these problems, if needed, and with luck I could be back to normal, or close to it, in only a few months.

The worst-case scenario was that I had a Grade IV, rapidly growing and malignant tumor. If so, not much could be done, and

I would have only a short time to live. Maybe only weeks. There were other possibilities with varying degrees or severity and requiring different treatments, and Jari hadn't explained them all to me, because the list was long. But those were the two extremes.

Kate took the news like a trouper, managed to stay calm. She started to cry a little but didn't break down. "How are you holding up?" she asked.

I had an awful migraine. After suffering from a near constant severe headache for a year, I was worn down, tired. Prolonged pain had sapped my strength and had left me in a permanent state of lethargy. Still, I'd continued working. "OK," I said. "I'm more worried about you having to deal with this than anything."

"Aren't you scared?" she asked.

Another consequence of prolonged severe pain is that the desire to end it supersedes everything else. "Not really," I said. "I just want this to be over."

She took me in her arms and held me for a while. There was nothing else to say.

Some time passed. "There's something else I need to talk to you about," I said. I didn't like bringing this up then, because I didn't think she would like it, and I felt like

I was using the possibility of my death as a way of manipulating her into getting my way. But I wasn't. I wanted to honor her wishes and not hold this back from her, and I had to give Jyri an answer about the black-ops unit now. He insisted on it. He said yes, I could possibly die, but he had faith that removing the tumor would be no bigger a deal than pulling a tick out of a hound's ear.

When our desires conflict, if possible, I try to put Kate's happiness ahead of my own. I promised myself I wouldn't let work interfere with our relationship again. I'm a romantic at heart. I told Kate that the national chief of police, Jyri Ivalo, had given me a job offer, and asked me to run a clandestine unit. It would use illegal methods to fight crime. I compared it to J. Edgar Hoover's COINTELPRO program, but more benign. Most of the illegal activity would be technological surveillance that violated privacy laws, and using that information to take cash, drugs, firearms, etc., from criminals, relieving them of the tools they need to ply their trades and using their money to fund our operation.

I told her what Jyri said about truly helping people, saving young women from being forced into slavery and prostitution. I told her I thought I could make a difference, save some of these girls from having their lives turned into hell on earth.

Kate shifted closer, pressed her body against mine. "Are you asking my permission?"

"Yes," I said, "I am, because I'll break laws and it's risky. And because if we're going to live in this country, I think I have to. During the Filippov investigation, I gathered a lot of dirt on people in positions of power. I know too much. If I refuse, they'll find a way to discredit and destroy me, to protect themselves. In a way, they're offering to let me join their boys' club. If you don't want me to take the job, we should leave Finland and move to America. I want you to make the decision."

"Do you want this?" she asked.

"Yes," I said, "I do. I feel that for the first time in my life, I have a chance to do something that makes a true difference. Most likely, I'll never have another opportunity like this again. But I don't have to make a difference. If you want me to turn it down, I will, without hard feelings or regrets."

She sat for what seemed like a long time, quiet. I watched her, admiring. Kate is a lovely woman. A classic beauty. Pregnancy had almost no effect on her figure, other than that her breasts were larger. She remained slim. Her long cinnamon hair hung loose. Her dove-gray eyes were far away, lost in thought.

"Take the job," she said, "but I want you to go on sick leave starting today."

"OK," I said, "but I want to play around a little bit starting up my new project, getting it functional, just to give myself something to do."

She nodded agreement, and at that moment, without realizing it, I became a dirty cop.

2

On Thursday morning, I had the biopsy. Jari used his superpowers as a highly respected neurologist and had the test results ramrodded through. I got an appointment with the surgeon who would remove my tumor the very next day. He was going to tell me whether I would live or die.

I insisted that Kate come with me and listen while the surgeon gave me the prognosis. I wanted her to have no doubts that, if the news was bad, I hadn't soft-pedaled it to spare her. It was January twenty-eighth, a bitter minus eighteen outside. The city sheathed in ice, snow banked up high by plows along every roadway.

I found, to my surprise, that I was calm. The possibility of death didn't frighten me as I thought it might. However, Kate's nerves were a shambles. She shook, could barely speak. Waiting outside the surgeon's office, she gripped the arms of the chair so

27

hard that her knuckles turned bloodless white.

The surgeon was businesslike. The news was good. I had a meningioma, about three by four centimeters, in my frontal lobe. He embellished on what Jari had told me about meningiomas.

It might have been growing there for as long as fifteen years. It had probably been affecting my memory, concentration, cognition, and possibly my behavior all this time, without me noticing be cause it happened so slowly, and of course, I had nothing to compare it to. As brain tumors go, he said, I was lucky. I had an outstanding chance of survival, and a very good chance of going on to lead a normal life afterward. As Jari said, there would be no follow-up treatments. He would cut it out, and that would be it. I'd go back to my life as if it never happened. He asked about the frequency and duration of the headaches. I told him constant and described the severity. "You have an excellent headache," he said, and smiled. His idea of a joke.

Then he moved on to unpleasantries.

After surgery, I might feel worse than I did then, but only for a short time. The intrusion would cause my brain to swell. I might possibly suffer dizziness, lack of coordination and motor difficulties, confusion, seizures, difficulty speaking, personality changes that could be quite severe, behavior that might baffle and even shock others. I might require therapy, but these effects should lessen over a time period he couldn't predict. Could be days, could be months. If an effect lasted more than a year, though, I could assume it was permanent.

"On the other hand," he said, "in two weeks it might be like this never happened at all. Any questions?"

Neither Kate nor I could think of any. The fear in Kate's eyes, though, told me she had a question, but he couldn't answer it. Would I really live through the operation, and if I did, what would I be like afterward?

"OK, then," he said, and opened his calendar. "How does Tuesday, February the ninth, work for you?"

"Just dandy," I said.

Twelve days and counting until they opened up my skull. I wasn't afraid until then. I had only thought about the possibility of dying. The surgeon's suggestion that I might be permanently damaged, either physically or mentally or both, turned into an invalid, scared the shit out of me. I tried not to think about it, stayed zonked on tranquilizers and painkillers. I spent a lot of time lying on the couch, listened to music, watched movies, read, kept Anu tucked under my arm. My thumb was her favorite toy.

Kate tried to be brave. She would have waited on me hand and foot if I let her. She made my favorite foods, came home one day with *muikun mäti* — roe from whitefish the size of my finger, that carries a price tag commensurate with the arduous work of cleaning the eggs out of those tiny fish, and to my mind better than beluga caviar — and a bottle of good Russian vodka to go with it, reindeer inner fillet for the main course, and we had a homemade cake for dessert.

There can be no normality in a home if a family member is gravely ill, but we did the best we could, and we managed moments of happiness, shared laughter, comfortable silences. As difficult as it is to have a newborn, Anu eased our burden. She kept us busy, kept our spirits up. I thought she looked like Kate. Kate thought she looked like me. I hoped, despite our dysfunctional relationship, that my parents would come to see their grandchild. Mom called to congratulate us. Dad didn't even come to the phone.

Kate was unable to make love because of recent childbirth, but she used an American expression I was unfamiliar with: "There's more than one way to skin a cat." I didn't ask what it meant, and remain uncertain of the relationship between the skinning of cats and oral sex, but I drifted off to sleep every night sated. Often, during the night, I heard Kate weeping. And at other times as well. When she was cooking, vacuuming, at moments she thought I couldn't hear her.

A few days before my surgery, Kate came home with a gift for me. A kitten. She'd gotten him at the animal shelter. I don't know what inspired Kate to give him to me. I had a cat once before, named Katt — Swedish for "cat" — and kept him for several years until I came home one day and found him dead. He tried to eat a rubber band and choked to death. I was truly fond of Katt, and his death hurt me. I named this kitten Katt as well, in memoriam.

He fell in love with me at first pet, wouldn't leave me alone for a second. He followed me to the bathroom and scratched at the door until I came out. When I sat or lay on the bed or couch, he climbed up, sat on my shoulder, kneaded his claws in my skin, and purred, used my neck and the side of my head for a scratching post. I let him. I looked like I'd been attacked and mauled by a pack of small but vicious animals. Anu loved him, too. The feel of his fur, tugging on its tail and ears. Katt took it all in good stride.

In that time before my surgery, Kate showered me in love, affection and kindness. Fear lurked behind it all. She radiated it. I wished I knew a way to calm her, to offer her some kind of reassurance and quell her dread, but I didn't.

3

On the evening of Friday, February fifth, Milo, Sweetness and I committed our first heist. As the national chief of police, Jyri is able to collate a great deal of information from police around the nation, and he also has a cordial relationship with Osmo Ahtiainen, the minister of the interior. Among his other duties, Ahtiainen heads SUPO. Ahtiainen also has amicable and cooperative relationships with his counterparts in both Estonia and Sweden. Through his own position and relationship with Ahtiainen, Jyri has access to a mountain of information.

Jyri had fed me dossiers on the Finnish and Swedish Gypsies and information on the drug deal. They were to meet at the dog park set on top of the hill in the neighborhood of Torkkelinmäki at seven p.m. It's a good meeting place. A wide-open area, plenty of people around letting their dogs run and play together.

I told Kate where I was going. She grimaced, told me not to get hurt, but made no attempt to dissuade me. Milo, Sweetness and I showed up at six and sat on park benches in a triangle around the park. My idea was to wait until the Gypsies arrived and for all of us to slowly amble toward them. We would have them surrounded, draw weapons and surprise them, take their weapons if they were armed, then just grab up their dope and money and get the hell out.

As I sat waiting, I decided it was an ill-thought-out and dangerous plan. I'm a lousy shot. Sweetness had never fired a gun. All four of the targets were hardened criminals, likely armed, and might prefer to fight. I pictured a gun battle at close quarters, stray rounds cutting down dogs and their owners. It ending with all of us lying dead on the ground, dogs sniffing our corpses. We had planned all along for Milo to attach global positioning system tracking devices to their vehicles before the heist, to make ripping them off again in the future easier. I called off the armed robbery and told Milo to just GPS their vehicles. We would B&E them later.

And so we did. We watched the men trade backpacks, shake hands, and drive away in

34

two separate cars. They drove about six blocks, parked, locked their cash and contraband in the trunks of their vehicles, and went together into a shithole bar to celebrate the event. We followed, Milo picked their car locks, and within five minutes, we had their money, dope and three handguns.

The following evening, we did the same again. This time, we B&Eed a luxurious home in the Helsinki suburb of Vantaa. The dealer was a dentist running a drug business on the side. Sweetness surveilled his house beginning in early evening. The dentist went out for a Saturday night on the town. We didn't know when he would get back, so we waited. He returned home, shit drunk, in a taxi at about four thirty a.m.

When he turned out the lights, we gave him a half hour to pass out and, using flashlights dimmed with red lenses, went through the house like we owned it. We found several grocery bags behind a shoe rack in a hall closet. They were filled with loose, used bills, mostly in small denominations. Milo booted up the dentist's computer and installed viral software so that he could monitor every keystroke, track his e-mails. Milo could use the computer as if he owned it from the comfort of his own home. He also installed software into the dentist's cell phone so he could eavesdrop on his calls and read his text messages. We now owned the dentist. These technological intrusions became our modus operandi.

When I got home, I changed Anu and fed her with breast milk we kept in the fridge. This became my nightly post-heist habit. I also usually manned the breast pump. It made me feel more like part of the process.

The next day, I asked Milo and Sweetness to help me sort, band and count the dentist's money. In early afternoon, they came over. Kate and Anu were napping in the bedroom. Sweetness wanted to play DJ, put on a Thelonius Monk album. We dumped out bills from seven grocery bags, sat on the floor and start sorting them. Milo and I went out to the balcony once in a while for smoke breaks. Sweetness uses *nuuska.*

The first time Kate saw Sweetness stick *nuuska* in his lip, she was both curious and disgusted. He took out a can of snuff, packed a syringe tube with it, and pressed it into his upper lip. I explained to her that it's like American snuff, but drier, and users don't have to spit juice. She asked why she couldn't see a lump under his lip where he put it in. I told her it had salt or some irritant in it, which abraded the tissue, so that nicotine would hit the user's system faster.

Over time, it cuts a hole deep through the gum. *Nuuska* users like it better after the hole cuts and rots through, because the nesting place made it unnoticeable and less messy. She was appalled. Sale of *nuuska* is illegal in Finland, so people buy quantities of it from the shop on the ferry to and from Sweden for themselves and their friends, and tobacconists keep it under the counter for preferred customers. Police ignore the infraction. Some of them enjoy their *nuuska* as well. I got hooked on nicotine with it when I was a young athlete. It's popular among hockey players.

Sweetness took breaks and went outside, he claimed, for fresh air. He was lying, and I wondered what he was hiding.

After a couple hours, I noticed that a car, an Acura, had been parked across the street for a couple hours, wedged in a slot cut by a plow in the snowbank. I thought I caught a glimpse of binoculars. I asked Milo and Sweetness to go out and investigate.

"Yes, *pomo* — boss," Sweetness said, put on his coat and made for the door. Milo trailed behind. I went out on the balcony to watch. I must have asked Sweetness not to call me *pomo* at least a dozen times, told him that if he has to call me anything, to call me Kari. Milo approached the driver's-side door, Sweetness the passenger's side. Milo held his police card up to the glass. The driver's-side window rolled down. The man reached toward an inner coat pocket. Milo drew his pistol so fast that I barely saw it. Milo hammered the man in the face and head with the butt of his Glock multiple times. I heard him scream.

The other watcher went for his pistol. Sweetness smashed the passenger's-side window with his elbow — protected by his overcoat — and reached through the window. He grabbed the man's shoulder with a massive hand and the man howled in pain. Sweetness held the man in check. Milo took their wallets, checked their identities. He tossed the wallets back into the car. The men drove away.

Milo and Sweetness came back inside. Milo laughed. "I just beat the fuck out of a SUPO agent," he said.

"I asked you to investigate, not rearrange his face," I said.

"He reached inside his coat. He could have been reaching for a weapon."

I didn't criticize further. Milo was right to stop him, even if he was overzealous.

So the secret police were watching us. I didn't know if it was a big deal or not. I had a meeting with Jyri the next day. I would ask him about it then. We finished counting the money. Two hundred and fifty-two thousand euros. We'd stolen almost half a million that weekend. A good start. I figured what the fuck, and tossed the boys packets of ten thousand each. "This is a onetime event, I'm not even taking one for myself, but these are bonuses for a job well done," I said.

4

It was a pleasant Sunday afternoon. I met Jyri for coffee at Café Strindberg, which overlooks Esplanade Park. Most of the customers at Strindberg are rich forty-something face-lift fraus with little manicured rat dogs. Jyri asked about the weekend.

I told him the total, minus a ten percent skim, not because I intended to steal it, but because he might take every cent, and we couldn't do without funding. In this scenario, he might just keep it all and tell us to fuck ourselves. He's not above that.

"All told," I said, "we took in about three hundred and fifty thousand. It's in the trunk of my car. I'll give it to you when we leave."

He smiled so wide I thought his face might rip. "Hang on to it for now. But three hundred and fifty thousand. Jesus fucking Christ. That's incredible!"

He's a snatch hound with a Casanova

complex. His eyes darted out the window at every woman that walked by. "Now that we know it works," he said, "let's discuss the details."

I had no doubt that the "details" had nothing to do with crime fighting.

He took a thin tri-folded sheaf of papers from the inner pocket of his immaculate suit jacket and pushed them across the table to me. "These will explain," he said. "The minister of the interior gave them to me himself. He just wanted to make sure I'm doing what I told him I would do."

EYES ONLY: INTERIOR MINISTER OSMO AHTIAINEN.

Document summarizing Operation Po-ronnussija — Reindeer Fucker (referring to me and my Arctic roots) — by agent Captain Jan Pitkänen, at the behest of the Interior Minister.

As the minister expected, extra-legal activity is being conducted by at least four men, one the national chief of police, two police officers under the direct authority of the national chief of police, and a man who is not a police officer. Only the most pertinent information concerning them and their recent activities for our purposes is discussed here.

JYRI IVALO:
DOB 16.10.46
SSN# 161064-4570
Height: 6'0"
Weight: approx. 165 lbs.

Ivalo has been national chief of police for eight years. There is no reason to consider Ivalo anything other than confident and astute. The investigation leading to this report suggests that Ivalo has developed a small but competent team to work, sometimes outside the law, to achieve objectives in those areas in which the national police force has had less then desirable results. Ivalo has vulnerabilities. A minor drinking problem. A desire to be in the social company of people of note, and especially a taste for beautiful young women are his major weaknesses.

KARI VAARA:
DOB 02.06.1968
SSN# 020664-2656
Height: 5'10"

Weight: approx. 190 lbs.

Vaara has the distinction of being the only current policeman to have been shot twice in the performance of duty. He is also one of only two policemen to have killed a suspect in the line of duty. The other is his partner from Helsinki Homicide, Milo Nieminen. They should be considered dangerous. Vaara has twenty-two years in law enforcement, including service in the military police. He has a reputation for acting alone and without respect for the authority of his superiors. Vaara is violent. He has shot and killed one perp and is rumored to have used extreme force against others. Whether that force was warranted is unknown. It is noteworthy, though, that he is capable of it. He inspires admiration from his underlings.

Vaara has few weaknesses. He has no significant vices, and is by and large a loner. He has a wife and infant daughter. The wife is American and living in this country on temporary residence and work permits. In September, his wife will have lived in

Finland for three years and may apply for permanent residency. If it is required to bring pressures to bear against Vaara, I suggest that it be done quickly, while the threat of deporting his wife may still be hung over Vaara's head. Vaara's relationship with Arvid Lahtinen might possibly lead to a charge of conspiracy to commit murder against him. See below. Vaara suffers from intense migraines caused by a brain tumor. He is scheduled for brain surgery on 9 February. It is unlikely, given the nature of his tumor, but he could possibly die or be permanently disabled, thus eliminating the need for further discussion concerning his illegal operation, as his colleagues, Milo Nieminen and Sulo Polvinen, lack the wherewithal to function without him.

MILO NIEMINEN:
DOB 23.04.1987
SSN# 230487-623L
Height: 5'7"
Weight: approx. 135 lbs.

After secondary school, Nieminen

served in the army, specializing in demolitions. He continued his training in Reserve Officer School. He has a measured IQ of 172. His computer skills are extraordinary. He has let it be known that he is an accomplished computer hacker. This suggests that his ego is such that he will brag, even though revealing such personal information could lead to a great deal of trouble for him. Like Vaara, he is for the most part a loner. He has no close relationships. His father is dead. His mother is alive, but telephone records reveal that he calls only on major holidays.

Nieminen's major flaw seems to be recklessness, and I tend to think that around-the-clock surveillance, rather than spot tailing, would lead to the discovery of acts that could be used against him. It seems likely that Nieminen could be convicted of computer intrusion and possibly computer theft hacking exploits.

SULO POLVINEN:
DOB 12.09.1987
SSN# 120987-357Y
Height 6'3"

Weight: approx. 265 lbs.

Polvinen's file has clearly been re-dacted. Computer files concerning his high school records have been changed, some grades improved and behavioral infractions eliminated. He also has a driver's license, which I believe is a fabrication, because I think it likely that his family lacked the money required for him to attend driving school. I suspect Milo Nie-minen did all this, but because of egotism was sloppy and thought it unnecessary to cover his tracks. According to his redacted file, Polvinen took a six-week course and became a certified security guard. This has been investigated and proven untrue. Cell phone surveillance indicates he intends to apply for a job with the National Bureau of Investigation. As he has no qualifications, it must be assumed that he expects to receive a job through nepotism. Polvinen's brother died in an altercation with two security guards at a nightclub. These bouncers were later stabbed, beaten to the point of disfigurement and hospitalized. Polvinen's father stabbed both bouncers to death in the hospital, also confessed to the attack at the nightclub, and is serving a prison sentence because of these crimes. However, it has been stated by some that Polvinen, who is easily recognizable because of his size, committed the initial assault on the bouncers, and as such, could be tried for attempted murder. Polvinen's mother is half Russian, half Estonian, and he earned high marks in English, Swedish and German in school. Those grades — I checked — are genuine.

ARVID LAHTINEN:
DOB 03.03.1920
SSN# 030320-259V
Height: 5'9"
Weight: approx. 150 lbs.

Lahtinen's record as a war hero is so long and familiar that I won't list it here. He is included here only because of his relationship with Vaara. Lahtinen recently lost his wife. Germany would like to extradite him for accessory to murder because of his wartime activities. Lahtinen is to be tried here in Finland because of his recent murder of a Russian businessman. Vaara was present at the murder, hence the possibility of prosecuting him as an accessory. Lahtinen claimed that said businessman was involved in the Arctic Sea affair and the sale of nuclear weapons. As such, Lahtinen's case falls under the National Security Act, and the case will likely drag on for some years. Vaara and Lahtinen have apparently developed a friendship. They speak on the phone frequently, and although he hasn't done so in monitored phone conversations, if Lahtinen does possess potentially damaging State secrets, he may well have shared them with Vaara. This might be considered another sound reason to deport Vaara's wife and get rid of him along with her.

Vaara, Nieminen and Polvinen committed breakings and enterings on both Friday and Saturday nights. They robbed drug dealers and made off with bags likely containing drug money and/or narcotics.

I regret to inform the minister that I

have blown my cover in this case. I underestimated Vaara because of his migraines, thinking they must impair his cognition and attention span. He sent out Nieminen and Polvinen to find out why we were surveilling his apartment. Nieminen approached, and I rolled down the driver's-side window. I reached for my ID and he drew his pistol so fast that I had no time to respond. He struck me in the face with it several times. It was my own fault, because I did not announce my intention to produce identification and so he was within his rights, as I could have been reaching for a weapon. My nose and cheekbone were broken, and my right eye socket fractured. My partner tried to draw his weapon in defense. Polvinen shattered his window, reached through into the car and squeezed my partner's shoulder so hard that his collarbone was crushed and his shoulder squeezed out of its socket and dislocated. I had no idea such a thing was possible. Nieminen took my police card. I said, "I'm a goddamned cop. What the fuck did you do that for?" He replied, "You're an errand boy sent by shopkeepers. I'm a pistoleer. Next time we meet, I suggest you remember that." I think it was a line from a movie, but I got the impression that Nieminen isn't all there.

As I said, my cover is blown, how should we proceed?

Best Regards,
Captain Jan Pitkänen

Reply from the interior minister to Pitkänen:

Operation Poronnussija terminated. Hope your face heals up.

Best Regards,
Interior Minister Osmo Ahtiainen

And lastly, I found two memos on a Post-it stuck to the last page. One addressed to Jyri. "Good idea. I want whatever you're getting."

The next Post-it was in Jyri's handwriting and meant for me. "Poronnussija: 15% each for me, you, and for the interior minister, 5% each for the maniac brainiac and the giant oaf. The rest for operational funding. Trust me, it's a good deal. Take it."

Giving Milo and Sweetness a bonus was a one-off. I never intended to become a crooked cop and do this for profit. "Thanks, but no, thanks," I said. "My paycheck will

50

suffice."

Jyri laughed at me. "Goddamn, you're naïve. You have to take the money. If you're not complicit, we can't trust you. Just consider it part of your paycheck. Trust me, you'll get used to it."

I didn't know how to respond for a moment. I stumbled on my words. "What happened to your speech about helping people?"

He shrugged. "Then help people." He snickered. "You know what they say the three biggest lies are?"

Disillusioned, I just shook my head no.

"I love you, the check is in the mail, and I won't come in your mouth."

"Wow, great joke."

"Actually, the point is that the joke is wrong. The biggest lie is that altruism exists."

I just stared at him.

"I'm moving you and Milo from Helsinki Homicide to the National Bureau of Investigation," he said. "You'll work directly under me and be out from under public scrutiny. And I'll make sure the oaf gets a job, too. Invent some specialization for him. There isn't a checkbox for giant attempted murderer on the job application. Why the fuck do you want him anyway?"

51

"Mostly to piss you off."

"I don't give a shit," he said, and got up. "Since you just got a big raise, you can pick up the check."

I got an idea. "Ask the interior minister if, in return for this fifteen percent, he'll do me the occasional favor, beginning with this one. Ask him if he can supply me with the dossiers of every known criminal taking the morning Tallink ferry to Helsinki on" — I pick a date at random — "Friday, February nineteenth."

"I'll ask," he said.

He started to walk away and then turned back to me. "And I want ledgers kept." He walked out, whistling the Irving Berlin song "Blue Skies."

5

I walked in the front door, knelt down in the foyer and took off my boots. Put away the money Jyri refused to take. Kate sat at our dining room table, nursing Anu. One of the advantages of my new position, so far, was that it was much like shift work for people with factory jobs. I was often home during the day and could spend time with my family, and when I worked at night, they were usually asleep, except for nighttime feedings. They were hard on Kate. I saw the fatigue in her face. When I was home, I helped out as best as I was able. We did normal things. Watched TV. Made meals. Took Anu for walks in her stroller. I hoped, once child rearing got easier for Kate, our life would be this way forever.

I walked over and sat beside them. "How are my girls?" I asked. Anu farted, smiled and cooed, as if to answer, "Just fine, Daddy." I leaned toward Kate to kiss her.

Said kiss wasn't returned.

"Little girl fine," Kate said. "Big girl not fine."

I saw that Kate was in a rage, preventing herself from screaming only to keep from upsetting Anu. Judging by the smell, Anu's coo signaled more than a fart. I took her to the other room to change her. She pissed in my face. I made myself not laugh aloud because of Kate's mood. After I cleaned myself up, I came back to the living room with Anu. Kate's controlled rage hadn't abated.

"My boss called me from corporate. She more or less called me an incompetent asshole and insinuated that whether I still have a job is an open question."

I started to move closer to comfort her, thought better of it. "Why?"

"Because I never resolved the matter of my maternity leave. I asked Aino" — Kate's assistant hotel manager — "if she could look after the hotel until we had settled things between us."

Kate didn't want to take the traditional nine-month maternity leave, wanted to do things the American way. Have the baby, take a few weeks, put the baby in childcare, and go back to work. Or alternately, for me to exercise my paternity leave, since I was less than enamored with my job anyway, but paternity leave is only a few weeks long, so I didn't really understand what her idea was in that regard.

But then there were family problems when her brother and sister were here, supposedly to help Kate when the baby arrived, in truth to escape their own troubles. Anu arrived early, we found out I had a brain tumor and might very well be incapable of taking care of an infant. Aino seemed to be doing fine at the hotel, and dealing with the issue in an official way went to the wayside. Under the circumstances, it was perfectly understandable.

"She ripped me a new asshole," Kate said. "She informed me that as head of the hotel, I was under an obligation to understand and obey the rules governing the treatment of my workers."

It didn't help that I pressured Kate to take the normal nine-month maternity leave. I had a feeling it just wouldn't work out otherwise. Anu switched nipples. Kate continued, "She said no one from corporate was there to look over my shoulder, and foreigner or no, I had better goddamned well learn the Finnish union rules and abide by them. Under no circumstances could Aino perform my job for an indefinite amount of time without being given a contract authorizing her to do that job and an adjustment in pay to reflect it. She said she wrote a nine-month contract and Aino signed it. My boss said, and I quote, 'We're fucking lucky she's good-natured. She could have complained to the union. I gave her pay retroactive to the last day you deemed to come to work.' The bitch closed with 'When you come back — *if* you come back — know what in the goddamned hell you're doing.' And then she hung up on me."

"Damn," I said. "Happy fucking Sunday."

"Yeah. Happy fucking Sunday. Look at us. We're sitting at a dinner table that seats ten that we bought so we could have dinner parties, except we don't have any friends to have a dinner party. I don't know if I have a job. I'm going to sit here playing milk cow for the better part of a year, and my husband may die on the table in surgery two days from now."

She realized the ugliness of what she just said and the cruelty of pushing that truth in my face. I thought she was going to cry, but she didn't. Instead, we stared at each other for a long time. Her expression was blank. For the first time, it struck me that part of her was furious at me for being sick. It made me sad. I imagined myself in her position, overwhelmed by anxiety, trepidation, anger, fear of the unknown and of being left alone.

I felt guilt for being sick, for doing this to her, especially because I looked forward to brain surgery, because whether I lived or died, the pain would be over. I'd learned to hide it well, even from Kate, but my migraine throbbed hard and constant. I scarfed drugs, slept as much as I could, sought oblivion to escape the agony. It had been going on now for about almost a year continuous. The toll it had taken was so great that if it weren't for my responsibilities and the possibility that surgery might end the suffering, I would have ended it myself. Just two more days. Two more days.

Anu had fallen asleep. We took her to her bedroom and put her in her crib. The closet door was half open. Kate noticed an unzipped backpack, cash spilling out of it. Grocery bags full of cash sat beside it. Her voice was calm. "What's all this?"

"Proceeds from the weekend," I answered.

She opened the door wide, plunged both hands into the backpack and tossed money into the air like confetti. She looked inside it again, reached in and pulled out a Bulldog revolver we had stolen. She held it up in front of her face and stared at it.

"Careful," I said, "it's loaded."

She put it back into the backpack and this time pulled out a clear plastic bag of Ecstasy. "So this is the new you."

"I was honest with you about everything."

"You think stuffing your daughter's closet with dope money and guns is OK?"

"I tried to give the money to Jyri. He wouldn't take it. It's to bankroll our project, and I just haven't gotten rid of the other stuff yet." This was not quite, but mostly true. I was keeping some of it. "And I'm pretty sure Anu doesn't know what any of it is, and she can't even roll over yet, so I can't picture her overdosing or shooting herself."

She whisper yelled. "That's not the point and you know it. Get this shit out of my house."

I didn't know what the point was, but if she wanted it, in the mood she was in, that was enough. I called Milo, asked him if he would come over, get the swag and keep it in his place.

"You've seen how small my place is," he said. "Where am I supposed to put it?"

"Please," I said. "And if you're not busy, could you come over now?"

He got it then. Domestic bliss had been disturbed. He lives only a ten-minute walk away. "OK," he said, "I'll just be a few minutes."

58

I went out to the balcony, smoked two cigarettes and waited on him. Kate needed some time to cool down, and I had more to tell her.

Milo came over with two gym bags stuffed inside a third. I helped him pack it all up except for a hundred thousand, which I kept for emergencies. It was a heavy load, and I asked him if he wanted me to help him carry it home. He understood that I needed to talk to Kate, and staggered out the door, weighted down with guns, dope and nearly half a million euros.

Kate had gone to our bedroom to be alone. She wasn't angry anymore. She just looked wretchedly sad. I said I had some things to tell her about my meeting with Jyri and asked if we could talk. I suppose because of the way she had spoken to me, because she'd tried so hard to be kind to me and finally lost control of her emotions, she looked contrite. She needn't have. Almost anybody would have done the same under so much pressure. She nodded and patted the bed. I propped up a couple pillows and lay down in a semi-recline.

"I'm leaving Helsinki Homicide, and so is Milo. This little black-ops unit of ours is moving to the National Bureau of Investigation."

59

"Which is?" she asked.

"The NBI is a national police unit that fights the most serious organized and professional crime. It provides a lot of specialized technical services — forensics, technical intelligence, operational analyses. Assists local police forces in their more difficult cases. It offers more expert services. Financial and money laundering crime. IT crime. More difficult homicide cases and more complicated cases in general. It also takes care of international police co-operation and exchange of information, a big help to me, since I want to focus on cross-border transportation of girls forced into slavery and prostitution. You can think of it as being like your American FBI."

"So it's a step up for you? A promotion?"

"In a manner of speaking. It's less public. I'm well-known, and it keeps me out of the public eye. And I'm fighting high-level organized crime, so our project fits in with the NBI mandate. Plus, they don't have educational requirements, only areas of expertise, so Sulo can get an official job there, too." This was before Kate hung Sulo with his nickname, Sweetness.

Kate laughed. "And his area of expertise is what?"

"Whatever we invent. The minister will

rubber-stamp it."

I didn't say that my role was to be similar to Hoover's uglier machinations. It appeared to me that, although during our meeting it went unsaid, the subtext was that I was to be used for heists and shakedowns, extortion and instilling fear, probably collecting dirt on perceived enemies of the establishment. I was now Jyri's enforcer, and before I had even begun, I had to find a way to extricate myself from this situation. It occurred to me that Jyri didn't even wish me luck with my surgery. If I died, he wouldn't mourn my loss, just find someone else to do the job.

"Congratulations," Kate said. "I shouldn't have complained about the things in the closet. You were up front about what you were going to do and asked my permission. I had a chance to say no."

Guilt renewed itself. She wanted to say no, but acquiesced because I might be dead soon, and she would deny me nothing. I squeezed her hand. "It doesn't matter. And all this isn't as good as it sounds. Jyri presented this operation as if we would steal from criminals out of need for funding. For the good of the public. It was a lie. We've been moved to the NBI in part because it's headed by the minister of the interior, and

61

he and Jyri have some kind of illicit partnership. Not all of the money we've stolen goes to funding the unit. Jyri gets a cut, the minister gets a cut, and they insist that I take a percentage as well."

Kate's jaw dropped. "That makes you a dirty cop."

I nod. "Yep, it does. I said I didn't want it. He said I had to take it because if I didn't, I wasn't complicit, and if I wasn't complicit, I couldn't be trusted."

"You can't do it," Kate said.

I sighed. "You can't imagine how disillusioned I am. I'm so fucking stupid and naïve. Maybe I should just resign."

"No," she said, "not yet. Remember, you have evidence on the national chief of police that would end his career. He's at your mercy and he knows it. He can't force you to do anything."

I was at a complete loss. "What do I do then?"

"You have surgery. You come home. You let me take care of you and heal. Then we figure it out together."

It made me smile. I rolled over and gave her a hug.

"Mä rakastan sinua," she said.

Her Finnish was getting better all the

time. "I love you, too. I'm sorry about your job."

"It doesn't matter."

She took Anu from her crib, brought her into the bed with us, and we all took a nap together.

6

That evening, Milo and Sweetness came over for a planning session. I wouldn't see them again until after my surgery. I asked them here to issue edicts, to make everything clear. When I was back in action, working under the assumption that I would be, I wanted everything running smoothly.

They sat at the dining room table. Katt perched on my shoulder. Kate sat on the couch breast-feeding Anu, her back to us. I didn't ask her for privacy during the meeting, in the spirit of my new policy of honesty.

Milo and Sweetness showed up wearing thousand-euro suits. "Plans for the evening?" I asked.

"Yep," Milo said. "We're going out for a night on the town, beginning with the casino. I have a feeling Lady Fortune is with us."

"Nice suits," I said.

Sweetness said, "I've never had one before. Milo helped me pick it out. It's a Hugo Boss. They don't make them in my size and they had a hard time altering it. Do you think they did a good job?"

"You look great," I said and meant it, "but you can't go to the casino."

Automatic, Milo went angry and defensive. The dark circles under his eyes narrowed to black pits. I wondered if he ever sleeps. "You can't tell us what to do with our money."

I shouldn't have given them the money. It was bound to result in them showing it off.

Helsinki has a major casino downtown. First-class. Big money. "Have you ever been to the casino?" I asked.

"No."

"They're going to take your pictures so they can register you and give you membership cards. Then video cameras will record every move you make, such as plunking down a grand on a roll of the dice. Swanky entertainment on a cop's salary. If you're ever charged with being a dirty cop, which you now are, you can rest assured your trip to the casino will be found out and used as evidence against you. That SUPO agent you beat half to death needs his face rebuilt. You think that will be forgotten, that you won't be watched? We can all count on being spot tailed now. Assume everything you do is known to the secret police." I pointed at Sweetness. "And technically, you're unemployed. You don't even have a source of income, which in large part is why I gave you some money, not to fritter it away. How do you intend to explain your sudden rise to the high life?"

He didn't answer, stuck some *nuuska* in his lip instead.

"Then what the hell is the good of having the money?" Milo asked.

"Money is always good. Just keep it invisible."

He scratched his head, puzzled. "If we're watched, how are we supposed to pull off these dope dealer robberies?"

"It's taken care of. Don't worry your pretty little head about it. And handsome though you are in them, don't make it a habit of wearing expensive suits. Just don't do things that call attention to yourselves."

Milo and Sweetness looked at each other and traded grins.

"What?" I asked.

Sweetness laughed out loud.

Milo said, "Where should I begin? Let's see. You and I were in the headlines just weeks ago for stopping that school shooting

66

and killing a man. Your limp makes you noticeable from a mile away, and that bullet wound scar on your face is fucking scary. You're a walking billboard that screams 'Look at me!' And our giant colleague makes quite an impression on people as well. You're just being silly."

The crew had taken up the habit of speaking English in Kate's presence, out of politeness.

"They're right, you know," Kate said, and I saw it dawn on them that she must be privy to everything. She looked at Sulo. "Sweetness," she said, "would you be a dear and bring me a cup of coffee, with a little milk in it?" Sulo translates to "sweet," and so it seemed natural to her to call him that. She had no idea what she'd done.

Milo hee-hawed. "Sweetness, that's great! Sweetness, could I have a cup, too?" And thus, Sulo became Sweetness forevermore. He maintained his dignity and pretended as if nothing had happened. He asked me if I would care for a cup. He served us all, even Milo.

"Thank you, Sweetness," Milo said.

Sweetness stood up, walked over to peruse my CD collection, kept his back to us so we couldn't see his face turn red. "*Pomo,* do you mind if I put on some music?"

I told him to go ahead, and we all sat without speaking and listened to Charlie Parker blow saxophone. The group had a strange dynamic. Milo and Sweetness both emulated me, vied for my attention, and I got the feeling I had taken on some kind of father figure role for them. They spent far more time in our home than necessary, stopped by under any pretense. *They were just in the neighborhood and popped in. Did we need anything from the grocery?*

Their demeanor toward Kate carried something with it that suggested mother-hood, and her quiet dignity and bearing, especially when she held Anu, reinforced it. Despite Kate lacking the lush figure commonly portrayed during the period, she and Anu together often called to my mind Renaissance images of Madonna and Child. Milo and Sweetness bickered and insulted each other constantly, but then Milo took Sweetness out and helped him shop for clothes, reminiscent of the behavior of brothers. And finally, Arvid Lahtinen called me every couple days, and the tone of our conversations were much like grandfather and grandson.

I'd only known Arvid a few weeks, and our relationship was forged by criminal activity and murder. Among other things, his wife had cancer, he helped her to die, and I covered it up for him. Plus, he knew my grandpa during the Second World War. They were friends and killed many men together.

And now we were phone friends. I'd never had a phone friend before, but I enjoyed his calls.

My relationship with Sweetness also began with an act of violence. Two bouncers accidentally killed his brother. He repaid them by stabbing them with a box cutter and hitting them repeatedly in the face with a key ring, the keys protruding from between his fingers, causing awful puncture wounds and disfiguring them. I gave him a chance and offered him a job on a drunken whim, because he had a shitty upbringing and I felt sorry for him, and because I thought his capacity for violence would be of use to me.

I picked up my phone and called my neurologist brother, Jari. He picked up. "Hello, big brother," I said to him, even though he's half my size, because he's four years older than me.

It was two days until brain surgery, his voice radiated concern. "You OK?" he asked.

"Yeah, I'm fine, but I made a decision. I'm going to be out of action anyway. I want to take care of all my problems at once."

"Such as?"

"I want to check into the hospital early. Tomorrow. I want the scar on my face removed, and surgery on my knee to repair it as best as they're able."

He laughed at me. "Hospitals and surgeons don't offer one-day service, and you need tests on your knee to find out how to best repair the damage, how much of the damage can be repaired, or even if it can be repaired at all."

"My appearance interferes with my work as a detective. If I can get them all done at once, I won't have so much downtime from work, and I have a baby to take care of. I know you can get it done if you call in favors. I'm asking you for a favor."

Kate still had trouble believing that medical care is essentially free here. Brain surgery, all the attendant tests and the hospital stay would cost me nothing. The police have private insurance, so I get preferential care. I forget, maybe I pay a fifty-euro-a-year deductible. Nothing more. For an uninsured citizen using the public health-care system, a hospital stay costs fifteen euros a day. A doctor's visit about the same. Specialists cost nothing extra. Tests are cheap or free. Medicine can be expensive, but most people can easily afford to be sick here.

"Well, the scar removal could be called a procedure as much as a surgery. We can have your knee assessed, and if your tumor removal goes well, it's possible to do them both in a short time frame. I'll make some calls and get back to you," he said.

I rang off. Everyone gawked at me, too shocked to question my decision, even Kate.

Sweetness changed Charlie Parker for Charlie Christian and sat down again. I issued my edicts. Milo was in charge. There would be no robberies, heists, B&Es, or any such activity while I was away. Robberies made enemies, they might cause problems. Milo would commit no acts of violence, because he enjoys them. If violence was necessary, it would fall under Sweetness's domain, because he doesn't enjoy it. Also, Milo was famous, Sweetness was unknown. He would be our front man, the face of the team, if we needed one. I suspect Sweetness has sociopath tendencies, doesn't care if he hurts people or not. Milo got a carrot on a stick. He was to teach Sweetness computer skills. In return, he would slowly get to take more part in the exciting, meaning violent, aspects of the job if they were required. I sensed resentment between Milo and Sweetness. Neither liked the arrangement, but they nodded agreement.

"That includes your hobby," I said to Milo. "No B&Es for voyeurism. I don't want you to get in any kind of trouble."

Milo's hobby is breaking into people's houses for fun. He doesn't steal. Just looks around, prowls, goes through their things. He told me he just enjoys seeing how people live, what kinds of secrets they're hiding. It's some kind of fetish. His face went red and he glanced over his shoulder to check Kate's reaction. She pretended as though she heard nothing.

"You're not to skim or steal," I said. "You don't have to. Both of you get five percent of the take. You'll continue to get it as long as you don't flash it around."

I told them that while I was out of action and recovering, Milo was to get us outfitted with everything we needed to cut the legs out from under the criminals of Helsinki.

"Go heavy on surveillance gear," I said. "We're not going to war with the criminals of Helsinki, we're going to steal them broke and put them out of business."

"I know what we need," Milo said. "It's going to cost a fuckload of money."

"Then spend the fuckload of money. We have plenty." I continued, "I don't trust the people we work for. Sweetness, I want you to surveil Jyri, the national chief of police, the interior minister, and also the leadership of Kokoomus" — the conservative party to which they belong — "and whatever other politicos you find they associate with. Just spot tail them at random. See what turns up."

I had an idea of who was crooked from my conversations with Jyri and bits and pieces of info I picked up during the Filippov investigation. Sweetness isn't built for surveillance. He stands out from a mile away. "Get a camera with a long telescopic lens," I said, "and don't let them see you under any circumstances."

Milo said, "I'll get you a shotgun mike and rig so you can record their conversations."

"And, Milo," I said, "get us about ten safe-deposit boxes in different cities and banks. Kate," I asked, "would you go with him and co-sign so we have access?"

She registered surprise, but nodded.

My phone rang. Jari said, "My office, seven a.m. I'll escort you to the appropriate places and spend the day with you."

"Why?" I asked.

"Because I want to."

Milo and Sweetness shook my hand and

wished me luck before they left. Sweetness couldn't help himself and gave me a bear hug, almost choked the life out of me.

I sat down on the couch next to Kate. "Should I have discussed tomorrow with you before planning the other surgeries?" I asked.

She put an arm around me. "No. I was thrilled. You wouldn't have done it unless you believe you're going to live."

Maybe I was addled because of the migraine. We had a newborn in the house. It didn't occur to me how incredibly unfair to her it was for me to choose to have knee surgery and cripple myself, on top of whatever damage brain surgery might cause. I placed a terrible burden upon her.

7

The next days remain blurred wisps of images. It was Monday morning, the eighth of February. Not too cold, just below freezing but windy. I took the tram to Jari's office downtown, not far from the railway station. Tomorrow's brain surgery deleted most of the coming days' memories.

The gunshot scar on my face was removed with laser resurfacing. There were tests, X-rays. Surgeries. Nights in the hospital, waking and not understanding where I was. I have a blurry image of Kate's face as they put me on a gurney and wheeled me off to an operating theater.

The thought of surgery made me think of all the autopsies I'd witnessed. The whine and smell of an electric bone saw at work. The hushed murmur of a scalpel carving flesh. I was dizzy, woozy, confused.

Eventually, I came back to myself. A surgeon came in and informed me that the knee surgery was a success. After several weeks of physical therapy, I would have full range of motion to the limits of the prosthesis, meaning only a slight limp. I should have full weight bearing with a cane within six weeks.

Another surgeon came in and told me they got the whole tumor. No complications. I remember seeing Kate, Anu, Jari. I remember asking Kate to let me look at myself in her makeup mirror. With the scar gone, and a small bald spot with a stitched-up incision on the front of my head, I barely recognized myself. Mostly, I slept.

When I awoke the next morning, the symptoms of the previous day had mostly passed. My headache was gone. It had tortured me for a year, and now it was as if it had never existed at all. And great changes had occurred within me. I felt like a different person. Despite the medication I had been given — painkillers and tranquilizers — it was as if my thoughts had been muddled for my whole life, and now, suddenly and miraculously, I was clear in the mind, sharp as a razor.

Jari warned me that some of my perceptions and attitudes might be altered, that it was typical for brain surgery post-op patients, sometimes for a considerable length of time. I wondered if this feeling that my thinking was no longer diminished was false, the result of surgery, or if I truly was more intelligent now. Along with this new sense of clarity, I felt a sense of certainty, as if when they removed my tumor they cut away my angst and remorse along with it.

I felt a complete and utter lack of emotion. No love. No hate. Nada. Kate and Anu visited. I felt nothing, I smiled and pretended that I was glad to see them. Pretending was hard. I was glad to see them leave. Over the coming weeks, I practiced smiling to hide my lack of emotion. I knew that I must love them, because I remembered loving them. I could feel the yearning affection and desire for them that I did only a couple of days ago, but only as a memory.

This lack of feeling changed my attitudes. I lay in bed alone and psychoanalyzed myself. My overriding emotion in life had thus far been remorse. My life had been a constant struggle to make up for what I perceived as my failures. Every day, for more than thirty years, I mourned the loss of my sister Suvi and blamed myself for her death, because she was under my care when we were skating and the ice broke under her on the lake, even though I was only a year older than her. No longer.

I bore no responsibility for her death. Our father was the responsible adult. He, however, was busy sucking down a bottle of whiskey and ice fishing rather than tending to his children. In fact, I remember now that I didn't even like Suvi. I resented her because, even though our age difference was slight, I was often given the responsibility of looking after her, when I wanted to be out playing with my friends. After her death, my father began beating me for the slightest infractions, an unspoken punishment for failing to safeguard her. He beat my three brothers as well, and my mother on occasion, but not with the same severity as he did me.

I remember taking a slice of a pie left cooling on a windowsill. As punishment, he made me eat the whole thing and I vomited. He made me eat that, too. And he laughed.

I thought I had forgiven my father for beating me as a child. Why should I forgive him? My father has never even apologized for his abusive treatment of me. I had forgotten the frequency and severity of the beatings. The memories came flooding back. I thought I should go to his home in Kittilä, pull his pants down as he did mine, bend him over the same chair as he did me so many times, and, as he did to me, beat him with a belt.

He never beat me so severely at any one given time, but I would hit him hundreds of times until blood feathered the walls, to make up for all those beatings at once. That would only make it about one hit for every hundred times that Dad hit me, but still, the symbolism would be there. I should make my mother watch, as she watched and did nothing while Dad beat me. Maybe I should gather the whole family for the event and let them watch, like they watched him thrash me. I realized they were afraid of him, but collectively, they could have stopped him.

As a young boy, we had no indoor plumbing. I hated going outside in winter to take a piss, would hold it as long as I could, and once in a while would wait too long and wet myself. Once, he made me walk to school in pissed-on pants. It was twenty below, and as I walked, my crotch hurt, burned and then went numb. When I got to school, I went to the bathroom and looked at my dick. It was gray, a first sign of frostbite. And as the day went on and my pants warmed up, my dick hurt like hell and I stunk like piss and didn't live it down for months. I considered that I should make him drink several liters of water, deliver his beating before his work shift, wait until he pissed himself and then force him to walk to work. A shared experience between father and son.

I felt no anger, no nothing, while I formulated this plan. It wasn't revenge I contemplated but simple justice. A punishment born of rational logic.

Jari visited to check on me. He tested my basic motor skills and pronounced them sound, asked me how I felt. Without going into great detail or relating the nature of my thoughts, I told Jari I had gone emotionally numb. Jari said not to make too much of it, it would likely pass. He said it was a common symptom of tumor removal called "going flat." Where there once was tissue in my head, there was now only empty space about the size of a small egg. It took time for this space to fill back in, and this was sometimes the result.

"How long does it last?" I asked.

"There's no way to know," Jari said, "probably one to six months. Your emotions might return gradually, or they might come rushing back in a single moment. That moment could be sparked by an event, or it could happen for no reason at all."

"Or it might never happen," I said.

He sat down on the side of the bed, solemn. "Or it might never happen."

"I'd like to keep this between ourselves," I said. "I can't tell my wife that I feel nothing for her or our child."

"I won't try to tell you how to handle your recovery, but understand that this problem is the result of illness. It's not your fault, and the support of your family is important while you get through it. Keeping secrets, hiding your symptoms" — he put his hand on my shoulder — "is inevitably a mistake."

"Maybe. But I just can't put that on her. It would be cruel." It struck me that I wanted a cigarette. "Take me outside for a smoke," I said.

"It's not a good idea. Just stay in bed. You can smoke your brains out in a few days."

I discovered the second primary symptom of the surgery's aftermath. I'd entered into a childlike, binary existence. Want or don't want. Will or won't. Take or leave.

"If you don't take me outside, I'll wait until you leave, hang all this IV shit on the thingamajig you use to walk with them and go by myself."

He cocked his head and stared at me for a long moment. I saw it hit him that my hardheaded attitude was because of my surgery, and he spoke to me like a child. "If

I take you out for a cigarette, will you stay in bed for the rest of the day?"

"Yes."

It was a bit of an arduous process, with IV tubes, the mobile carryall and wheelchair, but I got my cigarette.

He put me back to bed and rearranged my medical paraphernalia, told me he would check on me again as soon he could and left.

I lay in bed and pondered the meaning, the worth, of life without emotion. My remorse was gone, but also my passion. If my remorse and sense of failure were gone, what had replaced them? I was emotionless, or nearly so. What would motivate me in life now? Maybe the same things that always motivated me. A desire for balance. Justice. Perhaps now I could even pursue those goals with a feeling of equanimity. For me, duty and love had always been closely related. Something I doubted Kate would understand. I reached one decision. I would take Sweetness under my wing and help him find himself and discover, for good or bad, who he really was, and help him become whatever it was that might be. As I wished my father had done for me. I lay in bed for two days, practiced my fake smile, and contemplated the changes that had come over me.

I thought of Gregor Samsa in Kafka's *The Metamorphosis,* who awoke to find that he had become a monstrous insect. Was I a morphed Gregor Samsa, or a surgically enhanced Kari Vaara?

8

I came home on Friday. Despite all the work done to me, I had spent only four days in the hospital. I lay about, ate narcotics and tranquilizers as instructed, watched crappy television shows, played with Anu and the cat. I felt fine but a little tired and napped a lot. I was on a one-month sick leave, to be extended if necessary, but I was free to go back to work in two weeks if I chose. On Saturday I caught up on the news.

Parliamentary elections were a little over a year away, and a dark horse was gaining ground fast. The Real Finns Party. It was officially headed by Topi Ruutio, an experienced politician and member of the European Parliament. It had a second leader, Roope Malinen. He held no office, but his blog was the most popular in Finland. The Real Finns agenda was unclear, except that they were anti-foreigner and anti-immigration. The Real Finns had invented a euphemism for racists. They staunchly denied charges of racism and dubbed themselves *"maahanmuuttokriitikot,"* critics of immigrants. Our population was aging, our birthrate low, and without immigrants to work and pay taxes, there would be no pension money for our retirees. The Real Finns' answer: Finnish women must bear more children, out of patriotic duty.

Other than hate, their agenda wasn't clear. They wanted a return to traditional Finnish values. I'm unaware of what traditional Finnish values are, and I don't think anybody else knows, either.

Real Finns believed that government should decide what qualifies as good art to receive government support. They looked to nineteenth-century-style Finnish classic works as ideals. They made wild promises to spread the wealth that couldn't possibly be met. They wanted to leave the EU. Their rhetoric reminded me of early Nazi propaganda. Like I told Kate, Real Finns are like a more virulent strain of American Teabaggers.

Real Finns have skyrocketed in popularity because the global financial crisis, coupled with greed by our own leading financiers — despite manipulated statistics indicating we have the world's strongest economy, leading the world to believe that Finland is some kind of financial paradise — has driven our economy into the shithole. Nearly twenty percent of Finns now live beneath the poverty line. Their jobs are being out-sourced to other countries. Inflation is high, wages stagnant. People are frightened, and they're focusing that fear, placing their blame, on immigrants.

I don't believe they're actually pro–Real Finn. I think they're terrified and protesting the establishment that made them feel this way. I kept up with Real Finn antics because their policies changed daily and, when I felt emotions, it amused me. It's not funny, though, because since the other parties are suffering mass defections to Real Finns, those other parties are taking positions to stem the tide. Keskusta, a center party, adopted the slogan *"Maassa maan tavalla"* — "in the the way of the country" — but left the well-known phrase unfinished: *"tai maasta pois"* — or "get out of the country." Hate directed at foreigners.

Ruutio is charismatic and at least projects an image of being a good guy with strong if somewhat confused beliefs. He shies away from discussions about immigration and foreigners. Malinen writes well. In his blog, he makes convoluted racist arguments seem reasonable. He's a good hater. In person, he's almost unable to speak, and what he does manage to say is aggressive, defensive and often incomprehensible. Interviews give the impression that he's a maniac in dire need of medication. Ruutio pretends to distance himself from Malinen and his extremism, but in truth, they work in tandem. Neither can do without the other.

I slept in the next day and the door buzzer woke me. It was Valentine's Day. A detective handed me a thick envelope, a packet of dossiers on drug dealers and their upcoming events. It contained no note to me. The unspoken message: You're on sick leave, but do as you will. After waking up and having coffee, I called Milo and asked him to come over. I didn't want to talk on the phone, because ours had likely been tapped.

Kate was less than pleased to see Milo's face on Valentine's Day, on my second day of sick leave. He looked hung over. The black circles around his eyes were puffy. His eyes bloody red.

I gave him the envelope. "These are potential heist material," I said. "You can carry them out at your discretion. But you're not to take risks. If you act impetuously and someone gets hurt because of it,

I'll fire you."

I wished I could go. He's good at black-bag work. Thorough. And he's slick with a lockpick set, can get through an average door in under a minute. I could learn from him. I hate to think how many B&Es he pulled off while satisfying his voyeuristic desires to develop that kind of skill.

His jaw jutted out, defiant. "The chief wanted me on this team. You can't fire me."

"Try me."

He hangdog acquiesced. "We don't need to have this conversation. I don't intend to be impetuous."

"Good." I clued him in to leave. "Let me know what happens."

"I'm getting everything together so when you're back on duty, we can really rock. I want to have a welcome back party for you. You OK with that?"

I put on the smile I'd practiced in the mirror. "Sure. We'll set the date later."

He grinned, happy now. "Great. This party will be so much fun, you'll want to take it out behind the middle school and fuck it."

Going through the motions. Pretending to feel, to care. Without emotions, life lacks meaning. I learned a life lesson from my loss. Nothing has intrinsic meaning. We give meaning to the things important to us. It seems the other way around, that loved ones, material possessions we enjoy, our perceived successes, give meaning to our lives. Not so. Those things have meaning because we have emotionally injected meaning into them. Emotions keep us walking, talking, functioning, striving.

I promised myself that I would keep living life as if I felt emotions, in the hope that one day I would feel them again. I promised myself I wouldn't forget that although I felt no emotions, others did, and theirs remained important. That the most important things in life lie outside my inner being. I had duties to fulfill, whether I found meaning in them or not.

But I was running on sheer desire. Childlike. That meant I had some form of emotion left, but base, almost animalistic, primitive. I tried to squelch it. The childishness that was now a part of me, however, had a blurred sense of right and wrong. It had no interest in them. I had to guard against that part of myself, be wary of it, suppress it. The trick, I realized, was to act through the memory of emotions. In that way, I could at least outwardly be the same person I was pre-surgery.

In early afternoon, Kate went grocery

shopping. Anu slept. I had promised to cook that evening, was going to make linguini carbonara. Nothing quite like salty American bacon was available in Finland until recent years, and so carbonara is a relatively new dish for me. Bacon. I love the stuff.

I was gimping across the floor on crutches, a newspaper tucked under my arm, on my way to the couch to sit down and read it. Then I lost it, went incoherent, got dizzy and light-headed. My chest got tight. The world went slow motion. I felt myself going down. A few minutes later, I came to, sprawled on the floor. It scared me.

I followed my first instinct and called Jari. He said I'd suffered a seizure, but told me to stay calm. Especially in the first week after surgery, this could be a onetime event. To be on the safe side, though, I should start on anti-seizure medication and, depending on how things went, stay out from behind the wheel of a car for three to six months instead of just the standard one month following non-problematic brain tumor removal.

I nixed that idea automatic. I wanted my freedom, wanted my car back. I told him if it wasn't an anomaly, I'd take the medication, but wanted to wait and see first. He said that was OK.

But I was afraid to pick up Anu, in case I had a seizure while I was carrying her. Kate would be home soon, I had to think fast.

Mobility was difficult enough already. I had a baby carrier that fit in the front, against my chest. I put her in it and then walked around on crutches. I couldn't believe this was happening to me. First, I lost feeling for my own child, and now I was afraid to pick her up.

I went with my first idea, called Arvid and explained the situation, omitting the lack of emotions part, and told him I didn't want Kate to find out about the seizure because she would try to insist that I take the medication. This total truth thing with Kate didn't seem to be working out for me.

"Can you come here and stay for a few days?" I asked.

"What will it help, and on what pretext?"

"It will help because I don't want to fall with the baby. You carry her for me. The pretext is you say you were in Helsinki and just decided to drop by and visit. You seem dispirited, so I invite you to dinner. You accept, and then later, old man that you are, pretend to nod off on the couch."

"I doubt I'll have to pretend," he said. "I'm two days older than dirt. I nod off frequently."

"I'll suggest putting you up in the spare bed for the night. Then, in the morning, you just don't leave. You help out with the baby, carry her to me or for me, and I point out how much easier this makes life for me. I say you're probably just lonely, that you just lost your wife after fifty years of marriage."

I waited for a response, but none was forthcoming. I shouldn't have said that, it cut too close to the bone. He was so lonely and sad that it was unbearable for him. That's why he called me so often.

"I can spare a few days," Arvid said. "What am I supposed to do about bringing clothes, though? I can't exactly show up with a suitcase."

"When it becomes apparent that you'll be staying, I'll send one of the boys to pick some things up for you."

"All right. I won't be long. I'm coming by taxi."

"Why? A taxi is a hundred euros."

"I've been meaning to visit anyway. I've got a couple things for the baby and can't carry them to the bus stop."

"That's nice of you to think of her. I'll pick up the tab."

"No, you won't." He rang off.

Kate came home loaded down with groceries. After she put them away, I said, "I've got a Valentine's Day gift for you."

She smiled. "I have one for you too, but I thought we would wait until after dinner to exchange them."

I'd planned in advance, bought them weeks ago, and I wanted to give them to her while we had a private moment, before Arvid arrived. I put on my practiced smile. "I want to do it now." I hobbled off to the bedroom to take it from its hiding place in the closet and came back with a small, gift-wrapped box.

She had a dozen white roses in her hands. "Just a small expression of love," she said. "I have something else for you too, but it's physical in nature. You have to wait, though, to let the anticipation build."

A blow job. About the most thoughtful gift she could give me at the moment. The way I'd felt since surgery, if I couldn't eat it, drink it or fuck it, I didn't want it.

My knee hurt. We sat on the sofa. She opened her gift. A Kalevala necklace with a silver oak leaf, and matching earrings.

I put the necklace on her. She stood in

front of the foyer mirror and tried on the earrings. "They're lovely," she said. "Delicate and feminine but with a Viking air about them."

"They're about as traditional Finnish as you can get," I said. "Kalevala jewelry is based on ancient Nordic combined with modern designs."

The door buzzer rang. Kate answered. Arvid stood there with the taxi driver, who had helped him carry the mountain of packages up the stairs. The driver left. Arvid extended his hand to Kate. "I'm Arvid Lahtinen," he said. "I've heard so much about you, it's a pleasure to finally make your acquaintance."

"And yours," Kate said. "Kari has said nothing but good things about you." She gestured at the piles of gift-wrapped packages. "What is all this?"

His smile was shy. "Some odds and ends for baby Anu."

I was unable to help them. Arvid and Kate moved the boxes into the middle of the living room floor.

"Good to see you, Kari," Arvid said. "You look well. And younger. Without that scar, you look like somewhat less of a thug."

"Kind of you to say so."

Kate also said it makes me look younger.

It wasn't entirely gone, but almost. The skin was smooth, but there was a slight red discoloration, barely noticeable. The surgeon said the results are seldom this good. Also, I hadn't been to the gym since well before the beginning of the year. I was slimmer as well.

"Please," Arvid said, "open the boxes."

Kate and I were both awestruck. There were clothes of different sizes to last Anu for a year. An antique musical mobile decorated with wooden fantasy animals. A jumperoo. A variety of stuffed animals. Everything designer brands. The best money could buy. After the last package was open, Arvid took one more from his coat pocket and handed it to Kate. Inside was a silver box with Anu's name and birth date engraved on it. It's to keep Anu's baby teeth in. Arvid had spent a grand, maybe two, on all this. I was taken aback. Kate was moved to tears. The old man knew how to make an impression.

He was actually eighty-nine, not ninety as he habitually stated. I knew, from reading his secret police dossier while investigating him for murder, that he would turn ninety on March third. His appearance and movements, though, suggested a well-kept man in his seventies. Despite his advanced age, mentally he was sharp as a tack, and he had a good sense of humor. The three of us sat down for coffee and *pulla,* sweet rolls flavored with cardamom. He asked to hold Anu, and bounced her on his knee while we talked. He told stories from his life and travels. He had the social knack, spoke neither too much nor too little. He was charming the pants off Kate. If he were fifty years younger, I wouldn't have left him alone in the same room with her.

With a powerful blat, followed by a giggle, Anu announced that she needed her diaper changed.

When we were alone, I asked about feeding Arvid's four cats while he stayed here.

"That won't be necessary," he said.

It was hard to imagine that he gave them away after his wife, Ritva, died only weeks ago. They were all the company he had left, and they had been with him and Ritva for many years.

"How come?" I asked.

"They mourned Ritva and meowed nonstop. You ever read the Edgar Allan Poe story 'The Tell-Tale Heart'?"

"Yeah."

"It felt like that. They never stopped crying for her. I felt like I was going out of my mind. I couldn't give them away. They belonged to Ritva. So finally, I put them in a burlap bag and drowned them in the bathtub. Next to helping Ritva die, it was the hardest thing I've ever done."

And he's killed hundreds of men in war, so that's saying a lot. Arvid must be the toughest man I've ever met. The image it conjured was horrible. The cats choke, gag and struggle while he holds them under the water. Bubbles rise to the surface of the water as their lungs empty, until finally, they go limp.

"I built a wooden box for a coffin," he said, "and buried it in the snow. In the spring, when the ground softens up, I'll dig a grave out back behind the house for them."

"Why did you buy all those things for Anu?" I asked.

"I told you, I think you're a good boy. You remind me of your grandpa, my friend. I felt like doing something nice."

"That was more than nice," I said.

He just smiled.

After a while, I didn't have to prod her, Kate asked Arvid to stay for dinner. He played his role well, changed Anu himself once, with deft movements. He told Kate that he and Ritva had two boys, but both died before adulthood. One from cancer, one from a car crash. The story brought tears to her eyes. After a meal, a cognac and a little more conversation, it was as Arvid said. He drifted off to sleep. It had been a much more action-packed day than he was accustomed to. I prodded him awake and asked if he would like to spend the night in the spare bed. He nodded agreement, made it into Anu's room and was asleep again within minutes.

Before bed, I asked Kate if she would mind if I invited Arvid to stay with us for a few days.

"Why?" she asked.

"Because he's lonely, and I think the company would help him get past the death of his wife. They were together for fifty years. He's suffering."

"He's got too much pride. You can't say that to him."

"I can say he can help me out with Anu and give you a little more freedom, and that would be true. Carrying Anu around while I walk on crutches is hard."

"Is he really a mass murderer?" she asked.

"Yes."

"He's so sweet, and he's wonderful with Anu, but he killed a man in cold blood, in a restaurant I manage. I suspect he's a charming sociopath. And now he's sleeping in our house. The situation is bizarre. I have . . . reservations about this."

"He only kills Russians, not babies. Not even baby Russians," I said.

The joke combined with the strange situation made her start to giggle. "A few days," she said. "I don't want a permanent house-guest."

"Thanks," I said.

She kissed me, and gave me my Valentine's Day present.

9

The next morning, in front of Kate, I made a show of asking Arvid to stay with us for a few days. After a couple refusals for the sake of pretense, he reluctantly agreed.

Sweetness was to be my chauffeur for the day. First, a trip to NBI headquarters to fill out his job application, then to Arvid's to pick up some clothes for him, and then to my physical therapy, which I loathed, because it hurt like hell.

We took Sweetness's car, a 1998 Toyota Corolla with a hundred and twenty thousand miles on it. He was new to driving. Milo broke into the registry computers and created a license for him. Sweetness was so proud when he received it. Completing all the courses necessary for a license: normal weather daylight driving, winter driving, nighttime driving, et cetera, is a lengthy process and before all is said and done, costs some thousands of euros. Poor people can't afford one. The car had been his father's, but since he was doing a long stretch for double murder, he had no use for it.

He picked me up in front of my building. On crutches, on the ice, even making it from our steps to his car was difficult. We went straight, banged a left onto Helsinginkatu. We stopped at a red light by Vaasanaukio — Vaasa Square, often referred to as Piritori, Speed Square — because it's an infamous hangout for the alkies and dopers in Sörnäinen, not far from our house, that haunt the area.

Finland's number one killer is alcohol. According to statistics, despite our small population, we also have more heroin users than the rest of the Nordic countries put together. I don't know if that's true or if we're just better at keeping statistics, at which we excel, than the other countries in the region. We also have problems with amphetamine and tranquilizer addiction. Plus, about a quarter of us use or have used anti-depressants. And studies show that depression remains severely undertreated. What is it about this place that causes so many of us to seek oblivion and be so miserable?

In the square, it's quiet in winter because

of the cold. Minus ten and a little windy that morning, but thriving in summer. Druggies and drunks hang out and sip beers, listen to boom boxes. Police often park their vans in the square and keep watch, but don't often interfere with anything non-violent. A big S-market grocery store dominates one side of the square, a subway station the other, and a porn shop called Seksipiste — The Sex Point — sits off to one side. It's been there for many years. I never see anyone go in or out of it. It must do the majority of its business via the Internet.

Kate and I often shop in the S-market. It's interesting how quickly we adjust to things in life. The druggies don't harass us, and so become invisible unless they fight or cause scenes. Like much of Helsinki, normal middle-class inhabitants, even the well-to-do, exist side by side with the scum.

A bank ATM is attached to the wall beside the S-market. A little squab bones of a girl inserted her card. The machine spit her card out instead of money. A young man in a black bomber jacket with a bloated alcoholic face slapped her. I told Sweetness to pull into the square. We watched.

Squab Bones was underdressed in a tattered coat, had little ears and a low forehead, small pointy teeth inside a scarlet smear of a mouth, sores on her face. Crystal meth or heroin had whittled her down to nothing. Best guess, she buys whatever it is from him. The man looked simian and his mean eyes were glazed. She tried to speak. He grabbed her by her short dirty hair and jerked her head to and fro. She slipped, fell to the ice, started to sob.

Something should be done. I couldn't do it myself. "Sweetness," I said, "go over there and punch that guy in the head. Hurt him."

"OK, *pomo.*"

He reached in his coat pocket and took out a flask, had a pull from it and put it away. I checked my watch. Ten forty-five a.m.

Sweetness meandered over, the simian paid no heed. I rolled my window down to listen. Sweetness hit him with a right hook, lightning fast. So fast that at his size, I wouldn't have thought it possible. Simian's teeth were clenched in anger. I heard Simian's jaws both crack broken. His mouth hung funny. Blood shot out of his mouth like a burst water balloon.

Somehow, he kept on his feet. Teeth flew. He spat bridgework. He gagged on a tooth he swallowed that went down the wrong way. He hacked and coughed it out of his airway, spit it out, started crying, and the expression on his face asked Sweetness why. He leaned over, put his hands on his knees. Blood drooled from his mouth in a thin stream and puddled on the ice at his feet.

Sweetness hit him again. A straight jab angled down to the face. Simian's front teeth broke out. His nose crunched flat. He flew backward, hit the ATM and collapsed.

I called out. "Go through his pockets."

Sweetness took his wallet. Dope in eight-ball packets. A switchblade.

"Any money in the wallet?" I asked.

He pulled it out and counted. "Three hundred and sixty."

"Give it all to the girl except the switch-blade and the wallet. Throw it in a trash can." To force Simian to go to the trouble and expense of replacing the cards and ID.

Squab Bones snatched the drugs and money and, dope greedy, didn't bother to say thank you. Wounded animals are like that. She ran into the subway station.

Sweetness got behind the wheel, hit the flask again and we pulled out.

"You're fast," I said. "Have you trained?"

He grinned. "Naw, just another of my natural gifts."

We rode in silence for a while. Something rolled back and forth under my seat. Judging by the sound, it was a bottle of booze to refill the flask throughout the day.

"How much do you drink?" I asked.

He shrugged. "I don't keep track."

"Been drinking hard long?"

"More since my brother got killed. It's not so much that I like to get drunk. It just steadies my nerves."

Sweetness is one of those rare juicers. You never know when they're tanked: they never slur, their eyes don't droop. He always seems sober. He drove fast, wove in and out of traffic along the icy roads with careful precision. I said nothing, wanted to give it some thought. What I said wouldn't make any difference anyway. Sometime there would come a point when he'd have to choose whether to self-destruct or build a life for himself.

At NBI HQ in Vantaa, he filled out his application for a job as a linguist. He got the job through nepotism, but it wasn't a sham. Our team needed a linguist with exactly his abilities, for translation of electronic eavesdropping on foreign criminals. He only lacks Dutch. We could use someone who speaks it, because so much pot and Ecstasy comes from Amsterdam. We got it done and started out toward Arvid's. We wouldn't be taking his Toyota again. The shock absorbers were worn out, and every bump in the road jarred my knee, sent pain shooting through it. I have a Saab 9-5, 2007 model, which I love. We'd be taking it from now on.

On the way, I asked him about his plans for an education. Since he was now an NBI employee, he didn't have to go to the police academy in Tampere. He could stay here and attend the University of Helsinki or a polytechnic trade school.

"I got a job," he said. "What do I need school for?"

"That was our agreement when I hired you," I said. "I expect you to earn a degree. What you study, though, is up to you."

"I don't care," he said. "You can pick for me."

Then I got it. He would apply for whatever I suggested, then fail the entrance exam but claim he tried and acted in good faith.

"No," I said. "It's your life, and what we're doing now won't last forever. You make a decision, and you study like hell for the entrance exam. If you don't go to school, you can't work for me. End of story."

This made him mad. He didn't speak to me for the next hour.

After we picked up Arvid's clothes, I asked him if Milo had been teaching him some computer skills. "No. I don't like being around him if I don't have to. He calls me names, makes fun of the way I talk and tells me I'm stupid. I'm not stupid."

Sweetness has an East Helsinki accent and uses the area's slang. Sometimes I don't get what he's saying. Helsinki is funny that way. Dialects vary so much that you can often place a person's roots to within half a mile. East Helsinki dialect screams lower class.

"I'm not going to take much more of that shit from him," Sweetness said.

"You want me to speak to him about it?"

He scoffed. "*Pomo,* I don't need you to fight my battles for me."

"Just don't hurt him like you did the dope dealer." I was curious. "Did that bother you?" I asked.

"Naw, he deserved it. I couldn't care less." He switched topics. "Milo taught me a little about surveillance, though. I got some good pictures to show you."

"I told you to stay in the car and out of sight."

"Milo said that was bullshit, that I had to learn to be — what do you call it? — surreptitious. I gotta say, he was right. I got some great pics."

After physical therapy, Sweetness took me home, and I invited him to eat with us. It was like watching a pig at the trough. He ate at lightning speed, watched with an empty plate to make sure we had our fill, then devoured every last bite left on the stove. Why did I think my relationship with Sweetness was going to equate to Henry Higgins and Eliza Doolittle in *My Fair Lady*?

10

February eighteenth, Thursday. Nine days since my brain tumor was removed. My luck was extreme. My headache disappeared. I suffered no common physical side effects. No weakness, motor control or problems with coordination. No difficulties with speech. No more seizures. No mental deficiencies. Quite the opposite. Each day, I felt that my powers of cognition and memory increased. I remained, however, emotionally flat.

I continued my one-month sick leave. It didn't go as Kate and I had imagined: quiet time together, just us and our child. Milo and Sweetness were always underfoot. Arvid, though, knew how to make his presence unobtrusive. Kate liked him more and more over time. He mostly kept to himself, listened to music with his MP3 player, tended to Anu, grocery shopped and often cooked. He was an excellent chef, and taught Kate much about traditional Finnish cuisine. As a longtime world traveler, his English was good.

Sweetness played chauffeur, took me to physical therapy three times a week, stopped by to see if we needed anything approximately every ten minutes. At night, he surveilled politicos. He bought a good camera. He showed me his videotaped victories with pride. He had a close-up of Hanna Nykyri, head of the Social Democratic Party, with a dick in her mouth. A wider shot proved said dick didn't belong to her husband. He had a picture of Daniel Solstrand, minister of foreign affairs, with a dick in his mouth. Owner of said dick appeared underage. Sweetness had pics of the national chief of police and the minister of the interior with a variety of women, a veritable bevy of quail.

The minister, Osmo Ahtiainen, is an overweight pig not choosy about his quiff. A video showed the fat fuck minister in the saddle of a woman who looked like she might be the village blacksmith. She changed the TV channel with a remote control. The sound was off. He didn't notice. He came, squealed and grunted. She fake came with him, gave him the "Oh, baby, you're the best" patter.

110

One morning, while we were alone, I had a talk with Arvid. I asked him if he would like to be our bookkeeper, since Jyri wanted ledgers kept. "The murder you're accused of falls under the National Security Act," I said. "If I get caught, and you have the books, they can't be used against me."

"You won't get caught for the simple reason that police corruption, at least in the public consciousness, is so rare here as to be non-existent, and you're the most famous cop in the nation, so no one would believe it. It would be like trying to convince them that Jesus was a pedophile."

It's true. After being shot twice in the line of duty and being decorated for bravery both times — and especially since Milo and I stopped a school shooting and were glorified in the press for saving the lives of children — I'm a nationally respected figure.

"But sure, I'll do it," he said. "It will be fun. I'll keep them in a code from the war and teach it to you, make it feel like the old days."

Most of Arvid's time in the war was spent in Valpo, our secret police during those years.

Then I brought up what I really wanted to talk about, and told Arvid about going flat and feeling no emotion. "I'm afraid I

111

won't be able to keep up the pretense, and it will cause me to wreck my marriage," I said, "or it will cause me to make an error in judgment in my work and get somebody hurt."

I had already told him about my black op, ripping off drug dealers, taking money.

"I already told you, boy," he said. "You inherited your family blood. You're a killer, you just need the right justifications so you can pretend otherwise. There have been times in my life when I felt nothing. It started during the Winter War. I felt no fear, no joy or misery, no guilt. It went away over time, but sometimes, when I'm under stress, I still go numb inside. Our circumstances are different, your problem is neurological and mine is post-traumatic stress syndrome. I'm just saying I have an idea of what you're going through. You love your wife. Just because you can't feel it right now doesn't mean it isn't so. And this black-bag operation — you've been lying to yourself — people are going to die and you knew it when you took it on. Maybe you're better off if you don't feel anything for a while."

Arvid had become a mentor to me. My first and doubtless last. He's the only man I ever met that I trusted and respected enough to look to for wisdom. I didn't say anything, just sat there and tried to process what was doubtless true. He patted my knee and went to the kitchen to do the dishes. Left me to my thoughts.

Milo called. He was building surveillance gear and a new computer, said he didn't have room to work in his tiny apartment, and asked if he could use one end of my dining room table as a workbench.

He lives in squalor in an apartment barely big enough to turn around in. Our dining room table is huge, and he was doing this for the group. It was hard to say no.

"Are you going to trash my house?"

"No. I just need one end of the table for a couple days."

He showed up an hour later with boxes of components. Started stacking them in the corner. It was a big pile. He was going to trash my house. Arvid walked into the room. Milo saw him and a look came over his face like he just saw the girl of his dreams. So he had an ulterior motive for asking to work here. He wanted to meet Arvid.

Milo considers himself patriotic above all things and is fascinated by Finland's role in the Second World War. He reads incessantly about the Winter War of 1939–40, in which Finland slaughtered Russians by the droves.

Arvid is one of the great heroes of the Winter War and personally killed hundreds of Russians, as well as taking out six tanks, charging at them with Molotov cocktails.

Milo raced across the room, grabbed Arvid's hand and started pumping it. "It's a pleasure, sir. A great honor. As a Finn, let me express my personal gratitude for your bravery and sacrifice."

Arvid sighed, jerked his hand free. "For God's sake, stop kissing my ass."

Milo's euphoria was short-lived. He hadn't considered that Arvid might not enjoy the sum of the continual and uncritical admiration of everyone he came into contact with. "I'm sorry, sir. It's just that . . ." he could only stammer.

Arvid spared him further humiliation. "It's all right, just get over it."

Wisely, Milo kept his mouth shut and started unpacking his boxes.

Kate walked in. She saw the mess and it pissed her off. "What in the name of God is all this?"

I said, "I told him he could work in here, because his apartment is so small."

Kate looked put out in the extreme. "What, then, may I ask, are you building?"

He kid-in-candy-store smiled. "Can you please just wait one minute?" He unpacked an oblong box-shaped gizmo with dials and such on it. Plugged it in, made some adjustments. "This is a bug sweeper," he said. "It detects radio signals and info-burst packets used to monitor mains-powered transmitters, telephone transmitters, video transmitters, cell phones, tracking devices, you name it. It sniffs out mains carrier low-frequency and infrared laser-emitting devices. It also picks up signals from more sophisticated devices that only transmit momentarily and notify you that a signal has been detected: burst transmitters that accumulate information and fire it off in a fraction of a second."

"You realize," I said, "that, to the rest of us, your explanation was just a half minute of incomprehensible ratchet noises."

The black rings around his eyes crinkled with delight. "Allow me to demonstrate." He walked around the room with something that resembled an oversized mobile phone with an antenna and a plethora of control gizmos. As he neared Kate's purse, it emitted a beep that pulsed faster and faster the closer he got. He asked her to take her cell phone out of her purse. Steady beep.

The door buzzer rang. It was Sweetness, just checking to see if we need anything.

As Milo neared him, the beeping started again. And again got stronger as Milo got closer. Milo reached into Sweetness's coat pocket and pulled out his phone. Steady beep. It was the same for all of us. Even Arvid.

"The apartment is clean," Milo said, "but SUPO tapped all our phones."

I wasn't surprised. Arvid laughed. Kate's mouth gaped. Sweetness hadn't taken in the ramifications yet.

Milo ripped the tape off another box. It contained new Nokia phones. "These are N95s loaded with encryption software. The encryption," he said, "is certified by the Israeli ministry of defense. There are no back doors. The encryption keys are randomly generated by the software and can't be provided to anyone, either private organization or government. It's a dual combination of asymmetric and symmetric encryption with end-to-end protection, from phone to phone, for both audio and text messages. A one-thousand-and-twenty-four-bit random master key is automatically generated per contact and replaced at every call start, and a two-hundred-and-fifty-six-bit random session key is replaced every second."

He paused, waiting for us to cheer at our good fortune.

"That's great news," Sweetness said.

Milo didn't get it that Sweetness was teasing him. "Just insert the SIM cards from the phones you have now, and your privacy is ensured. We can even have conference calls if we like."

"I get one too?" Arvid asked. "What for? I just change diapers and cook."

"Sir," Milo said, "what is ours is yours. I have another gift for you as well, but I'd like to wait until we have Kari's 'Welcome back to the world' party, when he officially goes back on duty to give it to you."

I forgot to mention it to Kate.

"Party?" she asked.

"If it's OK with you," Milo said, "I'd like to have it here on the twenty-eighth of March. I need time to get everything together. It'll take a few weeks. I have — or will have — gifts for you as well."

Her curiosity was piqued. "Sure, we can have a party."

She was miffed because the house was full of people. Violent and criminal people at that, even if they all worked for the police — or, in Arvid's case, used to. Later, she told me she felt as if she was trying to raise a child in the lair of a terrorist cell. But Milo had proven the value of his undertakings and won her over for the time being.

"What else are you working on?" she asked.

"I'm building three synthesizable VHDL models of exact solutions for three-dimensional hyperbolic positioning systems," he said.

"More ratchet noises," she answered.

"They're mobile stations for eavesdropping on cell phones, so we can do to the bad guys what was done to us. They're not that great. The range is only a couple miles and they can only handle three or four phones at a time, but they're the best I can do. And I'm building a new computer to suit our purposes. There isn't one commercially made that has the exact components I want, and it saves a lot of money, too."

"Here's the deal," she said. "My husband is recovering from two major surgeries. He needs quiet. We have a newborn infant. She and I both need quiet. You can spend a limited amount of time here to build your toys, but I want the house kept neat and your presence unobtrusive." She turned to Sweetness. "You really are sweet, and you have our gratitude for driving Kari around, for shopping and just being generally helpful. But from now on, call before you come over, and don't call three times a day. This is our home, not your squad room."

Milo and Sweetness stared at the floor, hands in pockets, and waxed regretful.

"Kate, should I go home?" Arvid asked.

She walked over and put her hand on his shoulder. "Please, stay a few more days. You've been a great help to us, and we're grateful."

He flashed the smile that charmed her and nodded assent.

Kate left the room, went to tend to Anu.

I asked Milo, "How many heists have you pulled since I gave you that packet of info?"

"Two."

"How did they go?"

He and Sweetness shared an awkward glance. "Last night, we cased the apartment and the dealer was gone, so I picked the lock and we entered. A woman was asleep in her bed. She heard the door open, woke up, came out of her bedroom and saw us."

"What happened?"

"I found a roll of duct tape and mummified her. She had on pajamas, but still, it would have hurt like hell when it got pulled off, so Sweetness stood her up and held her up in place, and I rolled it around her backwards, so the sticky part faced out. Only her mouth was taped shut, and we tied a scarf around her eyes. Then we stuck her to the kitchen wall. And after all that, we only got twenty-three thousand euros."

"Can she ID you?"

"No. We wore balaclavas the whole time."

It must have made an interesting picture. "Milo, work on your contraptions for a while if you want. Quietly. Sweetness, go home for a while or dig some dirt on politicos or whatever. Both of you be back here tomorrow at three p.m. Milo, what weapons have we confiscated?"

"Four handguns, a sawed-off shotgun, and a Daddy MAC."

We would save the MAC-10 for something special. Illegal possession of fully automatic weapons carries more jail time. "Bring a couple pistols," I said, "for a frame-up."

Sweetness left. Milo unpacked his goodies, placed the components in orderly piles in the corner and threw out the boxes, so the dining room did indeed look neat. He left for the day, and according to Kate's wishes, we passed a quiet evening.

11

In the morning, Aino, Kate's assistant, who was taking Kate's place while she was on enforced maternity leave, stopped by our apartment to drop off some papers. Her gorgeous blue eyes were framed by a mop of messy blond hair. She's built the opposite of Kate. Short and lush instead of tall and thin. A long and sexy upper lip. Her sweater accentuated magnificent breasts. I got an insta-hard-on. All I could think about was fucking her.

It took me by surprise. I'd never wanted anyone besides Kate since I first laid eyes on her, and I hadn't had this kind of reaction to a woman since I was a teenager. I tried not to stare, to act natural. I was sitting on the couch and covered my crotch with the morning newspaper. I had found a new dimension to my post-op symptoms. My primitive desires included other women.

Jyri called. There were a number of big-money drug deals going down over the coming weeks. He knew I was weak and on crutches. How much could I do? Could Milo and Sweetness work independent of me? Could we get the jobs done? He didn't know how much they had already accomplished. I wanted to participate. I was bored shitless. I said we would find a way. Unless I was on death's door, I would participate. I counted the days. Two weeks until I could drive again. A month until I ditched the crutches.

Aino stayed for coffee, hung around for about an hour. She and Kate had a blossoming friendship. I was glad when she left. Her presence made me feel like my dick was going to burst.

A packet of dossiers arrived about two p.m. They contained info on criminals culled from the ship's manifest of the *Baltic Princess*, the ferry from Tallinn due to arrive in Helsinki at four thirty. I agreed to participate in this black-ops project because I wanted to help people. This day marked my first attempt to do so.

Milo showed up around noon and started assembling his new computer. The circles around his eyes were so dark, he looked like he wore camo stick.

"How many hours do you normally

sleep?" I asked.

"Two or three."

"Why?"

"It's all my body requires."

He has problems I didn't even want to contemplate.

While he worked on his electronics, I memorized the faces of the criminals entering the country aboard the *Baltic Princess.*

The ferries are cruise ships and offer all the amenities. The larger ones offer nightclubs and big stage-production entertainment. Cabins of various grades. Pubs. Shopping malls. A variety of restaurants, including fine dining. A buffet that offers at least fifty dishes. The main attraction is buying goods at Estonian prices. Alcohol, tobacco and luxury items, especially perfume and makeup, are offered at about half of Finnish rates. The trips are inexpensive, and the usual trip entails groups having parties at sea and drinking themselves into cut-rate comas.

They also transport about a hundred criminals a day from Tallinn into Helsinki. There is no airport-type inspection. The ferries bring thousands of people back and forth between the two cities every day, but have almost no security. The criminals bring drugs, guns, women pressed into prostitution. The border police safeguarding the harbors were recently cut by eleven percent, so they're by and large lawless zones.

We took Milo's Nissan Sentra. Not suitable for Sweetness the baby-faced ogre and a large man on crutches. My plan was to strong-arm a couple pimps, frame them up, stick them in a Finnish jail, and send their hookers back to Estonia.

It was a cold, blustery day, flurries of snow on and off. The full parking lot was filthy gray ice. We parked and leaned against the car. Milo and I smoked. Sweetness injected *nuuska* into the hole in his gum and took a hit from his flask. He offered it to us. We declined.

The ship landed. Passengers disembarked. Most bore heavy loads from shopping in Estonia. Some got in the taxi line. Some made for the tram. They were no good to us. We couldn't shake them down in a crowd. Others made their way to the bar on the other side of the lot to keep the party rolling. I watched faces. For a while, it seemed I would be disappointed. No criminals from the rap jackets appeared. Then finally, when the ship was almost empty, two pimps with four girls headed toward the bar. All were well dressed, young, good-looking.

Sweetness held my arm to keep me from falling, and we met them in the center of the lot. We drew guns. We flashed police cards. The men swore, protested, threatened. The girls stayed quiet. Milo and Sweetness threw the men up against a car, kicked their legs apart, patted them down and took their passports. I took the passports from the girls, wrote down their names, DOBs and passport numbers so I could check up on them later, and gave their passports back to them. Two of them were underage.

Milo took the pimps' flash rolls and handed them to me. I counted out about seven thousand euros, divided it into four, and gave it to the girls. Sweetness translated for me. "Go back to Estonia. Get out of Tallinn. If you don't want to hook anymore, disappear. Get a job. This is your start-up money."

They just stared at me. "Scram!" I shouted and Sweetness repeated, shouted, after me. They ran back to the terminal.

Milo took two pistols out of his coat and held them out to the pimps. They got the idea. Frame-up and jolt in Finnish prison. They refused to touch them.

We pressed Glocks into their chests. I said, "We put them in your hands while you're

alive or after you're dead. Same difference."
Sweetness translated. They took the pistols,
reluctant. We called the border police and
handed the pimps off to them. We helped
the girls. Strong-arm, extortion and frame-
up. It seemed right. Mission accomplished.

12

The next night, I made a call to the police in Estonia, gave them the ID info from the hookers we'd sent back there to get a new lease on life. Three were in the hospital, raped and beaten, used rubbers stuffed in their mouths. One was dead, killed in her apartment. Her hands in a kitchen sink filled with water. A toaster tossed in. Electricity fried her face glossy black. She was fifteen. They had gone straight from the boat to a whore bar hangout. Word of the pimps' arrest made it there within hours. They took the blame. I tried to do good. Their blood was on my hands. It was an experiment I wouldn't try again. Arvid was right, people would be hurt. I was a fool.

Milo finished building his toys. His laptop and the mobile eavesdropping devices' stations were slaved to the computer he had built. By this point, Milo and Sweetness had attached GPS tracking devices to the vehicles of most of the major criminals in Helsinki. We could watch them travel on a computer screen.

The capabilities were limited by range and the number of phones they could monitor at one time, but Milo set up his mobile eavesdropping stations to monitor the phones of criminals on our upcoming heist list. Their calls were recorded, as were their SMS messages. If they were in Russian or Estonian, Sweetness translated. Milo could set his phone up to ring when a particular criminal's phone was in use, handy if we planned to rob said criminal at a particular day and time. The criminals told us where they were, what they had, and when to rob them.

We burgled, heisted, robbed, almost nightly. My role, because of my lack of mobility, was to sit in the car and watch, cell phone in hand, to make sure no one walked in on Milo and Sweetness. Since the B&Es were almost always in the wee hours of the morning, I left after Kate was asleep and was home before she woke. My family life was at least outwardly unaffected. Kate knew. I hid nothing. I sensed her disapproval, but she didn't complain.

During B&Es, Milo mirrored the hard drives from criminals' computers, stole their banking codes, lifted their financial info, inserted viruses so that he could manipulate their computers from his own. We emptied their bank accounts, left them penniless. We continued in this way for weeks. A small fortune accrued.

There were consequences, some foreseen, some unforeseen.

I believed, and at that point rightly so, that no violence would be necessary. These thefts would be seen as betrayals among criminals, who would then go to war because of them. Foreign criminals are reticent to kill each other in Finland. Russian and Estonian criminals prefer to kill each other in their home countries, where corruption is rife, because they have little fear of prosecution, whereas in Finland, they almost certainly will be caught and incarcerated. The Helsinki Homicide history intimidates them. No murder had gone unsolved in Helsinki since 1993.

However, in the criminal world, to come up missing a large quantity of cash or drugs leads to mistrust. Theft isn't an acceptable excuse. Mistrust and uncertainty, like as not, end in homicide. In Tallinn and St. Petersburg, mafia wars raged. The body count, both cities combined, numbered seventeen. And of course, that only counted the bodies that had been found. This was OK with me.

Milo listened to the threats made during their telephone conversations. When the thieves were caught — meaning us — we would be tortured for days, slowly destroyed physically but not allowed to die. They would cut off our dicks, make us eat them. And so on.

If I wanted criminals locked up, either Finnish or foreign, I had various options. Drugs or guns discovered during B&Es could be left in place, or moved to the home of a criminal I had a particular disdain for and used for a frame-up. A simple phone call to the police would lead to an arrest. I had yet to exercise this option. Gangsters running free could be robbed again.

Unforeseen consequences. We did our job so well that we ran Helsinki dope dry. Junkie suicides and pharmacy break-ins reached astronomical proportions. A pharmacist was shot to death.

Milo and Sweetness stopped any pretense of comradeship. Milo called Sweetness "the court jester," "doofus," "clown," "the other half of a halfwit." Sweetness responded with a long list of insults suggesting Milo was effete: "Mary," "sissy," and my favorite, "Miss Froufrou."

On March third, I went to Fazer, the best bakery in Helsinki, and bought the fanciest cake they had. Fazer makes some of the world's best chocolate, and this was Karl Fazer's first shop. He opened it in 1891. I had a coffee and a pastry while I was there, because the back room is built under a dome that echoes. You can eavesdrop on conversations around the room from reflecting voices.

Then on to Alko, the state-run liquor monopoly. I had special-ordered a bottle of Rémy Martin Louis XIII cognac. Price: one thousand five hundred euros. The youngest cognac in the blend is fifty years old. The oldest, about a hundred years. I hid them until the evening, then set them on the table. Kate and I waited until Arvid ambled in. "Happy ninetieth birthday," I said, and we sang to him.

It moved him so much that he almost shed a tear. He opened the cognac box and took out the crystal decanter. "It was the only gift I could find that's older than you," I said. It made him laugh and we passed a pleasant evening.

On March seventh, Anu was christened and officially named. Winter hung on as if it would never end. The temperature was minus ten that day. We asked my brother,

Jari, and his wife, Taina, to be Anu's godparents. They're good people, have two fine boys of their own. I invited Jyri Ivalo to the ceremony, and to our house afterward for coffee and cake. He took it as a sign of respect, a gesture meaning that I wanted to solidify our relationship. He attended and gave Anu the traditional gift of a silver spoon set.

Milo didn't attend. During the ceremony, he was busy black-bagging Jyri's home. He made a mirror copy of Jyri's hard drive and photographed relevant papers. We now had the user names and passwords for all information available to the national chief of police. Milo said Jyri was so fucking stupid he didn't even password protect his home computer. He also planted a MAC-10 and eight balls of heroin and cocaine in various places around the house. More insurance, should Jyri choose to betray me.

On March fifteenth, my sick leave officially ended and I returned to duty, whatever that meant. I supposed I had an office at NBI headquarters with my name on the door. I had no intention of ever going there to find out. The date, the Ides of March, struck me as a harbinger.

13

Wednesday, March seventeenth. It was late morning. I lounged around in bed. Katt had crawled inside my shirt, shredded my chest with his claws and fallen asleep. Anu chewed on the little finger of my left hand. I was doing nothing, thinking nothing. Just existing. My cell phone rang. I reached over, careful not to wake Katt, and took my phone from the nightstand. Jyri Ivalo was calling. To answer or not to answer? I answered.

"Good morning," I said.

"And good morning to you. I have a job for you."

We'd heisted the town dry. I had nothing to do, wanted to do nothing. "I'm covered up in work," I said.

"Lisbet Söderlund was murdered. Her head was sent by mail to the Finnish Somalia Network. It was sent by normal post, packed in Styrofoam peanuts and newspaper. A note composed of letters cut from headlines of a newspaper said 'nigger lover.' Forensics is there now. The case is yours. I need you to go over there right now."

I turned the relevant facts over in my mind, considered the ramifications of taking the case. The Finnish Somalia Network, as the name suggests, is a political group that represents Somali immigrants in Finland. Söderlund was a Swedish-speaking Finn — and so, needless to say, white — politician belonging to the Swedish People's Party. Söderlund was a member of the European Parliament for about a decade. After the 2007 elections she was chosen to be the new minister of immigration and European affairs. She had come to be a symbol in her self-appointed role as a champion of immigrants' rights, far beyond the call of duty of her post. As the government's foremost advocate of immigrants' rights, she became the object of contempt and hatred of the extreme right and racists. For a time, until it was removed because of its illegality, a Facebook page existed called I Would Give Two Years of My Life to Kill Lisbet Söderlund. The page attracted some hundreds of members.

Her head in the mail was an escalation over a previous event involving the Finnish

Somalia Network. During the last holiday season, they were sent a pig's head, along with a note reading "Merry Christmas."

I said, "It's political, it's high-profile. Her assassination will be remembered by history and the eyes of the world will be focused on the investigation. It will draw attention to me that I don't need. It doesn't serve your purposes, either. It's a bad idea."

"It's the most significant murder in the region since Olof Palme was assassinated in 1986. I agree, and I don't want you involved. However, the president does."

"Why the fuck does Tarja Halonen think I should investigate this?"

Jyri sighed, aggravated. "It goes back to the Sufia Elmi murder. Immigrants are going to be up in arms over this. There will be protests, maybe retaliatory crimes. You solved the only case in our history of a high-profile black person's murder. Therefore, Halonen believes your involvement will give the immigrant community confidence that the government is committed to solving Söderlund's murder, and help assuage their anger. And she's probably right."

"Then I suppose there's nothing to be done about it," I said. "The president gets what the president wants." There was no possible argument to the contrary. "But let's do it like this. You say this is a matter of national security and I can't speak to the press until the case is over. You take the limelight and attention away from me."

"That was my plan. The address is Kuninkaantie 38. Let me know what happens. I have to keep the president apprised." He rung off.

I thought about bringing Milo, decided against it. He would talk incessantly and have strong opinions on every detail. I didn't want to hear them. I called Sweetness and he drove me to the crime scene. It had been five weeks since my surgeries. In a couple weeks, after I gained just a little more strength in my knee, I could trade in these crutches for a cane and drive again.

On the way over, I tried to impress the gravity of this case on Sweetness and repeated Jyri's comparison to the murder of Olof Palme.

"Who's he?" Sweetness asked.

I couldn't fucking believe it. Had this boy been to school? Did he spend history classes sniffing glue?

"He was a Swedish prime minister and was assassinated in 1986. He was a harsh critic of both the U.S. and the USSR, among other governments. The murder

136

went unsolved. Conspiracy theorists claim that either the CIA or KGB assassinated him. The point is that these two murders will be compared, and the whole world will be watching to see what happens."

"Are we going to be famous?"

"Probably."

"Cool."

The city streets were still lined with high banks of snow and ice, but we hadn't had much fresh snow for a while, so they were dirty and gray, the edges fringed in black filth.

A large crowd, mostly black people, had formed outside the Finnish Somalia Network. Sweetness pushed our way through and helped me walk until we made it inside. Two crime scene techs and a pathologist were examining Lisbet Söderlund's head. The cardboard box it came in was on another table. I imagined the shock of whoever opened it. Heads are heavy, the package must have generated curiosity. Digging through Styrofoam peanuts and wadded-up newspaper to find a severed head would add a new dimension to anyone's morning. The note was in the box. It looked like the letters were cut out with scissors and stuck to a sheet of printing paper with children's glue stick. "Nigger lover."

Lovely sentiment.

I asked the techs if I could touch Lisbet's head. The pathologist said it was OK. I picked it up by her hair, dark, with a thick shock of gray in the front. She was an attractive woman in her fifties. I spun it in a slow circle. Nothing unusual. Her eyes were closed. I flipped it upside down to look at the decapitation wound. It looked clean and neat, not a hack job. I borrowed a magnifying glass and took a close look at the spine. It was cut, not snapped, and I discerned saw tooth marks. Whoever killed her was well prepared, had the proper tools, took their time and did a good job of it. Sweetness examined the head with me. He asked if he could hold it. I handed it to him. He stared at it long and hard.

The cutting said a great deal about the murder. Few people can remove a head and keep their calm, not make a mess of it. I asked the pathologist if she had any insights she might share with me. Not yet. I'd seen all I needed to and we left.

I went home, fired up the laptop and checked the Internet site of *Helsingin Sanomat,* the nation's leading newspaper. It was already announced that I would lead the investigation. There was an article on me, my strength and determination, taking

138

on the nation's most pressing crime despite recent brain surgery. It cited other cases of international interest I've handled. I turned on the tube. The case — and my face — were on all the news broadcasts. My change of appearance now seemed prescient.

Several articles detailed Lisbet Söderlund's career. They discussed her bravery and resolve, leading a life of public service that culminated in giving up that life for her beliefs. I was more interested in the reader comments on the articles than the articles themselves. They ran about two to one, those glad she was dead, stating that she got what she deserved, and those mourning her loss. The site was supposed to be moderated, but opinions weren't censored. There were already a couple hundred, so I skimmed. "Niggers out. White men unite." "Killer white man's hero and patriot." "Immigrants parasites on the Finnish taxpayer." "Gang rapists."

I checked out some racist sites: the most popular, Finnish Pride, and other lesser ones, some permanent, some on Facebook. The permanent ones can only go so far, but since publicly inciting racial hatred is a crime, many of the more virulent hate tracts are on Facebook. When someone complains and a desist order is issued, the site is closed and reopened under another name until the next complaint and desist order. On these I found talk of murder and creative propaganda. "The spreading nigger cancer." "Pus from the nigger pig order." "Finnish whores breeding mud babies with criminal nigger scum must die."

Sweetness sat beside me and read along with me. Arvid came out with his bag packed. He looked at Sweetness. "Mind giving me a ride home?"

He had originally come for a week and stayed for a month, but he had become part of the family. In the back of my mind, I knew better, but it seemed a permanent arrangement.

"Why so sudden?" I asked.

"It's not sudden. I wore out my welcome long ago."

I started to protest.

He shook his head. "You're back in the spotlight, and having a murderer you arrested as a houseguest will be hard for you to explain away."

He was right. "Thank you for all you've done," I said.

"It was good for me." He extended his hand and I shook it.

"Have you said good-bye to Kate?" I asked.

"She's asleep. Tell her I'll see her again soon. I'll call, and come to your party."

He left. I called Milo. "You hear about the Söderlund murder?" I asked.

"Of course I did. Why didn't I get a look at her fucking head?"

I lied. "Sweetness was here and I was in a hurry. Trust me, before it's over, you'll know more about her head than you can possibly imagine. Right now, I need info. There was a Facebook site dedicated to murdering her. Are you able to hack Facebook and ID the site members?"

"No. And nobody else is, either."

"Haven't you told me any site can be hacked?"

"Give me a year, and if I dedicate my life to it for that time, there's a small possibility I can get in."

"My feeling is this," I said. "Whoever killed her did it for prestige, to brag to his hate buddies, and it's an open secret among that group. We have to find out what circle the killer moved in and apply pressure until somebody rats out the murderer. Our best bet is the members of that site."

"Probably so. We find one, scare the shit out of him, he gives up the others. It might not be that hard."

"Maybe, but until then, we have to do

police grunt work. Plan on devoting your life to looking at rap sheets until something turns up."

I told him I'd call in the morning and rang off.

Next call, Jyri Ivalo. "I need you to use your superpowers to get me sheets on every known racist in Finland. That includes anybody who's committed or been accused of committing a hate crime in the past few years, and the membership rolls of every racist organization in Finland."

"Since you're calling me, apparently you own a fucking phone. Get off your lazy ass and make the calls yourself."

"I would if I could. If I call, racist sympathizers on the force may suppress information or drag their feet. If the national chief of police calls and says jump, they just ask how high."

"Anything else I can do, Your Highness?"

"I'll have to look at thousands of people. If I have paper files, it will be almost impossible. Get it all scanned so I can build a database."

"So you want an army of secretaries."

"No, the president wants the case solved."

"Fair enough. You think it's going to be a tough one?"

"Depends." I explained it to him the way

I put it to Milo. "I need somebody to roll over. I can't do that if I play nice."

"In my experience," he said, "playing nice rarely accomplishes much. You'll start receiving the files tomorrow morning. I'm starting to see your reasoning behind hiring the oaf." He rang off.

14

At five thirty the following morning, I got a call from Colonel Alexander Nilsson of the Finnish Defence Forces. He was instructed to call me because one of his soldiers had been murdered while on guard duty. The killing might be related to the murder of Lisbet Söderlund, and although, as he emphasized, the murder fell under the jurisdiction of the Finnish military police, as a courtesy, I could examine the crime scene if I wished. It was in a wooded training area near Vantaa. I thanked him and told him I would be there as soon as possible.

I called both Milo and Sweetness. Milo because he might be of some value, as despite his annoying ego and overconfidence he was an astute detective, and because I hadn't taken him along to examine Lisbet Söderlund's head, he would be justifiably offended if I excluded him again. Sweetness, because hiking through the deep snow in the forest might prove impossible on crutches, and I might need him to more or less carry me.

Army conscription takes place twice a year, in January and July, but conservatives in the government are determined that Finland will join NATO. As such, they were holding maneuvers that they ordinarily wouldn't, to prove their zeal to other countries. There are several large training areas around Finland. That the maneuvers were being conducted near Helsinki was good fortune.

We took my Saab. When we arrived at the training area, military police at checkpoints guided us in the right directions, and we arrived about seven thirty. Colonel Nilsson greeted us, then stepped out of our way, indicating that he would leave us to our own devices.

The sun had been up for only an hour and cast long shadows. The crime scene techs were done with the body and combing the surrounding area for evidence. Snow is a double-edged sword in a homicide investigation. Fresh snow is every cop's investigative dream. Even the smallest objects, unless white themselves, leap out and announce themselves. Trampled snow, the policeman's nightmare.

This area, in a stand of birch, had been stamped on by hundreds of soldiers for the past couple days. The snow was gray, most of it mashed up, and full of pockets created by footprints beside the main walking paths. Even a detailed, thorough search would yield only the most obvious evidence. A squad had occupied this small area. After the murder, they had been ordered to vacate it, with the exception of a soldier who was on guard duty when the attack occurred. Only their empty tents and a rifle rack made of crossed tree branches remained. Two rifles remained on the rack.

This was all new to Sweetness. He'd exercised his right to choose civil service over military duty. After he graduated from high school, while most of his male classmates were performing their mandatory nine months in the army, he spent a year working in a kindergarten. He preferred crayons to hand grenades, even if it meant an additional three months' service for being — in the eyes of most men — a sissy. The victim was a young man with his throat cut. The corpse seemed to mesmerize Sweetness. He couldn't stop staring at it.

Milo knelt down and examined the wound. "Nothing special," he said. "The throat was cut from left to right with a single motion. The weapon had a long, sharp blade. He was probably grabbed from behind, and it was all over before he knew it even happened."

The remaining soldier sat on the trunk of a felled tree, chain-smoking. He flicked ashes and put extinguished cigarettes in his coat pocket, so as not to further contaminate the crime scene.

I was right. Sweetness had to pretty much carry me around. It was a bit on the humiliating side. The military pathologist told me to have a look at the body. His preliminary examination was complete. The murder was self-explanatory, he said. The victim had been placed faceup on a stretcher. His arms crossed. They were only waiting for me to view him before taking him away. The cut across his throat was deep, nearly to his spine. His tongue flopped out through the laceration.

I sat down on the tree trunk beside the soldier, introduced myself and the others. Milo and Sweetness stood in front of us, listening.

"What's your name," I asked.

"Harri."

"Can you relax and tell me what happened? We're not here to judge or blame you for anything. We just want to find out who did this."

We all lit cigarettes except for Sweetness. He hit his flask and injected *nuuska.*

Harri pointed at the corpse. "Me and Rami were taking our turn at guard duty. Everybody else was asleep in their tents. I got tased and everything after that is blurry. I guess I got hit with a lot of volts and a couple times, because the burns on my back and neck are bad. When I got my senses back, I was duct-taped to a tree, and Rami was dead."

He pointed at the tree. Much of the tape was still hanging from it in tatters, where he'd been found and cut free.

"My mouth was taped shut. Two men were dressed in black military clothing and balaclavas, but they were definitely black. I could tell from the areas around their eyes. The squad's rifles were stacked on the rack. They packed all they could into duffel bags. There are two left, so they took ten. One of them got up close so our faces almost touched. He had a thick accent and really bad grammar, but I guess he knew it and spoke slow to make sure I understood. He said, 'I allow you to live so you will deliver this message. We pray that Allah gives us the strength to use these weapons to do His will.' Then they just walked off, and about half an hour later, somebody got up to take a piss and found us."

"What kind of unit are you in?" Milo asked.

"A mortar squad."

Milo walked over to the rack and picked up one of the two remaining rifles, gave it a once-over. "This is an Rk 95 Tp," he said. "Most people just call it the M95."

A Kalashnikov AK-47-style rifle made by Sako, the Finnish arms manufacturer. "And the significance is what?" I asked.

"There aren't that many of them. A lot of them went to mortar units. Most soldiers are still carrying the old Rk 62. That means if we come up with a suspect in possession of an M95, as compared to an Rk 62, the odds of him having stolen it from here are quite high."

I asked Harri, "Is there anything else you think I should know?"

He shook his head. "Just that I feel responsible. Safeguarding this area was my duty, and now Rami is dead."

He wasn't still a kid. His uniform was almost new. He's probably only been in the army since the last cycle, in January.

"I've been a cop for twenty-two years," I said, "and my experience is that when a man turns predator and you're the target, you don't know you're being hunted and you don't stand a chance. There was nothing you could do."

His face said my pep talk, which was a simple truth, made him feel no better.

A reasonable assumption was that black immigrants had taken the murder of Lisbet Söderlund as a declaration of war and begun arming themselves. Somalis have a semblance of political organization and gangs that occasionally commit violent race crimes against whites, and vice versa, so their desire to acquire arms wasn't entirely surprising, especially given the threats and violent rhetoric that were now daily directed against them. But blacks armed with AK-47s would terrify many Finns. The extremist Real Finns preached the inevitability of a race war between Finns and immigrants. I had an ominous gut suspicion that it might be coming true.

This lent a new sense of urgency to the Söderlund murder, and I wondered how many would die before I solved it.

15

It was almost noon by the time we got back to Helsinki. I figured Jyri Ivalo would have put out the nationwide call to police forces, and also to SUPO, requesting that all information concerning racists be sent to me. I asked Milo to come over to my house so we could start the sorting process and begin looking for potential suspects in the murder of Lisbet Söderlund.

We stopped at his house, around the corner from mine, to pick up his laptop, and set up shop on my dining room table. My Outlook in-box was jammed and more e-mails were coming in by the minute. We networked our computers and set up a database. In 1977, the differences between towns, cities and municipalities were removed, and we now have a hundred and nine municipalities. This makes things a little easier in a nationwide search, as previously there were between four and five hundred towns that we would have to deal with separately.

We created a method, tried to sort groups with racist beliefs from moderate to extreme, and then members of those groups from moderate to extreme, red flagging any person accused or convicted of committing a race crime. Sweetness passed the time looking over our shoulders, trying to learn police work. He played errand boy, brought us coffee. Kate ignored us so we could work in peace.

Real Finns, despite the anti-immigrant stance of many of its members, was the most moderate of our target groups, and also the hardest to investigate. In the 2008 municipal elections, they took around a hundred fifty thousand votes. Those records are of course sealed. They have their own magazine, published every three weeks. The circulation is twenty-five thousand. There were insufficient grounds to subpoena the list of recipients. The list would have been valuable, as this murder was political, and I could have cross-checked against known racists. They had around five hundred municipal councillors in office, but in fact, only seven or eight people were the true organizers of the movement. Most of them were from the other end of the country, but

I could at least have them questioned. Not that I thought that any of them were likely murderers, but their known associates could have been.

I got an e-mail that contained compiled statistics of crimes committed by and against foreigners. It interested me.

Two point five percent of the population is foreign or naturalized.

Foreigners commit nine percent of all crime.

Foreigners commit twenty-seven percent of all rapes.

The majority of crimes by foreigners are committed by Estonians and Russians, not by people of color — blacks, Turks, Gypsies, etc. — who bear the brunt of racial hatred. Turks, for instance, have a near monopoly on the pizza shop industry. Their storefront windows are frequently smashed out.

Race crimes against foreigners were up twenty percent in 2009, and numbered over a thousand.

Race crimes against Swedish-speaking Finns were on the rise. Nationalist Finns were beating up other Finns for speaking their mother tongue.

The organization Finnish Pride ranks high in virulence. The seven-hundred-member organization is xenophobic, anti-immigrant, and many members hold neo-Nazi beliefs, including Holocaust denial. Many were also Real Finns, had political aspirations, and had toned down their rhetoric as those aspirations increased. Still, it was poisonous. Some had been involved in race crimes. I thought I could get their membership role subpoenaed.

Neo-Nazis were well organized in many cities. They had several dozen full-time activists and large memberships, especially in the Joensuu area. The neo-Nazi demographic had changed. The movement was growing by leaps and bounds among university students. Academics had joined them. They were discussing forming their own political party, which requires five thousand signatures, and were close to getting them. They embraced the swastika. That kind of confidence speaks for itself. "If a party's leader wants to be a führer, then so what?" said a leading neo-Nazi.

The police and department of corrections began sending records of those convicted of hate crimes in batches, usually sorted by municipality but not by crime. There were thousands. Each one had to be looked at individually.

SUPO had jackets on hundreds of hate activists. The sheer number of them intimidated me. Even if I assembled a large team of investigators, how could we possibly look at them all in sufficient depth?

Each so-called hate crime had to be considered. Was the crime committed because of a person's ethnicity, or was that incidental? For instance, the beating of bus drivers. Some black bus and taxi drivers had been beaten, but so had white ones. Those crimes weren't necessarily racially motivated. Legally, however, if the victim had been attacked by a person or persons of a different ethnicity than his or her own, they were almost always considered hate crimes. There were no instances of racially motivated decapitation or anything like it. As the hours passed, neither Milo nor I saw anything that might make any individual stand out enough to be considered a suspect.

At about five p.m., news of the murdered soldier and the theft of the AK-47 rifles hit the Internet. Every newspaper pumped it up on its Internet page. Someone had taken a close-up of Rami, the boy whose throat was cut, his tongue flopped through the incision. The image captured the nation. And young Harri had told — or sold — his story.

Real Finns Party leader Topi Ruutio remained silent on the subject.

Roope Malinen wrote a hate tract gloating over his prescience. His every word and thought had been vindicated. His blog received fifty-four thousand hits that day. A new record for him.

Hate coalesced.

Anti-foreigner animosity roared through the media. In the moderated newspaper commentary sites, readers voiced their opinions following the articles on the soldier's murder. All blacks should be immediately deported, stripped of Finnish citizenship if they possessed it. We took them into this country out of the goodness of our hearts and now they waged jihad against us. Blacks and Muslims should be placed in concentration camps. Finnish Gypsies are scum. What the fuck kind of Gypsies take up residency and don't move around nomad style. Finnish Gypsies go back and forth from Sweden to Finland on the ferry, claim residency in both countries, and draw on the welfare systems of both. Finland was a white man's paradise, now destroyed by the black man's seed. If they won't go home and stay there, drive the Gypsy beggars into the sea.

Un-moderated bloggers and social networking sites ran wild. Sterilize blacks and Arabs to prevent the dilution of Finnish blood. The mud people make mud babies. Tar babies. Burn mosques. Fuck Lisbet Söderlund, the dead nigger dick licker got what she deserved. Niggers destroy order, breed chaos.

Finland roiled with hatred. Race crime threats abounded.

In Joensuu, five neo-Nazis wearing bulletproof vests, presumably in case police shot them with rubber bullets to quell the riot, attacked a left-wing candidate and her supporters during a speech. The anonymity of social networking generated straight talk. Facebook pages sprang up and discussed the pros and cons of sending the niggers back to Africa versus feeding them to gas chambers and ovens. They discussed eliminating more politicians from the left with bullets.

Plus, there were two more junkie suicides and one more pharmacy robbery.

I got a call from SUPO. The country's major newspapers had all received a fax. It appeared constructed in the same way as the note accompanying Lisbet Söderlund's severed head. It read, "For every crime committed by blacks against whites, we will kill a nigger in retribution."

They sent me a scan. The angles at which the letters had been cut out looked like work by the same hand.

Milo shook his head, disgusted. "You know, they brought a lot of this on themselves."

If I'd felt emotions, I don't know if I would have been angry, or laughed at his ignorance, or both.

"And why," I asked, "do you think that might be?"

"Because our Muslim immigrants breed like rats, and they make little or no attempt to assimilate. Suomen Islamilainen Puolue — the Muslim political party — calls for Sharia law. With the rise of political Islam, what many term Islamofascism, by which fundamentalist Muslims pervert their religion and attempt to build a worldwide caliphate and impose Sharia law on all of us, it's our natural inclination to be opposed to it."

It had become our habit to speak English when Kate was present, out of politeness. Her ears perked up.

Milo continued, "If they succeeded, they would take away all our freedoms, force us to change our way of life, take away our right to free speech and all the basic rights of women, such as education. Do you want Kate to be forced to wear a veil? Our criminal justice system would no longer include fair trials and our limbs would be amputated as punishments. Those possibilities scare a few people."

"And after a few generations," Kate said, "all the little Finnish babies would be chocolate colored instead of Aryan snow-white."

Milo hesitated, he knew he couldn't give a non-racist answer. "I like Finland as it is. Finnish people living the Finnish way."

"Milo," Kate said, "for a bright guy, you can be a real fucking dipshit."

She turned on the radio so she could tune him out. I was glad she didn't understand the words to the song that was playing. It was a hit from the early nineties, when Somali immigrants first began arriving, by Irwin Goodman. It was about getting rid of the mud people and licorice clowns.

16

The following day, Sweetness and I set out early and went to post offices to see if any postal workers remembered the person who mailed the box that contained Lisbet Söderlund's head. The box was uninsured and required no receipt signature, so we knew only, from the ink stamp, that it was mailed in Helsinki. We began at the neighborhood post office that services Kuninkaantie 38 and so the Finnish Somalia Network. No luck.

However, after receiving the pig's head in the mail just before Christmas, a worker there invented a Finnish pseudonym and set up a Hotmail account. Fearing a more violent attack, she joined every anti-immigrant Facebook group she could find, including I Would Give Two Years of My Life to Kill Lisbet Söderlund, in order to gather evidence in the event that the Finnish Somalia Network was targeted again.

She printed out all the posts daily. She made me copies of all of them. A valuable gift for the investigation. No criminal justice authorities had done the same.

We moved on to the main post office downtown and got a copy of the work roster for March sixteenth, the day the package was mailed. The place is a madhouse, always busy. We interviewed every worker who had been on duty that day in person if they were on-site, or by telephone if they weren't. Too many customers. Just faceless cattle in long lines. We got zilch.

We stepped outside, I lit a smoke and my phone rang. The caller was Detective Sergeant Saska Lindgren, from Helsinki Homicide. He was at a crime scene investigating the murder of two black men. A note at the scene, the letters clipped and glued to a sheet of printing paper, read, "For Rami Sipilä," the soldier whose throat had been cut the day before.

I'd consulted with Saska before, and he's sharp, considered one of the best policemen in the nation.

The murder scene was in East Helsinki, a district with a bad reputation and a high immigrant population. Sweetness grew up there, and so knows the area like the back of his hand. We headed over. It was a little below zero, but we had twelve hours of sunlight a day now.

We arrived at a single-family home with a yard. There weren't many around here. The area is dominated by apartment buildings, most of them built in the 1970s, when functionality was the style and ugly was the result. The area was cordoned off. Television news vans and reporters lined the street. They waved microphones and shouted. Saska and I exchanged greetings and ignored them. I introduced Sweetness. He usually takes people aback because of his massive size, but Saska appeared not to notice. Half-Gypsy, he's taken a lot of racial shit in his life, and I've noticed that he's non-judgmental about people, or at least reserves judgment until given cause to form one. "Have a look," he said.

Two young black men had been poisoned in a makeshift gas chamber. They were taken to their garage and made to lie on the floor under the rear of a station wagon. A blanket was draped over the exhaust pipe, the bumper and the men. The engine was left running until they died of carbon monoxide poisoning and the car ran out of gas.

"They're brothers," Saska said, "Dalmar and Korfa Farah. Somalis. They lived here

162

with their mother and sister. Their father was killed in Somalia. I don't know anything about them yet."

Milo, Saska and I went to the front lawn to smoke. Sweetness tagged along, looking back over his shoulder. Corpses have a strange effect on him. I notice he can't stop staring at them. "I called you because of the note," Saska said. "Some blacks and whites are playing tit for tat. White racists murdered Lisbet Sönderlund. Angry blacks stole rifles and murdered a soldier. The same racists probably killed these guys. It won't stop here. Reprisals are inevitable. I'd like for us to stay in touch, share relevant information."

"Yeah," I said, "let's do that. This country is already in a hate frenzy. It could lead to places we never thought possible."

He ground out his cigarette. "That's my fear."

"Where are the mother and sister?" I asked.

"Hiding in the house. They're afraid to come out. They were asleep, didn't hear a thing."

"How's the Saukko case going?" I ask.

Maybe I shouldn't have asked. The case is a kidnap-murder involving Finland's richest family. It went wrong. Almost a year has passed and it's gone unsolved. A source of embarrassment. The case belongs to Saska.

"It isn't going," he said. "I'm going to have to start from the beginning, re-read every document and report. I've missed something."

I tried to commiserate. "The Söderlund case isn't going any better."

Of course, I'd been working on my case less than a week, and he was coming up on a year, but he knew I was just trying to be politic. "Let me know when you get some background on those guys, will you?"

"Yeah," he said. Sweetness knocked reporters out of my way so I could get through them on crutches, and we left.

17

I went to physical therapy, got my knee tortured and went home. The surgery and therapy worked, though. My knee hadn't had this much mobility since I got shot, and its range of motion increased daily. Pretty soon, I could say good-bye to the crutches.

Sweetness and I tossed Lisbet's home and office. I went through her correspondence, looked for threatening letters. Her purse was missing, and her mobile as well. Her office was neat, orderly. It spoke of efficiency. I noted that there were no personal touches. No photographs. No awards or signs of achievement, and given her success, she must have received many. This told me she was private and modest.

Having processed hundreds or thousands of crime scenes, I've been in countless Finnish homes, and what has always struck me the most is their similarity. Almost everyone uses the same styles of cups and saucers, furniture. Most homes are nearly inter-changeable, and hers was the same. I noted that she liked plants. There were almost two dozen plants of various kinds throughout her apartment. And she had a large temperature-controlled fish tank. The fish looked exotic — no goldfish — so I assumed they brought her pleasure. I fed them, and made a note to have them removed and cared for.

Her wardrobe was commonplace business-woman boring. She had workout clothes. Shoes for aerobics and jogging. She took care of her physique. As with her office, she had few knickknacks or photos displayed. She believed in functionality.

Once home, I got her phone records, called every person she had called or had called her for the past couple months. She was single, had no romantic interests. Her work dominated her life. She was well liked, hadn't spoken of threats or enemies, other than the website that wished her dead. She didn't take it seriously. I spoke to her col-leagues. They told me the same. She was last seen leaving work on the day of her death at about six p.m.

She used public transportation, owned no car. Officers were posted at the bus and tram stops she normally used. For several days, every person who used those stops would be queried and asked if they remembered seeing her. But if they didn't, it meant nothing. Helsinki public transportation passengers seldom look around, avoid eye contact.

Milo and I worked from our own apartments. There was no need for us to be in the same building. Our computers were networked, the database set up, and we had split up the files to sort through them. We could videoconference with webcams if needed. I sat for a long time, thinking about a practical way to search for her body. In this large, metropolitan area, I could think of none. I could only hope that it turned up in a Dumpster or some such thing. In Helsinki, at this time of year, anyone with half a brain would weigh her down and give her a burial at sea.

"It's good to see you being a detective again, instead of a thief," Kate said.

"I like it better, too," I said. And I did. I had no moral problem with taking down dope dealers. I was just more at home in an old and comfortable role. I couldn't focus on the mountain of material detailing every racist in Finland, though. Kate and Aino talked on the phone. Their friendship was deepening. I kept picturing Aino's blue eyes and blond hair. The way her sweater accented her breasts. Thoughts of fucking her were far more interesting than those of Lisbet Söderlund's decapitated head. I couldn't work until Kate hung up the phone and ended their conversation.

I sat at the table with my laptop for two more days. Katt slept in my lap or sat on my shoulder, dug his claws into my neck. The pain kept my mind from wandering. Yes, going through this morass of material, routine police investigation, and following up on hundreds of most likely possibilities would eventually lead to Lisbet's murderer, but how long would it take? People were dying daily. Routine work wouldn't do. I went through the Facebook pages given to me by the woman at the Finnish Somalia Network. I felt the answer lay inside them.

I joined every Finnish social networking hate group I could find. One, Auttakaamme Maahanmuuttajarikolliset Takaisin Kotiin — Let's Help Send the Immigrant Criminals Back Home — had over twenty-six thousand members. Another needle in a haystack. But the group on Facebook that directly threatened her, I Would Give Two Years of My Life to Kill Lisbet Söderlund, had a member with a user name and picture of Heinrich Himmler who on multiple occasions expressed a desire to send all of Finland's black immigrants to the gas chamber. And now two brothers were dead, murdered in a homemade gas chamber. Many members of the group went by Nazi user names: Goering, Ilse Koch, Joseph Goebbels, Adolf Eichmann, but the tone of the rhetoric of the member that called himself Himmler told me he was the man I wanted to locate. If he hadn't himself murdered Lisbet Söderlund, I thought he knew who did. But how would I find him?

Saska Lindgren called me. The murdered young men were known low-level drug dealers. They sold everything from hashish to heroin. Their bank cards indicated they had taken a train to Turku on the day of their murder. Bought one-way tickets. They ate at McDonald's in Turku. That was the last trace of them.

I watched the news. Assaults and beatings, white and black youth gang clashes. Attacks on apostate Finnish white women, converted to Islam because of their marriages to Muslims. Their mixed-race babies spat upon in their carriages. Close-ups of tears streaming into veils. The media used to bury these stories, often not reporting gang fights. Police often broke up clashes but made no arrests. A concerted group effort to hide racial tensions. Now the media is minimalizing and downplaying them, reporting them in the most neutral of tones, but they can't be ignored.

On Friday night we pulled a heist, B&Eed both ends of a drug deal after the fact. It didn't make sense to me, as we were in the public eye, but Jyri insisted, told me I'd be glad I did it. It was odd, though, because we were to steal over half a million euros, plus the drugs, then take them to another address and hide them in the apartment. We exercised extreme caution. Milo had their cars GPS tracked, their phones tapped. We drove around for an hour first, made sure we weren't tailed. It went off without a hitch.

We went for a drink after the heist, as had become our habit. As we sipped our beers, paranoia and mistrust finally boiled over. One gangster finally killed another, stabbed him to death and left him in the trunk of his car. Milo learned of it when the killer called his boss to tell him what he had done. If a mafia war started and Helsinki Homicide investigated, everything would unravel and the trail would lead back to us. I decided we had to dispose of the body in the morning.

18

We met outside my apartment building at seven a.m. The media had honored Jyri's wishes that they deal with him, as I dealt with the investigation and matters of national security. There were no reporters outside my home, no tagalongs as we drove around the city. The only calls and e-mails were from news agencies outside Finland, and I ignored them.

Body disposal fell into the category of subjects off-limits in front of Kate. My keen intuition told me she wouldn't approve.

The thermometer was on the plus side now, and I noted that the series of grimy icebergs lining the street was shrinking. Not the result of global warming, but of spring. The first tiny buds were appearing on the trees.

We went to a kiosk around the corner and got coffee. A small high table meant for standing rather than sitting made for a good spot to converse, sotto voce.

"Ideas?" I asked.

"I ain't cuttin' up no fuckin' bodies," Sweetness said.

Milo and I agreed. None of us had the stomach for something that disgusting.

"The head and hands have to go," Milo said. "I made a thermite bomb last night, and I have enough gunpowder from my reloading outfit to pack his mouth. We can put the bomb in his hands. It will burn at about three thousand degrees. His hands will disappear, along with most of the rest of him when the bomb goes off. When the gunpowder ignites, his teeth will be reduced to powder. The car will explode and there won't be anything left but a smoking black frame."

"How did you make the bomb?" Sweetness asked.

"It's mostly just aluminum and iron oxides. Stuff you can get at hardware stores. I had some lying around."

"Isn't there a less dramatic way to get rid of him?" I asked. "We just need to make him disappear. No body, no murder."

Sweetness takes some *nuuska* and jams it into his gum. "Dad worked as a welder at the shipyards. He got me a job there one summer. They got barrels of acid in shipping containers. They're for industry, like paper and nuclear factories. We could just stick him in one and seal him up."

Milo's eyes sunk deeper into their black pits as he pondered. "Do you remember what kinds of acid?"

"Hydrochloric and hydrofluoric are two that I remember."

Milo half grinned. The less-than-gentle giant knew such big words.

I tried to sip my coffee. It was still too scalding to drink. "There are workers around the shipyard. And we have to dump out part of the barrel so he fits in it. So we need an empty barrel. And those barrels are big and heavy. We need something to pick it up with so we can tip the full barrel and pour part of the acid into the empty one. And we need protective clothing, head to toe, in case we slosh it and get it on us. The concept is right, but we can't do all that at the shipyards."

Milo slapped the table, slopped everyone's coffee and burned Sweetness's fingers. "Goddamn it," he said.

Milo laughed. "I got it. Filippov Construction. Everything we need is there, and we have the privacy."

Filippov Construction had been closed since Arvid murdered its owner, Ivan Filippov, a few weeks ago, and his wife, Iisa Filippov, disappeared. The business specialized in industrial waste disposal. Work there had ceased, the site stood empty.

"How do you know they have acid, and the right kind?" I asked.

"I read their inventory." He looked at Sweetness and, for the sake of one-upmanship, because Sweetness knew big words, said, "I remember almost everything I read. They have sulfuric acid. It's not as effective as hydrochloric or hydrofluoric for our purposes. The body will take some weeks to dissolve. It will turn to goo, then viscous liquid, and eventually just be gone. Not even a trace of DNA will be left."

"And the other problems I mentioned?" I asked.

"There are six two-hundred-twenty-gallon barrels of sulfuric acid, and four empty barrels designed for storage. Closed-loop portable tanks that meet safety requirements. Reusable three-eighths-inch-thick stainless steel construction with extra protection for valves and fittings. Minimum one-hundred-psi pressure design meant to be handled with a forklift, so Sweetness can use one and tip the forks to pour acid from one container to another. And of course, all the protective clothing is there, too."

"Maybe after, we should take the car to the woods and burn it up with your bomb," Sweetness said.

"I can't picture the place re-opening within the next few weeks while the gangster decomposes to goop," I said. "Sounds like a plan."

I drove for the first time since my surgeries. It was no problem. My knee was more than strong enough to depress the pedals without bad pain. We took my Saab and located the Ford with the body in the trunk. Milo has master keys that fit almost any vehicle. He and Sweetness took it — I was trying to make them spend more time together — and I followed them to Filippov Construction, in an industrial park in Vantaa.

Milo picked the gate lock. Sweetness hit his flask. The area was surrounded with a heavy chain-link fence topped with two strands of barbed wire and lined on the inside with corrugated green fiberglass, so no one could see in.

We drove into a spacious asphalt lot filled with small-grade heavy equipment. A couple Bobcat dozers, a cherry picker, a forklift and other machines, along with industrial waste, yet to be disposed of, and containers to hold it. I stayed outside in the morning sunshine while Milo and Sweetness suited up.

They came out looking like mad scientists from a bad sci-fi movie, covered head to toe in everything from respirators and goggles to rubber aprons. They carried tools to open the barrels and set to work. They decided the best method was to dump the gangster in the empty barrel and then cover him over with acid.

They backed his Ford up to the tank and popped the trunk. Lifting him out was no easy task. He had been dead just long enough for rigor mortis to hit its peak. He was ironing-board stiff. Luck was with them, though, because he had lain in the trunk in a near fetal position. Otherwise, they would have had to break nearly every bone in his body to make him flexible enough to fit in the barrel. Luckily as well, Sweetness was with us. He lifted the gangster by himself from an awkward position, using only his arms, as there was no way to angle himself so he could get his back into it. Milo and I never could have accomplished it.

They opened the barrel of acid and the empty barrel, too. Sweetness fired up the forklift and, slow but sure, began drizzling sulfuric onto the gangster.

I wore no protection and leaned against my Saab, a good thirty-five yards away, to keep from breathing the fumes.

"I hope I haven't interrupted you at an inopportune moment," a quiet voice said to me.

It scared the shit out of me and I jumped. Sweetness must have seen sudden movement in his peripheral vision. He kept cool and eased the forks back, stopped pouring. He gestured with a black-rubber-glove-covered hand to Milo and pointed in my direction. They came toward us, taking off their headgear and gloves as they moved. I saw Milo rip a hole in the back of his paper suit, and saw what was coming.

The man beside me waited without speaking. He wore a black cloth bomber jacket, jeans and boots. His head was shaved. He had large and ornate French paratrooper wings tattooed on the sides of his head. He looked like the devil incarnate.

Milo smiled as he neared, and reached into the hole in his paper suit. He drew down on Satan, but the man produced his pistol so fast that it seemed magical. "Deputy Dawg," he said, "will never out-draw Yosemite Sam."

Milo scowled and lowered his Glock, beaten. "Who are they?"

"American cartoon characters. I have a great affection for classic American cartoons. My favorites are Wile E. Coyote and Road Runner." Satan paused. "I don't think guns are necessary," he said. "Shall we put them away?" He made the first gesture by replacing his Beretta in the holster at the small of his back.

"Who are *you?*" I asked.

"A man of wealth and taste." It was as if he'd read my mind and thought about Satan and came up with the Stones riff.

He introduced himself as Adrien Moreau. He was a French policeman, Finnish by birth, but spent fifteen years in the French Foreign Legion, hence his name. He'd exercised his right as a Legionnaire and taken French citizenship and identity. He asked if we could have a private conversation while my colleagues finished disposing of the body in the barrel of acid, and I agreed.

The looks on their faces said they didn't like missing out on the conversation with this interesting new character, but they respected my wishes and went back to sloshing acid without complaint.

"I believe you and I could have a mutually beneficial relationship," Moreau said.

"And how might that be?"

He tried not to laugh, but the upturned corners of his mouth reflected amusement. "I've been following you for some days. I watched you commit a robbery last night. You looked like a bizarre version of the Three Stooges turned criminal. Your trigger-happy friend fumbled with lock picks. You stood nearby on crutches, and the big man reminded me of the monster Grendel from the Beowulf legend. I could help you improve your technique in this regard, but I have a more specific and practical matter in mind."

"Under whose authority?"

"I am employed by Direction Générale de la Sécurité Extérieure. The DGSE is France's external intelligence agency. It functions under the direction of the French ministry of defense and works in conjunction with the Central Directorate of Interior Intelligence, DCRI, in providing intelligence and national security, including paramilitary and counterintelligence operations abroad. I am a superintendent in the Action Division. We are responsible for planning and performing clandestine operations and other security-related operations."

Moreau was about my age, perhaps a little older. He spoke perfect Finnish, but as if it was long out of use. It lent credence to his story. Despite his jacket, I saw that his carriage and muscular frame suggested a lifetime spent in the military. His manner was easygoing and confident in a way that was somehow reassuring. He spoke in a blithe way that suggested he was a man at peace with himself. His appearance and manner were at such odds with each other that it disconcerted. In every way, he seemed an unusual man.

"And this specific and practical matter you spoke of?"

"My hope is that once you have concluded your business here, we could perhaps have coffee and discuss it in leisure and at length."

I lit a cigarette, considered it. He made me a little too comfortable. That might lead to a lack of wariness. Always a mistake. "At the risk of seeming rude, I'd prefer if you began with a concise explanation."

His smile said it bothered him not at all. "As I am sure you will recall, the Saukko family had two children abducted last year. The ransom was paid as per instructions. The daughter was released, but shot in the head by a sniper three days later. The son never resurfaced. I am in Finland at the request of the father of the family, who has connections with the French government via the armaments industry. He suspected the boy might have escaped and run to Switzerland, where the stepmother now resides, as it is possible they had a, shall we say, ongoing Oedipal relationship. The Finnish police were reticent to search Switzerland, and the task fell to me. The son is not in Switzerland. He has ties to racist groups in Finland, as does the father, but the father had a falling-out with them because they believed his monetary contributions not sufficient to prove his devotion to the cause of hate, and hence a possible reason for the kidnapping. I am at once to search for the son and assess the racist situation in the Nordic area. The racists may have performed the kidnapping. If so, I will return the son and money to the father, and mete out justice to the murderers of the daughter."

" 'Mete out justice'?"

"In the biblical, eye-for-an-eye manner."

"And how do our interests coincide?"

"I search for racists who shot a woman's head off with a sniper rifle. You search for racists who cut a woman's head off. Few people in Finland are capable of such violence, especially for relatively unemotional motives such as money and politics. It is entirely likely that we're looking for the same man or men."

It was possible, even plausible. "Not coffee today," I said. "I need to burn a car at the moment. I'm having a party tomorrow. Come to my house around four, we'll discuss it then."

"Very well," he said. He extended his hand and we shook.

He turned and began to walk away.

I called after him. "My wife will be there. Don't mention this body dump in front of her. And bring me a present."

He turned and grinned. "A present. Why a present?"

"Because it's my party, and I like presents."

"And you can cry if you want to?"

"You never know," I said.

He slipped out through the fence gate, chuckling.

I had the sneaking feeling that I was about to make some kind of Faustian bargain.

Milo and Sweetness followed me in the now liquefying gangster's Ford. I headed into the countryside, took a back road into the forest and drove without aim. The roads weren't plowed, and I slipped and slid, but they were passable. At last, a road ended and opened up into a field with nothing in sight.

I told Milo to drive to the middle of the field or until the car got stuck, whichever came first, and blow it up. He had made a thick, crude fuse, much like for a big firecracker, and said it was a rough guess, but we had about five minutes after we lit it. He and Sweetness looped it around inside the car so snow wouldn't snuff it out, then pulled off the license plate, lit the fuse and ran.

I couldn't go into the field because of my crutches, so I turned the car around and waited for them. Another small post-surgery revelation. My conscience was gone, or nearly so. A gangster died because of my actions, we desecrated his body, and it meant less than nothing to me. And yet another revelation came to me. The famous Helsinki Homicide record. No unsolved homicides since 1993. A quick tally. They've investigated around twenty thousand deaths since then, but not one unsolved murder. *Not even one?*

I'd bet good money I'm not the first cop to make a body disappear. Further, I think maybe there may be a tradition of employing a small group to extort, strong-arm, or disappear people on occasion.

Or maybe not cops, but criminals allowed to act with limited impunity for the occasional favor. Rationale for said revelation: Jyri never mentioned the possibility that there would be no black-ops unit if I died on the operating table. He had no concern about the surgery. My conclusion: because he didn't care if I lived or died. He had someone else already chosen in the event that I shuffled off this mortal coil. None of this bothered me, but it interested me. It was something to look into. Collecting skank on Jyri Ivalo had become a hobby with me.

They ran across the field. To fuck with them, I made them buckle their seat belts: for safety, I said, before I would move. Then I hit the gas and we bolted. After a couple minutes, at a safe distance, we stopped to watch. The thermite lit up the day sky with a crack, and then the gas tank went with a boom. Flame and dirty smoke shot into the air. This job was becoming more interesting with every passing day.

19

Milo and Sweetness were curious about what Moreau wanted. I told them he would stop by tomorrow and explain it himself. I dropped them off and went shopping. Milo and Sweetness had complained that I demanded that they be subdued in their appearance and actions, so as to not attract attention to themselves. They chided me because my own appearance, limp and facial scar, made me stand out in a big way. I would set an example. Tomorrow was my "Welcome back to the world" party, an ideal time to unveil the new and improved, surgically enhanced and nondescript Kari Vaara. I bought a cane. Plain and cheap. My knee surgery was so successful that I wouldn't need it long.

Then I shopped for hair color. I had no idea the selection would be so large. Should I enhance my natural hair color, go subtle or dramatic? My natural color was now gray, and my hair has the feel and consistency of squirrel fur. I hadn't had it cut in two months and had gone from a close-cropped military look to unkempt and messy. Kate pestered me to do something about it. Tomorrow, she would see why I hadn't.

Afterward, I went home. Kate had come to accept that she must endure nine months of motherhood leave. The Finnish lesson was finally drilled into her: We do things a certain way because we've always done them a certain way, and we do them in that certain way because it's the way we've always done them. Attempts to change our accepted norms breed disdain.

Without the sociopaths that work for me lurking about, home was tranquil. Kate seemed content. She seldom asked about my work, but when she did, sometimes she called me Michael Corleone. She didn't smile when she said it. We got along well, though. My practiced smile carried me through the sham of emotion. We sat together for a while, talked the banalities of couples with a newborn, and then I told her I had to go back to researching my murder case.

I considered the Finnish French Foreign Legionnaire turned French policeman and figure of international intrigue and wondered if he was all that he said he was. I would grill him tomorrow. He spoke of a mutually beneficial relationship. I had all the resources of government at my disposal. What did he think he could bring to the table to entice me? I agreed with him, though. There weren't many people capable of calculated assassinations, far fewer with the skill and wherewithal to successfully execute them without being apprehended. And in a country with a population of only five and a half million, the pool of qualified suspects was small. We might very well have been looking for the same man.

I needed to acquaint myself with the Saukko kidnapping-murder. Saska Lindgren was in charge. I called him and explained that it was possible our cases intersected, and asked him to send me some files so I could get a handle on the Saukko case. While I waited, I skimmed the Internet, looked at almost year-old newspaper articles, and got a take on the press's views of the crimes. After reading Saska's files, I felt I had a reasonable picture of the sequence of events and the people involved in them.

Veikko Saukko: captain of industry, alcoholic, lunatic, art collector.

His collection includes more than five hundred pieces. Many are Finnish, but there are also works by Chagall, Dalí and Picasso, among many notable others. His estranged wife fled the country and is wanted for tax evasion, among other crimes.

Born in Helsinki on 22 April, 1941, into a prestigious and politically influential family, Saukko went his own way early and began building his career as a magazine publisher, specializing in scandal sheets. Launched in 1959, his best-known and most successful publication was *Be Happy* magazine. It focused on so-called human interest journalism. In the 1960s and 1970s, *Be Happy* achieved overwhelming popularity with indecent gossip about celebrities. The articles were sometimes fact, sometimes fiction, often a combination of the two.

Suicides, divorces, destroyed careers. *Be Happy* paid well for skank, and the skank was good. A teen idol gets tossed from a nightclub, the doorman sells skank. Teen gets tossed in drunk tank, cops snap skank photos. Said teen gets fucked in ass in drunk tank, guard sells skank story for big money. Such hard-core skank is never stated outright, but implied in a house style that always leaves the message crystal clear. A politician fucks a minor. *Be Happy.* A tough guy movie star sips fruity rum drinks in fruity swish bar. Finland knows. *Be Happy.*

Saukko got stinking rich because, better than anyone, he understood the Finnish zeitgeist. No one must try to rise above the masses. To do so is more than to risk contempt, but abject hatred. No one must try to accomplish something special. No one must be unique or gifted. The very attempt at virtuosity of any kind suggests that a person thinks he's better than others. Frequently heard: *"Kuka sekin luulee olevansa?"* — Who does he think he is?

Yet, when an individual does succeed, he or she is beloved by the nation until that fateful day when, as they almost always do, the celebrity suffers a humiliation, either large or small. And then, proven right in their contemptuous beliefs, the nation rejoices. How Finns love to see the mighty brought low. How we hate people for trying to make the most of their talents. "Who did he think he was?" We know. He is, and always was, good only for skank.

In fact, stars are often OK with this, because after being reduced to skank fodder, they often turn it around and use it to rejuvenate their careers. Finnish stars turn alkie, dry out or claim to, then tell their sob stories to the media. A celebration of humiliation. Public applause and adoration. A common ploy. The price paid for the admission that they were no one after all. Dumped wives of stars do the same, rebuild their lives and start their own careers based on *Oprah*-type "Boo hoo hoo but aren't I brave?" crap.

Finland was Skank Exultant. Finland was Skank Ecstatic. Daddy Saukko grew Skank Rich. Daddy Saukko is a good businessman and realized the limitations of wealth that can be accrued with Finnish skank, because it has no international interest. He sold *Be Happy* to a publishing conglomerate for hundreds of millions of Finnish marks, the equivalent of around a hundred million U.S. dollars.

Saukko invested part of this fortune in art and constructed his luxurious Villa Veikko, a mansion on a large tract of land fronted by the sea. Beside Villa Veikko is the family museum run by their foundation. Saukko diversified his corporation, Ilmarinen Sisu, and invested in the machine tool, ice cutter and paper industries, all of which flourished. After some years, Saukko foresaw the future. He divested his interests in the aforementioned industries and reinvested in securities and quantitative investment, the arms industries of various countries, investment fund management, technology and media.

He believed the future of fortune building lay in technology and media manipulation, and arming Third World nations for small wars. He bought heavily into Nokia and Sanoma. As of today, his corporation controls nearly a quarter of Sanoma Corporation, his interest in it is valued at more than three hundred million euros. Forbes recently named him the five hundred and fifty-sixth richest man in the world, and the richest man in Finland, with investments in around fifty nations totaling 1.7 billion dollars.

Saukko comes from a long line of landed gentry. His father, Juho Saukko, was a lawyer, a politician and foreign minister who negotiated with the Soviet Union prior to the Second World War. During the Continuation War, Juho headed the Prisoner of War Office. After the war, in 1946, Juho was tried in a court-martial, but the charges were dropped. Post-war, he was a CEO or officer in several corporations, and headed the supervisory board in one of the nation's largest banks. He also presided over the Finnish American Association. Juho was a devout racist, an admirer of Henry Ford's opinions on race, in agreement with Nazi beliefs about race, and was fascinated by eugenics and the concept of Finnish racial purity.

According to his children, Veikko Saukko was an abused child, both physically and psychologically. His father was stern, critical, and impossible to please. Saukko himself is profane, cruel and violence-prone, known for striking employees without provocation, and his enjoyment of drunken bar brawls has resulted in him being locked up in drunk tanks in various cities around the world. He smokes three packs of cigarettes a day, has been an alcoholic since an early age, and even today, at age sixty-nine, habitually drinks four gin and tonics per hour. Several years ago, he spent three months in jail for drunk driving. His known associates include influential racists and a number of mafiosi from various countries. Saukko inherited his father's racist views, and has no qualms about expressing them, either privately or publicly.

Saukko has a complex personality. Despite the above, adjectives used by friends and acquaintances to describe him include: charming, sensitive, droll, profound, open, timid, dreadfully shy, and a sophisticated and entertaining conversationalist. He's also one of Finland's most skilled open-sea yachtsmen. A picture emerges of a manic-depressive, even schizophrenic man.

His first wife, Anna-Leena, bore him five

children, three girls and two boys. He divorced her suddenly and without apparent provocation after thirty-six years of marriage. Three weeks later, he married Tuula Jaatinen, age twenty-six. Tuula was made director of the Saukko art foundation and began embezzling right away. Over the course of two years, she absconded with, at best estimation, 10.2 million euros. She was tried and convicted for embezzlement, but disappeared rather than serve her three-year prison sentence.

Currently, Tuula lives in Switzerland. Finnish authorities requested that the Swiss return her to Finland, but the Swiss prevented the extradition. She's wanted by Interpol, as requested by Finnish officials. Her location in Switzerland is known to Finnish police and press. Interestingly, she's still married to Veikko Saukko, even though, aside from the embezzlement described above, she's rumored to have been the lover of Veikko's son, Antti — also married with children — throughout the course of her marriage to Veikko.

Veikko's first wife, Anna-Leena, is in deep legal difficulties herself. As former director of the foundation, she was accused, via multiple lawsuits, of misappropriation of funds. In 2007, she declared bankruptcy, after being court-ordered to return 17.5 million euros to the foundation.

The five Saukko children all live at home, with the exceptions of Kaarina, deceased, and Antti, missing for nearly a year, in the mansion that stands two hundred meters behind the museum. Veikko insists that he stays surrounded by his children, whether single or married, and that they reside in the mansion. He enforces this through financial blackmail. His children are:

SON JANNE — member of corporation's board of directors. Age thirty-seven.

SON ANTTI — member of corporation's board of directors, but a less-than-serious person. He prefers yachting, snowboarding and surfing to working. Married. Father of four. Age thirty-nine.

DAUGHTER KAARINA — party girl. A Finnish Paris Hilton. She would have been age thirty-two.

DAUGHTER JOHANNA — married and mother of two. Lutheran priest. Age forty-two.

DAUGHTER PAULIINA — the troubled child. Engaged in prostitution as a minor, presumably to antagonize her father and defy him to publish her antics in *Be Happy*. Finally he did, after which she gave up prostitution. She did, however, become a heroin addict. She's now a recluse, seldom if ever leaves the mansion, and is addicted to methadone. Age forty-four.

His children despise their father and have made no effort, not even in the media, to pretend otherwise. Some of them believe he has a narcissistic personality disorder, and a total inability to feel empathy. They complain that he subjects them to late-night drunken monologues, and pits them against one another by constantly changing the provisions of their inheritances.

Veikko, for many years, put off choosing which of his children would take over the family business. Finally, apparently no believer in primogeniture and for reasons incomprehensible, Veikko chose Antti, the prodigal son, and transferred all power in the family company to him without informing his other children. This despite that Antti had for years called his father an asshole, a human monster, the worst sort of pig, and probably fucked his wife on a regular basis.

The children had formerly felt a solidarity. When Antti was chosen, that solidarity disappeared, and they began slagging one another in the media. Janne was sacked from his position on the board of directors. Each of the other children had held honorary positions in the corporation, to provide them with exorbitant incomes. They were also let go, and are now at the complete mercy of their father for income. This situation continued until August 2008 when Antti — in the same way that he was appointed, and equally unfathomably — was removed as chairman of the board, and complete control over the company reverted back to Veikko. This remained the family dynamic for the better part of a year.

Then in 2009, on May twenty-seventh, almost a year ago, two of the Veikko children, Antti and Kaarina, were kidnapped from the family home, and at the same time, paintings Veikko had recently acquired, by Cézanne, Lautrec and Mary Cassatt, were stolen. As the children came and went without notice for lengths of time, and although the theft of the paintings was realized the following day, the absence of Antti and Kaarina wasn't taken seriously by either the family or authorities for three days, and then only because they couldn't be located for questioning concerning the theft.

These two members of the Saukko industrial dynasty were kidnapped and held hostage for ransom. A kidnapping of such magnitude from such a powerful family was unprecedented in Finland. A long and complicated course of events unfolded.

May thirtieth: The brother and sister were declared by the police to be considered missing persons. However, the police didn't immediately assume kidnapping to be the reason for their disappearance.

June second: A ransom e-mail was sent, in English, to the family matriarch, Anna-Leena. It read:

Sender: Charles Brown
Sent: 2. June 9:47
To: Anna-Leena@gmail.com

Mrs Saukko.
Please note that this email concerns your daughter K. and son A. who we will from now on call merchandise.

Merchandise is in good shape, healthy and so on. There are certain rules to obey in order to make us deliver Merchandise back to you.

1. No contact to any authorities! Not to any third parties, etc.
2. 0400769062, your mobile, should

be on and ready to receive further instructions.

3. price will be paid in cash, used notes only. No new notes.

4. procedure. we instruct the payment delivery, you leave the cash there, and we will secure the payment. Please note that we will also check payment for any surveillance devices, etc. When payment is secured merchandise will be released. If surveillance devices are used to follow us, we will begin amputating the limbs of the merchandise, tourniquets used to prevent death, and will continue to do so until we have identified all surveillance devices and surveillance is discontinued.

5. ANY fault or trick, and you will never hear from us or the Merchandise again.

6. Price shall be 10,000,000 paid in euros, 6 in 500 notes, 2 in 200 notes, and 2 in 100 notes.

7. payment will be packed in two sports bags, instructions concerning delivery will be given later. Deliverer needs your mobile phone, a gps map and a car.

I noted that this was inconsistent with demand number two, as they had already stated that they had the mobile phone number. Were they careless, or working to give the impression of carelessness?

8. answer this email and let us know when you are ready to deliver.

Merchandise is out of the country of the moment.

You have now 12 hours to answer this email.

XM

Anna-Leena called her former husband, Veikko. He went against the kidnappers' wishes and called the police immediately. He also made the requested initial contact by e-mail. The police considered whether the kidnapping was legitimate, and if so, whether the kidnappers' use of English was a reasonable indication that Kaarina and Antti were truly now outside of Finland. Veikko Saukko made it clear that the police were to investigate, but should they fail to recover his children, the ransom would be paid according to the kidnappers' instructions, whatever their demands might be.

Over the coming days, hundreds of police

took part in the investigation, headed by the Helsinki Police Department, and the minister of the interior was kept informed of every action and development. The police had two significant clues.

1. Although the stolen paintings were valuable, artwork of far greater value was left untouched. Presumably, the kidnappings were perpetrated at the same time that the art thefts occurred. The stolen paintings were recently acquired and as yet uninsured. This displayed knowledge that insurance companies will continue investigations for years, long after police have thrown in the towel, thus demonstrating that the kidnappers and thieves were experienced and knowledgeable criminals. They devoted a great deal of attention to doing their homework, somehow accessing privileged information about which paintings were most prudent to steal.

2. The villa's security system was disabled. Investigation of the company that installed the villa's system revealed that the files detailing the Saukko security system were accessed on Sunday the ninth of May, almost three weeks prior to the crime. A great deal of time, thought and preparation went into the crime beforehand. The security company had noticed no signs of break-

in, a slick job, and the files were user name and password protected, so the criminals were technologically savvy. These were people to be reckoned with.

No effort or expense was spared. The kidnapping sparked a major operation involving the police, the Defence Forces, the Border Guard, and Finnish Customs.

June fifth: The small airfield at Kiikala was shut down to aid in the investigation of the kidnapping. Under the pretense of an exercise, civil aviation assisted police authorities by restricting the use of the airspace between Helsinki and Turku for nearly the next two weeks. Radio-controlled pilotless planes from the Finnish Defence Forces' base in Niinisalo were taken to Kiikala for use in discreet reconnaissance work. Equipped with powerful cameras, the diminutive unmanned aircraft were able to transmit high-resolution images from an altitude of two thousand meters or even higher. Police refrained from the use of traditional aircraft and helicopters in the search, for fear that they would alert the kidnappers and the result would have fatal consequences for the Saukko siblings.

On June ninth, authorities give up on the search from the sky. The Kiikala airfield was re-opened.

There was a gap in Saska's notes here. Saska doesn't make such mistakes. I took it that there was information he wished to hold back for reasons of his own, and he deemed that information irrelevant to my investigation. I trusted his judgment. I wouldn't question it.

June tenth: Veikko Saukko e-mailed the kidnappers and informed them that he had raised the cash and was prepared to make the exchange. He was given the following instructions. He was to park a car at one p.m. in a specific space in a parking garage in Helsinki. The bags of cash were to be in the trunk, the key taped under the rear bumper. An orange traffic cone should be placed in the adjacent space to the right to reserve it.

The kidnappers chose their parking spot well. Only one security camera picked up on them, and they were obviously disguised in wigs, sunglasses and false facial hair. In front sat a driver. In the rear, Kaarina Saukko and a man holding a surgical saw in one hand and a scalpel in the other. Kaarina's eyes and mouth were covered by tape. The driver moved the cone, parked, and transferred the sports bags of money to the front seat of his own car. They left the garage and were monitored by UAV aircraft until they entered a forested area near Turku under tree cover, out of view.

Twenty minutes later, the car exploded. Kaarina Saukko had been moved a safe distance from the vehicle, bound hand and foot but uninjured. The man in the rear of the vehicle beside her was discovered to be a mannequin fastened upright in the car. The lone kidnapper appeared to have left the scene of the explosion on a small motorcycle, probably a dirt bike. Kaarina reported that during the time she had spent abducted, she received good treatment in the basement of a home. During transport, her eyes were covered, but it had been a long journey. She also stated that she and Antti had been separated, and that she never saw him during the time of her abduction.

That evening, on the bank of the Aurajoki River, which runs through Turku and into the sea, the body of Jussi Kosonen was found. He had been murdered by a single gunshot to the back of the head. His body was near a speedboat that he had purchased in Turku, with cash, three days previously. The money and paintings were nowhere to be found. Multiple sets of Kosonen's fingerprints were found in the wreckage of the burnt-out car used in the crime. Fingerprints also proved Kaarina had been held hostage in the basement of his home, which he had soundproofed.

Investigation into Jussi Kosonen raised many questions but answered none. He had been a forty-four-year-old corporate lawyer employed by the University of Turku. Kosonen had studied in Turku and Stockholm and spoke several languages fluently. His profile bore no resemblance to that of a high-stakes kidnapper, and according to his employer, he didn't have money difficulties.

The Turku branch of the Social Democratic Party was flabbergasted by the revelation. Kosonen had stood as a Social Democratic candidate in the municipal elections in the autumn of the previous year. He lost the election. Kosonen was the father of three and in the process of getting a divorce. He was supposedly tending to the children while his wife was on a two-week vacation in Tenerife. The children hadn't attended school during that time. Kosonen had informed the school that he had decided to take the children and join his wife on holiday, in an apparent attempt at reconciliation.

Antti Saukko wasn't returned to his family and remains missing, raising the question of whether he took part in the crime or was murdered by his kidnappers. Kaarina

Saukko was assassinated with a high-powered rifle while strolling outside the family villa three days after her release. The bullet entered one temple, passed through her head, and exited out the other side. The bullet was never recovered. However, the wound channel suggested the bullet had been fired from a .308 caliber rifle with a full metal jacket. A simulation of the sniping, guesswork at best, and a calculation of trajectory based on it indicated that the shot had been fired from about seven hundred fifty meters.

If the killer were proficient enough, he could have fired a sniper rifle with the intent of passing the round through her head without hitting hard bone, and he would know what lay beyond her, and could have intended to ensure that the bullet came to rest in a place from which it would be impossible to locate and recover. For instance, in a patch of grassy lawn, where the bullet would bury itself and be impossible to find, or into the sea. Such an assassination would require a marksman of significant prowess.

No progress whatsoever has been made in the case since her murder.

I got an e-mail from Milo. He spoke with Ismo, the pathologist, about Lisbet Söderlund's head. Ismo hates to be called and asked for synopses of autopsies. He expects a detective either to take enough interest to show up at the autopsy, or wait for the transcription, which may take months. I'll send him a bottle of scotch. Grumpy though he was, he informed Milo that Lisbet was dead when she was decapitated. Her neck was severed through to the spine with a single ring-like cut, and then her spine was severed with a fine-toothed electric saw. The act was smooth enough to be worthy of a talented butcher. More expertise and professionalism. My talk with Moreau tomorrow seemed of growing importance.

20

Sunday, March twenty-eighth. The day of my "Welcome back to the world" party. It's a misnomer. I was only in the hospital for a short time after my surgeries and became semi-active almost immediately upon returning home. I had a feeling it was really Milo's party. It was his idea, and he decided the guest list. Just me, Kate, Sweetness, Arvid, and himself. Every time the subject came up — and he often mentioned it — he radiated exuberance. He set the time at three o'clock. I had invited Moreau to come at four, so Milo could unveil whatever treasures he had for us to behold.

Kate and I spent the morning in bed. We made love for the first time since Anu was born. Technically speaking, she had been able to have sex for a couple weeks, but she was nervous about it and we waited. Afterward, we lounged with Anu and Katt and talked. Just small talk. Her lack of work and reticence on both our parts to discuss mine limited our topics of discussion. But having both an infant and a kitten — both were growing fast — filled the void.

Around noon, the door buzzer rang. Kate sighed. "None of them would dare show up this early, would they?" she asked.

"No," I said, "it's something else."

Two deliverymen brought in massive boxes. I asked the men to open the boxes for me, and they unveiled a massive man's chair covered in soft blue-gray fabric, a stool, and a reading lamp.

Kate watched, astonished and amused, as I directed where they should be placed. I gave them a generous tip, and the deliverymen left.

I plunked down in the chair and put my feet up. The seat was four feet wide, had plenty of room for both of us. I patted the seat beside me. "Try it out," I said.

She sat snuggled up next to me and interlaced her feet with mine on the stool. She asked, "So, what prompted this?"

The dining and living room are one open space. Only a low dais separates the two rooms. Our couch faces away from the dining room toward a big flat-screen TV and entertainment center. A built-in bookcase composes the wall to the right. Besides these things, the living room contained only a couple chairs for guests. Usually, Kate sat on the couch beside me or lay on it in front of me, with my arm draped over her, especially if we were watching TV.

"It's just something I've never had but always wanted," I said. "I spend a lot of time at home. I can sit here with my laptop if I'm working, and it's big enough for the whole family to sit in together if we like."

She nodded her head in agreement. "Pretty cool," she said. "It's really high-quality. How much did it cost?"

I said, "Don't ask."

She didn't, just buried her face deep in my shoulder for a little post-coital dozing. Katt sat in my lap and purred. Anu lay in her crib, and I heard barely audible snoring. She was having a nap, and I did the same.

Around one, I woke and told Kate I had to get ready for the party, and that Moreau, a French policeman, would be coming at four for a brief discussion about the murder investigation.

"It takes you ten minutes to shower and shave," she said.

"I have primping to do," I said.

It was a strange word for her to hear come out of my mouth as a way of describing my ablutions.

" 'Primping'?"

"Yes, primping."

She scooted over so I could get up. "Far be it from me to interfere. By all means, primp."

I went to the bathroom, locked the door, and set about dyeing my hair. After I was done and it was dry, I realized I didn't own a comb, hadn't in over twenty years. My hair hadn't been long enough to warrant one. It was still pretty short, though, and I just sort of mussed it forward with my fingers and thought it looked all right.

I examined myself in the mirror. I was thirteen pounds lighter from not working out, was down to a hundred and eighty, but had no fat on me. My scar was gone. My hair was auburn. I wasn't sure who I was looking at.

I realized that my vision seemed sharper. Everything seemed sharper. Memories seemed muddled compared to my current perceptions. I felt my thinking had become more focused, more insightful. I wondered if the empty space in my skull was filling in, if I would regain my emotions anytime in the near future.

I walked out of the bathroom naked, without my crutches, forced myself not to limp, and found Kate in the kitchen, drinking a glass of water. She dropped it, and it shattered on the floor. She stammered out, "Oh my God."

"Is that a good or bad 'Oh my God'?" I asked.

Her stare was intense and she couldn't seem to stop. "I don't know. In my mind, I see my husband of three months ago, but I look at the man in front of me, and the two don't equate. You look like a different person. And ten years younger."

I flashed my practiced smile and started picking up shards of glass. "That was my intention."

Arvid showed up half an hour early. I had dressed in case someone did just that, put on jeans and a new sweater. He took off his shoes in the foyer, pulled a small gift-wrapped box out of his jacket pocket and looked me up and down. "Nice job," he said, "you're almost unrecognizable."

"Good," I said.

"Sorry to come early," he said, "but I need a few minutes to talk to you."

He walked into the living room. "Goddamn. Nice chair."

"Try it out," I said.

Arvid plunked into the chair and put his feet up.

Kate came in and moved to sit with us. I gave her a look that said we needed a moment, and asked her if she would be kind enough to make some coffee. She gave us privacy.

"Here." He handed me the box. "Open it."

I sat down on the couch at an angle from him and tore off the wrapping paper to find an old and worn hinged box. Inside the box was his Winter War medal. Only a few men left alive had earned one, and God knows how much blood was spilled and suffering endured to earn it.

I held it, turned it over in my hands, admired it, put it back in its box and tried to hand it back to him. "I'm honored, but I can't accept this."

His hands were on the chair's armrests, and he refused to lift a hand to take it back.

"I'm giving this to you, and telling you something now, because I can take advantage of your post-surgery condition. You're emotionless, and you won't protest or argue with me. It's true, that medal was my most prized possession, but it's symbolic of something else. I've seen a lawyer, had the papers drawn up, and made you my heir."

This confused me. "Why?"

"I have no family. My friends are all dead and buried. I just turned ninety. I needed to make a decision or when I die, my estate will go to the government, and they'll spend the majority of it on things I disapprove of. Your position is tenuous. You may not be a policeman much longer. My home is spacious and comfortable, a good place to raise a family, and it's paid for. Plus, I have considerable assets. They'll make you safe from the vagaries of political misfortunes."

"But still, why me and why now?"

"Don't make me uncomfortable. You know why. You're a good boy, I've enjoyed your friendship, and you've made me feel a part of your family. Why now? I'm ninety fucking years old. Don't be thick."

I sat for a moment, overwhelmed. I searched for words, but only found two. "Thank you."

He smiled. "You're welcome. Let's not speak of it again."

We enjoyed a comfortable silence. Kate didn't bring coffee. She had lived in Finland long enough to know we wanted peace, not caffeine.

The buzzer rang again. Milo and Sweetness arrived at the same time. They were weighed down with packages. They looked at me and gawked. Sweetness dropped his armload of gift-wrapped boxes. "Damn, *pomo,*" he said. "You look great, but I wouldn't have even recognized you."

"You two laughed at me when I told you to keep a low profile, so I decided to set an example."

"You did a good job," Milo said. "You look so . . . young."

They had to make three trips to get all the boxes into the apartment, and they piled them in the middle of the living room. They kicked off their boots and found places to sit. Arvid kept my new chair. Kate sat on the couch beside me, and Sweetness on the other side of her. Milo swept the house for electronic surveillance, then sat on the floor, in the middle of his treasure trove.

"Well, Kari," he said, "welcome back to the world."

"I never left it."

"You came close enough."

"Not really."

Milo had on an exquisite new leather jacket. Must have cost a fortune. Our talk about anonymity must not have quite taken hold. I didn't comment on it.

"Does anyone notice anything unusual about this coat?" he asked.

No one did, and he kept waiting, so finally

Kate said, "Well, it's very nice," so he would get on with it.

"It's custom-made to conceal this," Milo said, and drew an antique sawed-off double-barreled shotgun from a soft and thin leather holster sewn into the coat's lining. He handed it to me. It was the most beautiful firearm I'd ever seen.

"It's a 10-gauge Colt Model 1878 Hammer shotgun. When it first came out, it was the most expensive gun Colt made. It's a side lock, double-hammer, double-trigger gun with brown Damascus pattern barrels, blue trigger guard and break lever."

I looked it up and down. It was covered in gorgeous floral scroll engravings. The barrels extended just past the fore-end, and the buttstock had been cut down to the pistol grip with such skill that it looked as if it had been designed that way. The modifications to the checkered walnut and ebony were the work of a master craftsman.

"When it was manufactured, it had thirty-two-inch barrels," Milo said. "Before it was turned into this hand cannon."

I passed it around so the others could admire it. "Can it handle modern ammunition?" I asked.

"No. It would explode like a grenade. I got everything so I can make shells just like they were in the 1880s. The same gunpowder, paper shell casings, wadding. Everything is perfect. Cut down like this, the shot pattern is wide enough to take out a room full of men with a single blast if I let both barrels go. But you have to be careful. If you shot it with one hand, instead of keeping the other on top of it for ballast, the gun would rear up and backward, maybe break your wrist and split your head open."

My thoughts turned back to his apartment and his hand reloading outfit. When I was there once, he was loading shotgun shells with fléchettes, razor-sharp darts, instead of normal lead shot. In this weapon, they would cut a room full of men into fish bait. "Load it with rock salt," I said. "That thing's a menace. Even rock salt will tear through clothes and scorch the hide off somebody. Use birdshot at most."

The dark circles around his eyes furrowed and he wanted to argue, but he didn't want to ruin our fun today. Arvid handed it back to him. He put it back in his jacket and hung it up in the closet.

He came back and handed each of us a passbook and paperwork from a bank in Bermuda. Arvid, Kate, and Anu got them, too. "We all have offshore accounts now," he said. "I put seventy-five thousand in each of them to start. Go to your accounts on-line and change your passwords and you're all set."

I thought Kate might be distressed by killing machines and repositories for stolen money. Instead, she seemed fascinated. "Why Bermuda?" she asked.

"Because I didn't have to leave the country," Milo said. "Opening an offshore account in Bermuda doesn't require you to be present at the bank. An account can be opened by mail."

Milo was on a roll and about to embark on one of his biblical length rants, citing the mandate I had given him to be in charge of acquisitions. Kate escaped, went to the kitchen to cut a cake she had made for the party. He ranted and words zinged through my head: window mounts, suction cups on glass, audio surveillance, wireless video, wireless audio, Bluetooth stealthware.

Just when I thought he would never stop, he asked us to look out the window. He pointed out two vehicles. "Those are ours," he said. The first was a Crown Victoria.

I felt my eyes roll. "Oh, Milo, not a Crown Vic."

The cliché of all law enforcement vehicles. Aside from actually being used by many American police departments, Crown Vics

217

have also appeared in dozens or even hundreds of films and TV shows as cop cars. It's an embarrassment.

Milo laughed so hard that he held his belly, trying to stop. "I know," he said, "but I couldn't help myself. This isn't just any Crown Vic. This is the Ford Crown Victoria Police Interceptor. It's got heavy-duty parts and two hundred and fifty horses under the hood, plus a higher idle, and the transmission has more aggressive shift points and is built for firmer and harder shifts. For God's sake, it's even got Kevlar-lined doors for gunfights. It's only got twenty thousand miles on it, and I got it for four thousand euros. Besides, I'm going to be the one driving it most of the time."

I conceded defeat.

"Maybe everybody will like this one better." He handed Sweetness a set of keys. "You look like Gulliver in Lilliput driving around in your little worn-out shitbox."

He pointed down at a good-looking SUV. "Behold the 2008 Jeep Wrangler Unlimited Sahara. It's got four-wheel drive and four doors — I thought that would be handy for putting in Anu's car seat — and an extra-wide wheelbase. And it's a convertible, fun with summer coming on. It's high on safety features: an electronic stability program and seat-mounted side air bags, a navigation system and Sirius satellite radio. And a My-GIG multimedia entertainment system to make driving fun."

Sweetness crossed his arms and furrowed his brow, flummoxed, as if this were some sort of trick, afraid Milo was teasing him. "This is for me?"

"It belongs to the group, but I bought it for you to keep and be the primary driver, and I registered it under your name. So yeah, it's yours."

Still perplexed, he said, "Thank you."

Milo didn't acknowledge him. He turned toward me. "You like your Saab, so I didn't get you a vehicle," and then to Kate, "and I didn't know if you drive or want a car."

"I have a license, but I just use public transportation, since you really don't need a car in Helsinki anyway." She pointed at the small mountain of packages that still lay on the floor. "Should we take a break for cake and coffee?"

I said, "That guy I mentioned will be here in a little while. Let's wait on him."

Milo's face said *Goody goody gumdrop, now my circus won't have an intermission.* Four big and heavy boxes were in a stack. "These are care packages for all of us guys. They're all the same."

"Me too?" Arvid asked.

"Of course."

"Why?"

"You're one of us, one of the team."

Arvid smiled at him as he would a child. "I am? How so?"

"Kari said you're our bookkeeper. Anyway, we all think of you as one of the team."

Arvid's smile widened, indulgent, and he nodded assent. "All right. Then I'm one of the team."

Milo paused, cautious. I saw him consider whether he should vocalize something. "I've been thinking. The team should have a name."

When I felt emotions, I would have teased him without mercy. "What name do you suggest?"

"How about . . ." He paused again and pretended like he hadn't been thinking about it. "The New Untouchables. Or, since Arvid is one of us, the New Veterans."

Arvid looked at me. This last was an insult to him and the men who had suffered through the ordeal he and his brothers in arms had experienced. I felt certain he was considering ripping off Milo's head and shitting down his neck.

I tried to lighten the situation. "Remember the movie *Fight Club*?" I asked.

"Yeah," Milo said, and his tone told me he wondered where I was going with this.

"The first rule of Fight Club was 'Nobody talks about Fight Club.' What if they hadn't given Fight Club a name? It would have been *really* hard to talk about. The first rule of . . . is nobody talks about . . . Maybe we shouldn't have a name, so no one can talk about us. To name a thing is to define it. If we have no name, in a sense, we don't exist."

It was the truth and he realized it as such. "You're right, forget the name thing. It was a stupid idea."

I glanced at Arvid. He was placated.

"Would everyone like to open their boxes, or should I just open one and show you everything?"

"Arvid, Sweetness, and you need to take them home," I said. "Maybe it's better if you just open mine."

I checked the time. Four o'clock. Moreau wasn't the kind of man who would be late. He was a spook. He was watching us from somewhere, waiting for us to finish so he wouldn't intrude.

Milo took each item out, one by one, and gave us a running commentary on each as he did so. Our knives: "The Spyderco Delica Black Blade. Overall length, seven

221

and one eighth inches. Closed, four and a quarter inches. Blade length, two and seven eighths inches. The Delica4 has a non-reflective VG-10 flat saberground blade coated with black titanium carbon nitride."

He went on citing its virtues from memory, basically reciting the entire manual. He did the same with: night-vision goggles, Nomex coveralls, shoulder holsters, belt holsters, ankle holsters, gloves, Kevlar masks, zip-lock plastic handcuffs, bulletproof vests, utility belts, glass cutters, lock picks, electronic pick guns, key wax, ear protection, Maglites, saps that were extendable steel rods, Kevlar vests, Tasers, flash-bang stun grenades, double magazine pouches and spare magazines, Gemtech silencers that would render our weapons so quiet that we would only hear the clatter of our automatics' slides recycling, and in discussing these he hinted at the weapons that we would receive to go with them. In his mind, setting us up, sitting us on pins and needles of anticipation.

Kate tried to escape to be with Anu, but he called her back. Milo had a small box for her containing a Taser and pepper spray, because it's a dangerous world out there. The others were bored enough to cut their own throats with their Spyderco Delica

Black Blades, but I was fascinated. Each item had been chosen with utmost care. I had never seen such a display, such an act of love. This team was the most important thing that had ever happened — and possibly ever would happen — to him.

Next came our weapons. First, we all got new .45 caliber 1911 Colts with three-inch barrels. Backup guns to be worn in ankle holsters.

He handed all us men boxes. Sweetness got the biggest. He asked, "Should we take turns, or all open them at the same time?"

Milo didn't hesitate. "We have to take turns. I'll go first." He had bought himself a serious collector's item, a .45 Colt 1911, manufactured in 1918, with black walnut grips and engraving patterns on the frame and slide.

"How much did that cost?" I asked.

"Five thousand U.S. dollars."

We had a lot of money, but still. "Isn't that a little extravagant?"

He took umbrage. "When you asked me to join this team, I told you I wanted certain weapons and you agreed. Additionally, you appointed me armorer, and I did the job as I best saw fit."

Maybe it was a lapse from brain surgery.

"Sorry, but I don't recall naming you armorer."

"Before you went to the hospital, you told me to get the stuff we needed. Same difference."

I couldn't bring myself to destroy his day in the sun. "You're right. So I did. But one question. If you actually have to shoot someone with it in a situation that doesn't conform to law enforcement conditions to justify it, you have to get rid of it. It would be a shame to throw that down a sewer drain."

He beamed, triumphant. "I bought extra barrels and firing pins by the box. I just replace them and keep the pistol. In fact, I've already swapped them out, just in case. Barrels in bulk are sixty bucks apiece. And I got five thousand rounds of two-hundred-and-thirty-grain ammo."

Again, I conceded.

"Open yours," he said.

Guns don't interest me, and I'm a lousy shot. I opened the box. I admitted though, it was a pretty pistol.

Milo said, "It's a .45 Colt 1911 Gold Cup National Match. A competition-grade target pistol. I hoped it might encourage you to practice."

It won't. "Thank you," I said.

Sweetness opened his without asking. An unblemished walnut presentation case was inside the wrapping. He opened it. It was a two-gun U.S. 82nd Airborne commemorative set, adorned with 82nd Airborne symbols. The slides had never even been pulled. They were something truly special.

"You're ambidextrous," Milo said. "So I got you a pair. I'll teach you to shoot, and you can blaze away with both hands simultaneously."

Tears shone in the corners of Sweetness's eyes.

Arvid sat in my armchair with his box in his lap. Milo motioned for him to open it. Inside was the pistol Arvid had used to murder Ivan Filippov, that he had executed so many men with in the Second World War, that his father had carried before him in the Civil War almost a hundred years ago, and the only possession Arvid had that belonged to his father before him. He looked at it with disbelief, dumbstruck.

"I stole it from the evidence room," Milo said.

Arvid just looked at him, expressionless, for a good two minutes without speaking. Milo began to squirm, afraid he had done something wrong.

"You have my sincere gratitude," Arvid said.

"Sir," Milo said, "you are most welcome."

I saw then that Milo's motive for all this, the extravagance, the silliness of it, his obsession with our black-ops unit, was one that I doubted he himself was aware of. This wasn't about fighting crime for him. He wanted to be part of a family. My family. For all of us in this room to be one big happy family. He wanted our love. It was unfortunate. It was something none of us were capable of giving him.

Unbelievably, there was still a big pile of boxes, but Kate couldn't stand it anymore. "I'm dying for a piece of cake," she said.

21

Kate set the table and went to the kitchen. As if on cue, the door buzzer rang and I let Moreau in. He was forty-five minutes late. I recognized in him a man who was never late, never disorganized, always prepared, always in control. He had indeed been watching us from somewhere and made his entrance when it seemed most appropriate.

Kate came to greet him and, because he was down on one knee removing his boots, her primary view of him was of the large and ornate French Foreign Legion paratrooper wings tattooed on the sides of his head. They startled, even frightened her.

He stood, took her hand and introduced himself, and his pleasant demeanor offset her initial reaction. He went into the living room and introduced himself to everyone by turn, and then we all went to the dining room.

My mother had taught Kate to make a

traditional Finnish birthday-type cake —
my favorite kind — and she did it well, with
layers of fruit-based filling and a simple
frosting made of cream and sugar. The kind
of frosting many Americans are so fond of,
that comes ready-made in a can, is now
available in Finland, so at Kate's insistence
I once gave it a try. It's so sweet that it's
like eating rotten candy, disgusting to me. I
also find American coffee useless. They
drink it weak, like hot black water.

Moreau gestured toward the pile of gear
in the living room. "You are preparing for a
paramilitary operation?" he asked.

Milo loved to talk about our group. He
looked at me for permission and I nodded
yes.

I watched the storm come in as he talked.
The sky was first zinc, then black and heavy,
and then the rain came, wind-driven into
silver diagonals. Kate rocked Anu back and
forth in her carriage. Katt reclined on my
shoulder.

I waited for an appropriate moment.
"Adrien, tell us about yourself."

"I grew up in Finland, in Iisalmi — a
small town in the east," he said. "This is the
first time I have been back in over twenty
years."

Now we spoke English, but yesterday we

spoke Finnish. His manner of speaking our mother tongue made me believe him. It carried an odd intonation, unusual word choices and grammatical constructions. I've noticed this before about the speech patterns of long-term expats.

"I attended the University of Helsinki and studied philosophy, because I wanted to find out who I was and what I wished to be. By the time I completed my master's, the answer was clear, and I joined the French Foreign Legion."

"Why not the Finnish army?"

"I had already served in the Finnish army. It has been said that every young man needs his war, and I needed mine. Finland has not fought in a war for sixty-five years now. Finnish boys must seek their glory elsewhere. I have served in Chad, Rwanda, the Côte d'Ivoire, the Gulf War, Gabon and Zaire, Cambodia and Somalia, Bosnia and Herzegovina, the Central African Republic, Congo-Brazzaville, Afghanistan and, of late, in Mexico. You would be surprised how many Finns are in the Legion, for just that reason."

This is true. I've met several former Finnish Legionnaires, and several more who tried but washed out in basic training. Only one in seven applicants makes the cut.

"What interest does France have in Mexico?" Kate asked.

Moreau smiled. I looked around the table. His calmness of mien suggested an uncommon gentleness, and it set people at ease, despite his satanic appearance. "France has interest in all things international. The American government requested French assistance in Mexico to help reconcile the violence caused by friction between the drug cartels. That assistance came in the form of me."

That was quite a teaser for a story, and we waited for him to elaborate, but he didn't.

Sweetness waited until everyone had their fill of cake and then proceeded to eat the rest of it by himself. And then jammed *nuuska* into his lip. I sighed. I thought again that he was going to have to play Eliza Doolittle to my Henry Higgins if I was to make him presentable.

Then Moreau said, "It is little understood that the drug trade must be maintained, but controlled and balanced. Were the narcotics industry to suddenly cease, the economies of many countries, the U.S. among them, would be destroyed. I left the Legion a few years ago, am now a policeman, a superintendent in the Central Directorate of Interior Intelligence Action Division. I was helping to restore that balance."

He got up. "Which reminds me. I have brought a small gift for Kari." He had brought a backpack with him and left it in the foyer. He got up, took something out of it, came back and placed a clear plastic bag filled with white powder on the table. "This is a half kilo of uncut Mexican heroin," he said.

Kate's jaw dropped. The others looked on with interest.

"For what?" I asked.

"You have destroyed this balance I spoke of. Because of it, now people commit suicide and a crime wave is in progress. If you distribute this, it will restore the balance and repair the situation for a time."

"How did you get it into Finland?"

"In a diplomatic pouch. I travel on a diplomatic passport and am not subject to search."

I shook my head. "How the fuck am I supposed to move that much heroin?"

Sweetness cleared his throat. He had made several trips to the balcony and his hip flask must be near empty. "I wasn't exactly unemployed before I came to work for you. Me and my brother sold marijuana. Not a lot, just some, so we could have at least a little money. We never sold hard drugs, but I know some *neekerit* who do. I could front it to them, an ounce at a time or something like that. It's worth about a hundred thousand euros. If I gave it to them all at once, they would steal it and leave the country."

Kate flew mad. "First you steal drugs. Now you want to sell drugs. And" — she pointed at Sweetness — "don't use language like that in my home."

He was mystified. "I'm sorry. What language?"

I stepped in. "Kate, he meant nothing derogatory. Most Finns still say *neekeri*. It's always been the word for black people, and it's slowly changing, because the press and academics know how ugly it sounds and are now making substitutions for it, but they still haven't even agreed upon what the right word should be. Until black people started coming here in the 1990s, Finns had almost no exposure to blacks and had attitudes something like Americans in the 1920s. When I was a kid, in the 1970s, my school-books said *neekerit* were simple but happy. They liked to sing and dance. Sweetness meant no harm. And Moreau is right. We meant well, but we went too far and people got hurt."

She softened. "Let's discuss it later."

"OK."

"As to selling the heroin," I said, "that's not going to happen. Presumably, if junkies have the money to buy heroin, they have the money for a train ticket to another city. They can buy it elsewhere."

"Does that mean you do not accept my gift?" Moreau asked.

"No, I'll keep it. I might find other uses for it."

He grinned. "Such as planting it and framing your enemies? Inspector, your waters run deep."

I said nothing.

Milo jumped in. "I have more presents we could open."

Kate groaned. "Milo, I don't want to have to see any more guns."

"Well, how about the presents for you and Anu, then?"

That got her. Curiosity overcame her anger and she smiled. "All right, then. Adrien," she asked, "what inspired you to get those striking tattoos?"

His smile was warm. I saw that he liked Kate, and that she found him charming, heroin or not.

"I have jumped from airplanes eighty-seven times. On my thirty-seventh jump, my parachute failed to open. I thought I was a dead man, but it unfurled at about four hundred feet from the ground. I hit the ground like a rock, but was unscathed. I feared it was an augury of things to come. I felt that I needed protection afterward, so I took the wings of Icarus. As long as I don't fly too close to the sun, I am now safe."

As the others filed back into the living room, I asked him what he wanted for his heroin.

"At the behest of the French government, my goals are to find the son, recover the money and discredit the Real Finns Party. Were they to take power, Finland might leave the EU and upset the balance of things. Share information with me. Take me along when you conduct interrogations as you prosecute your murder investigation. I want nothing more."

"Agreed," I said, but felt certain that he did indeed want something more from me.

He cocked his head, inquisitive. "What did you do with all the drugs you stole?"

"I kept some for blackmail or unforeseen circumstances when I might need it. But we tossed most of it in Dumpsters."

He tut-tutted me. "Such a waste."

We took our places with the others again, and Kate was opening her gifts. She held up a pair of shoes. She giggled like a little girl. "Manolo Blahnik Nepala pumps," she said. She slipped them on and they fit her perfectly, meaning they were tight and painful, as Manolos are meant to be. She looked at Milo. "Did Kari tell you my size?"

Moreau said, "He has an IQ of one seventy-two and an advanced sense of spatial relations. He also knows your bra size and, if you smile, the length of your teeth to a fraction of a millimeter."

Milo turned red. Moreau had made his point. He knew things.

Kate then opened a package with a Gucci "marrakech" evening bag with woven leather trim and tassels, and finally a bottle of Clive Christian No. 1 perfume. She was in heaven.

"The bottle is handmade lead crystal with a thirty-three-carat diamond in the neck," Milo said. "Its ingredients include Madagascar ylang ylang, vanilla, orris, natural gum resin, sandalwood and bergamot. It was weird. I went to boutiques to find this stuff and the salespeople all spoke Russian instead of Finnish. Russian tourists buy them here and Finns can't afford them."

Kate brought Anu to see her gift: a huge Steiff teddy bear. She loved it, kept petting the soft brown fur and wouldn't stop. Arvid had fallen asleep in my chair. Sweetness was also sleeping. A flask of *kossu* — Finnish vodka — and half a cake had done him in.

"The last is for you," Milo said, and handed me a long and heavy package. I ripped off the wrapping and gawked at it, astonished. It appealed to my childish like-or-don't-like instinct, and I liked it very much. It was a cane, cudgel-thick. The handle was a massive lion's head made from several ounces of gold. I had gone to so much work to become anonymous, and this would make me stand out in any crowd. I didn't care. I loved it. I would carry it.

"Let me show you how it works," Milo said. "Gadget canes were once very popular. They were made with just about every device imaginable. Bang down on the floor with the tip. It spring-loads the lion's mouth and it snaps open. The teeth are steel razors. Sharp contact, like swinging the mouth against something, makes it clamp shut and bite with about three hundred pounds per square inch of pressure, the same as a Rottweiler's jaws. Pressing the eyes — one is a ruby, the other is emerald — disengages the spring and the mouth lets go. Unscrew the shaft, and there's a twenty-inch sword inside."

While he explained, Kate unbuttoned her blouse and, at a discreet angle to the rest of us, began breast-feeding Anu. While I admired the cane, I noticed Moreau admire my wife in a way I wasn't fond of. He picked up on my disapproval.

"Forgive me," he said. "You have a most lovely family. Your wife calls to mind someone I once knew, and she too had an infant."

I didn't know if I liked him or detested him, but was sure that if my emotions were as they once had been, my feelings toward him would be nothing in between.

I opened the lion's mouth and smacked the edge of the coffee table. Anu yelped. It bit so deep I couldn't pull it free, had to depress the eyes to make it let go. Kate looked at me with disapproval. I had disturbed the child and damaged the table.

My knee would be fully recovered soon. I would limp, but it would be almost unnoticeable. "Milo," I said, "this is the most wonderful toy I've ever owned. Thank you. It makes me almost sad I won't need it for long."

"You can always use it," he answered. "A man doesn't walk with a cane, he wears it."

Moreau turned to Milo. "I think everyone is tired, perhaps we should make our exit. Are there more weapons in the unopened packages?"

"Yes."

"Are they anything special?"

Milo grinned. "Extra special."

"Do you know how to use them?"

Milo laughed. "Not a fucking clue."

"I'm probably familiar with them. Why don't we drop off the others and have a look at them together."

Kate was off in her own little world, admiring her gifts, expensive and precious things that, when she was younger, brought up poor, she could never have conceived of possessing. She looked up at us. "Is this what comes of being a criminal's wife?" she asked.

Moreau answered. "No. This is what comes of being the wife of a powerful man."

Milo had thrown a hell of a party. Once the others were out of the house, we got Anu to sleep and made love again.

22

Milo came over the next day to finish his last "synthesizable VHDL model of exact solutions for a three-dimensional hyperbolic positioning system."

We sat at the dining room table. Kate lay near us on the couch, reading a book. I continued wading through files, a policeman's nightmare drudgery. I was firm in my belief now, though, that the identity of Lisbet Söderlund's murderer was an open secret, and the way to solve this case was through the application of intimidation and pressure, or maybe through the application of biographical leverage — blackmail — until someone ratted out the killer.

I viewed these files with a different eye now, deciding who to approach. I agreed with Moreau, and I was now looking for someone who not only was capable of decapitating a woman but was also an accomplished marksman. This narrowed down the field a great deal. The shooter likely had considerable military experience, well beyond that of a typical Finnish conscript.

It occurred to me that Moreau would fill the bill as the murderer. I made some calls, checked with the French police. They refused to provide details, but he wasn't in Finland at the time of Kaarina Saukko's murder. However, he was a policeman on a diplomatic passport, listed as an attaché at the French embassy.

The disappearance of Antti Saukko troubled me. It was entirely possible, given his relationship with his family, that his kidnappers released him and he chose to simply change his identity and disappear. Pursuing a missing person, unless there is some reason to indicate that said missing person is the victim of a crime, is trampling on that individual's rights. We have the entitlement to abandon our lives at will, hence the policy of no body, no murder. The fate of the three missing children of kidnapper Jussi Kosonen concerned me, but it wasn't my case.

My cane leaned against the table beside me. Milo nodded toward it. "You know, you could poison the teeth on that thing if you wanted to. Did you enjoy your party yesterday?"

"Yeah, I really did. And I meant what I said. The cane you gave me is my favorite possession. Do we have any money left after your spending spree?"

"Oodles. Robbing dope dealers is so lucrative, I'm not sure why more people like us don't take up the occupation."

"I'm sure some do, but have short-lived careers. Your sawed-off was a good idea. If you load it with something non-lethal, it could get us out of jams if we got stuck, say, pulling a heist and a few guys walked in. Just don't do anything weird, like load it with beehive rounds or rat-poisoned buckshot."

The dark circles under his eyes deepened. Always a sign of trouble. Milo was both obdurate and rambunctious, an often annoying, even dangerous combination. Now he wanted a fight. "Well, would it be fucking OK with you if I just fucking carry lethal ammo, should fucking necessity arise?"

I tamed him with the unexpected and then switched gears to disengage his temper.

"Sure. Did you spend much time with Moreau?"

I noticed Kate's eyes drift from her book to us.

"We dropped off Arvid and Sweetness. I don't know why he thinks he's fooling anyone hiding his drinking."

Now we had Kate's full attention. She hadn't caught on to Sweetness's drinking. It can be hard to tell someone is drunk if you never see them sober.

Milo fired up his machine and fiddled with it for a minute. "Goddamn it. These work, but not well enough. They pick up the cell phones but can't track enough at one time and the range is too short."

"What do you need?"

Asking was a mistake. Prolix Milo kicked into gear. "I can't get my hands on one because of its military-grade sales status, and I couldn't fake my way through it, and even by our standards, they cost a fortune. A GSM A5.1 Real Time Cell Phone Interceptor. It's undetectable, can handle twenty phones in quad band and four base stations."

It meant nothing to me and I wasn't interested. "What did you do after you dropped off the others?"

Milo doesn't have a raconteur's bone in his body. "We went to my place and looked at the weapons. A Remington 870 tactical shotgun to handle ballistic breaching lockbuster shotgun rounds. A Heckler & Koch UMP machine gun. It's much like the MP5 but state-of-the-art and made from the latest in advanced polymers. And a .50 caliber Barrett sniper rifle. It's like something out of *Star Wars*. The optical ranging system is an integrated electronic ballistic computer . . ."

He went on. Kate hated this kind of rambling constantly disturbing her tranquillity. This was what she had complained about. It made her feel as if she lived in a police precinct instead of a home, and she had also sacrificed a great deal of privacy having the team ginning around like they lived here.

Milo would have continued but I cut him off. "What do you think of Moreau?"

"He's a really cool guy. He told me he would teach me how to use the .50 Barrett. Why did you shoot down his idea about selling the heroin?"

"It's tricky and dangerous. We just keep ripping off dealers. Keep them beaten down."

Milo switched to Finnish, so Kate wouldn't understand. "So long as they don't start a drug war and we have to hide it by dissolving any more bodies in acid. That really skeeved me out."

But Kate *did* understand. She set Anu on a cushion, turned around, rested her folded arms on the back of the sofa and her head on her arms. "Pardon me. What was that again? Something about bodies and acid."

I explained to her what had happened. That one gangster killed another and we had to cover it up, or gangsters would start gunning each other down in the streets, Helsinki Homicide would get involved and inevitably would trail the murders and the reasons behind them back to us.

"We really had no choice," I said.

Since the beginning of the Cold War, because of its geographic location, Helsinki has been awash in spies. Out of survival instinct, these spies had made an unspoken agreement many years ago, early in the Cold War. Helsinki would be holy ground, a sacred city to which secret warriors could travel without fear. Even after the Cold War, Helsinki remained a city in which both its inhabitants and fringe dwellers existed in relative safety. I didn't want to be responsible for destroying that tradition.

"Apparently," Kate said, "I've been kept in the dark about some details, but it's gone something like this. You've committed a number of thefts, maybe dozens, I don't know. But because you didn't know what you were doing, you stole too much, and a lot of people have died because of it. You incited someone to murder, and you left the body to dissolve in a vat of acid. Am I correct here?"

"Yes."

Milo was already putting his boots on, making his escape. He needn't have. She wouldn't be angry at him. I gave the orders. I was her husband. And he had given her, among other things, a two-thousand-euro bottle of perfume yesterday, as an act of friendship and to make up for her inconvenience. I was alone on the gallows. He shut the door behind him with a soft click.

"This isn't my home," Kate said, "it's a gangster hangout. Has it occurred to you that I might like to have people over, like Aino, friends from the hotel, but I can't because Milo might slip and mention who's been killed or body dumped? I don't even know where Anu and I fit in your life. You've changed. You're colder, more distant. I don't know if it's because of your job or your surgery or both."

I sat down in my armchair and considered which truths to tell her and which not to. I didn't even know what the truth was. I still couldn't tell her that I was nearly without emotion and felt little or nothing for her or our child.

"I'm disillusioned," I said. "I was misled, turned into Jyri's cat's-paw. I'm no more than a bagman and an enforcer for corrupt and criminal politicians. Sooner or later I'll outlive my usefulness and they'll find a way to dispose of me. I have to find a way to destroy them first. I'll get money and passports. When the day comes, we'll disappear."

"This is insane," she said, "and can only end badly. We should leave now, take the money you've got and go to Aspen. You can use your stolen money and pursue hobbies: take nature photos, collect stamps, whatever."

"I gave you that opportunity," I said, "and you declined. I know it wasn't fair because you felt like you might be granting the last wish of a dying man, but now things are what they are, and I'll see this job through. I took the job because I wanted to do some good. And before I quit, I will. We may have to leave, but not yet. I'm sorry."

The news started on television, and we both almost missed it. The main story:

"Winter War hero Arvid Lahtinen committed suicide this morning . . ."

We were both dumbstruck. Our argument ceased and I turned up the volume. He shot himself outside his house, probably because he didn't want to decomp for God knows how long before someone found him. He put on a suit, carried a chair outside, and sat while he put the gun to his head. I suppose he thought it would be more dignified than being found in a heap on the wet ground. The reporter speculated on the reasons behind his suicide, discussed the murder charges against him, both domestic and international, and his achievements as a national hero.

Kate cried. "Why?" she asked me.

I thought what sparked his action was his time here, the remembrance of what it was like to be part of a family, the realization that he would be old and alone now, had nothing to look forward to but a slow death in an aged, soon-to-be-failing body. Before long, illness, the loss of his home and independence. And he would have to do it alone, without his beloved wife of half a century.

"Because he didn't enjoy life without his wife. Because he knew he had had a good run, but his time was over, and if he left now, he could die with his dignity intact."

"He was my friend," Kate said.

"Mine too. He told me that he was leaving everything to me. I should have known then."

"He did?"

"Yeah. House. Money. Everything."

Kate sat down next to me in the oversized chair. We were silent together for a while.

"Work with Moreau," she said. "You fucked up a lot of things because you didn't have the experience to know better. He does. If you learn, you can achieve some of the good that for some mystifying reason is driving you, and we can stop all this."

"OK," I said.

I was Arvid's heir and so responsible for his funeral arrangements. The service was held in Helsinki's magnificent and most prestigious church, Tuomiokirkko. It sits atop Senate Square and looks down upon both the city and the sea. The church was full, and the man and what he represented were truly mourned. I acted as a pallbearer. It seemed, after he was laid to rest, that nothing was ever the same again. Especially for Kate. I don't know if the suicide of a man she called friend awakened something inside her, or killed it.

23

Vappu — May Day, the heaviest drinking holiday of the year. In Helsinki, a good day to stay at home. It's amateur night, normal people reduce themselves to the level of dumb beasts. Children as young as ten or twelve pass out on the streets of downtown. May Day Eve fell on a Friday, so festivities would begin as soon as people got off work and continue for three days.

When I was a young man, the drinking culture was much different. People still got shitfaced, but with style. Men wore suits to bars, and doormen wore them also. The madding crowds didn't shriek about whose turn it was. They waited in line, humble. Patrons were required to sit at tables. They couldn't switch tables at will. If they wanted to move, they had to ask a server to move their drink to another table for them. Bartenders didn't sling drinks, they administered communion, and were frequently addressed as *herra baarimestari* — sir barmaster — and it wasn't until about thirty years ago that women were allowed in drinking establishments without male escorts.

Vappu, too, has changed. In a time that doesn't seem that far distant, Vappu had been a drinking day, especially for university students, but also a family day. People donned their high school graduation caps — still the tradition — but took their kids out with them, had family picnics. It lacked the tone of complete debauchery now attached to it.

It's a different world now. Banks would also carry more cash than usual, as people prepared to pour their bank accounts down their necks. A good day for a robbery.

Every year, the great hope is that Vappu will be warm, and the nation can sit on sidewalk patios, drink, and celebrate the rite of spring. This year was a disappointment. The temperature was just above freezing and rain drizzled. No matter, spring would be celebrated nonetheless.

At ten thirty a.m. on that dreary May Day Eve, with the tellers' cash drawers freshly filled, two men entered the branch of Sampo Bank in Itäkeskus, in East Helsinki. They wore black military-style clothing, ski masks, and carried AK-47-type rifles. Each had two banana clips fastened end to end with black electrical tape, so that when one clip was shot empty, the two-clip rig would only have to be flipped to re-load, eliminating the need to reach for another clip.

They fired off bursts into the air to make their presences known and began screaming in thick, grammatically poor English. One shot an unarmed bank guard dead. They didn't have to order people to lay prone on the floor. The few early customers flung themselves down in the hope of staying out of harm's way. No alarm was triggered. The robbers ordered the tellers to fill black plastic grocery bags with money. One teller, an older woman, too terrified to move, was also executed.

The robbery was over in less than three minutes. Before they left, one robber bellowed, "We strike against the enemies of God." The other laughed and shouted, "Lock your daughters up, you motherfuckers, we comin' to get you."

I was called within minutes of the robbery and told to come to the crime scene because, as with the young soldier whose throat had been cut, it was felt that the robbery was related to the murder of Lisbet Söderlund.

Milo living so close to me was a convenience. I called him, picked him up, and we were at the bank within half an hour. It wouldn't be my case, it would go to Saska Lindgren. Apparently, a race war was in progress, he would be given the cases related to it, and I would consult because of the presidential mandate concerning Lisbet Söderlund. We questioned all present. We looked at the videotapes. Although we couldn't be certain because the only exposed skin we had to go by was the area around their eyes, all agreed that the perps were black.

Milo rolled a tape back and forth a few times. "The rifles they used," he said, "are Rk 95 Tps, the type stolen from the training camp. An unlikely coincidence."

According to the rules of battle as set forth by the white combatants in this race war, the original decree was "For every crime committed by black men, we will kill a nigger in retribution."

That hadn't proven accurate. A number of crimes had been committed by blacks since then without retribution. My gut told me, though, that they had realized the difficulties behind killing a black person for *every* crime committed, but as was the case with the young soldier, murder would be answered with murder, and if we couldn't unravel this fast, more people would soon die.

Later that evening, Milo called me. He'd picked up something interesting on a cell phone tap. Helsinki was heroin dry, and Russians were going to try to re-lubricate. The Russians believed they were safe, as only two men knew about the deal, the seller and the buyer. One would bring five kilos to Helsinki tomorrow. It was worth a million euros plus on the street. The deal was for half a million, wholesale price.

The normal price of a gram of heroin was a hundred twenty euros. With the city bone dry, the buyer planned to sell it for more than twice that price. He would distribute by the ounce, and then one more rung down the ladder, smaller dealers would sell by the eight ball — three and a half grams — but end users would pay two hundred fifty a gram. Plus, this was eighty-eight percent pure Afghan heroin. Street heroin was usually fifty percent. He could step on it hard with lactose and sell it off as close to eight kilos. In Afghanistan, a kilo costs five thousand bucks. Five thousand becomes a million. The stuff entrepreneurial dreams are made of.

Tomorrow was Vappu. They would seal the deal and celebrate spring by having some drinks on the patio outside at Kaivo-huone — The Well Room — at five p.m., and then make the exchange in the parking lot. Milo asked if I wanted to take it on.

I considered it. What was my goal? To make Helsinki heroin-free or gangster-free? I wasn't a social worker, the answer was gangster-free. Stealing the city dry has been a mistake, but unleashing five kilos on Helsinki would mean a total loss of control, dealers back in business. Also, it might cause a number of overdose deaths, as junkies whose systems were nearly clear shot up doses that, when totally hooked, would only have gotten them high.

"Let's snatch it," I said. "It's an easy one. We just go out to the full parking lot and pop their trunks. People won't recognize me with my image overhaul. Nobody will even give us a second glance."

"It's Vappu for us, too," Milo said. "What do you say we have a few drinks while we're there?"

"OK. Why not? Let's have some fun."

"I'll call Sweetness and tell him to meet us," Milo said, and rang off.

24

Kaivohuone opened its doors in 1838, and began its life as a spa with a sea view for the Russian elite. It's now a national landmark, not far from embassy row. For many years though, the stately white building has served as a nightclub. Legally, it holds a thousand people inside and four hundred outside, but in summer the place is oversold, so jammed you can barely move. Its prices, from cover charge to drinks, are outrageous, and the people that spend a great deal of time there do so partly to show off that they can afford to. Kaivo is *the* place to be on Vappu.

Others go to rub shoulders with the wealthy, so that for a brief, shining moment, they can feel themselves one of them while they gawk around, hoping to catch a glimpse of a B-class star.

It has traditionally catered to the children of wealthy Swedish-speaking Finns. Young people, many of them students, who can afford three-hundred-euro bar tabs two or three times a week, drinking themselves stupid under the midnight sun, despite never having had jobs.

The city owns it. The neighbors hate it because the noise level makes it like living next to an airport with jets constantly taking off and landing during the summer months. It changed management a few years ago. It's falling apart, shaken to bits by years of abuse from the throbbing sound system. Through some sort of backroom deal, it came into the hands of a Helsinki nightclub tycoon, with the agreement that he would put ten million into its restoration and convert it into a fine dining establishment the city could be proud of.

Instead, he put about fifty euros into paint, gimcracks and doodads, made some cosmetic changes so that he could say he lived up to his word and renovated it, and kept operating it as a nightclub. The building still stands, the kids keep rockin'.

I went to the front of a hundred-meter line to the outdoor patio, showed the doorman my police card, said I was there on official business, and was ushered in ahead of the crowd, gratis. The place was oversold and I could have shut it down as a fire hazard if I chose to, and they knew it. They would have plied me with free Dom Péri- gnon for the evening if I asked for it. The patio was packed with beautiful young people weaving and staggering, their eyes glazed from their second-day drunk.

I saw Milo wave at me. He'd managed to get a table, a small miracle. He'd probably showed his police card, intimidated some kids and commandeered it. Sweetness was with him. I pushed and shoved my way over to them. They had saved a seat for me.

I noticed that Milo, Sweetness and I had all adopted the same style. Cargo pants. Clothes with lots of pockets for things like Tasers and silencers. Bowling shirts that didn't need to be tucked in, to cover the waistband repertoire: pistols, knives, saps, etc.

They had girls with them, a surprise in itself, because Milo and Sweetness aren't exactly ladies' men, but these girls aston- ished me. The official age for admission at Kaivo was twenty-four, but that in truth only applied to men, and it was discretion- ary, to enable the doormen to weed out young testosterone-tweaked troublemakers, but the legal age was eighteen.

These girls were young, one about twenty, the other maybe sixteen. Even that didn't really surprise me. Girls as young as fourteen made their way in if they were beautiful enough and with the right people. What got me was that these girls, on a patio jammed with gorgeous women, were so stunning that they made the others look like a coal miners' convention. They drew open stares, even from other women.

It was only about fifty degrees Fahrenheit, but the tables had heaters in the shape of beach umbrellas overtop them that made it hot sitting there. The girls introduced themselves as Mirjami and Jenna. They were tipsy and giggly. They sparked my six-year-old self in an adult body, and I had an insta-hard-on in moments.

I sat next to Mirjami, the teenager. She was tanned, told me she had just returned from vacation in Málaga. She was long and thin and dressed in a Hello Kitty outfit. A short pink Hello Kitty top with spaghetti straps showed a piercing in her belly button and golden nut-brown skin surrounding it. Hello Kitty regalia: handbag, cell phone cover, necklace, watch, earrings and bracelet adorned her.

Milo went to the bar to get us all drinks. He made it back fast with a full tray, said he cut the line, flashed his police card and held up a C-note to make his intentions clear. He dropped the bartender a twenty.

The girls got two cosmopolitans each. Milo, Sweetness and I got two shots of *kossu* each and a beer. I had little desire for alcohol since my brain surgery. I enjoyed my increased sharpness of thought and didn't like to dull it. Now, though, seemed like a good time.

Mirjami and I clinked glasses and said *"Kippis"* — cheers. She downed the cocktail in one go and I did the same with the *kossu.* Milo inserted an earbud connected to his cell phone. He was monitoring the dealers' conversations. I asked him if he heard about Arvid. He nodded. Neither of us wanted to talk about it right now, but we drank to his memory.

The almond shape of Mirjami's eyes made me think she had Sami blood. She made me think of cherry pie. Yum. She wore pink lip gloss, glitter polish with heart and moon designs on little brown fingers and toes. I imagined her small breasts were like scoops of chocolate ice cream with cherries on top. She had big, heart-shaped sunglasses over them, but I later saw that she had brown doe eyes with long lashes. She wore flip-flops and white pedal pushers, like she was ready to hit the beach. I could have wrapped my hands around her waist. I imagined my tongue in her belly button. She sat close to

Milo, and so I thought she must be with him.

Jenna. Apple pie. She had big, baby blue eyes in a round face. White perfect skin. Ruby lips that required no lipstick. A button nose. Waist-length white-blond hair. She was a snow queen. A blond Cinderella. She also wore a revealing top, but jeans and sandals. Even though she sat, from my angle to her, I saw she had a wonderful ample bottom. And huge high breasts like the proverbial ripe melons. Height: Five foot nothing, tops. Apple and cherry pie. A slice of each would be a great combination. It was Mirjami who really got to me, though.

A Dusty Springfield song came on. "Son of a Preacher Man."

"I love this one," Mirjami said. "Dance with me."

"I'd love to" — I tapped the lion's head on my cane — "but I can't."

No one else was dancing. "Then I'll dance for you," she said, got up and started swaying to the rhythm. Jenna joined. Then Sweetness. And finally Milo. The girls radiated sexy. Mountain-sized Sweetness was light on his feet, a good dancer. This was a day of revelations. Milo danced like most men, incompetent, but he made up for it with enthusiasm. The song ended.

The guys came back to the table. The girls didn't stop. They danced playful. They did the swim. The mashed potato. The twist. They vogued. They mimicked John Travolta and Uma Thurman dancing in *Pulp Fiction*. They did it well. People applauded. The girls grooved on the attention.

"The Russians are here," Milo said. Two men walked away from the bar. One carried a bottle of Smirnoff in a champagne bucket.

The girls came back, then went for so-called nose powdering.

"How in the fuck did you guys pick up those two girls?" I asked.

"Yeah," Milo said, "they're a little out of our league. Mirjami is my cousin. She's got a thing for cops. Plus, I flash my cop card and get us in places so she doesn't have to wait in lines or sometimes even pay, and she's my chick magnet. I like going out with her because it gives the impression that I'm cool enough to get a girl that gorgeous, and we're pretty good friends, too."

"And I guess they don't card her if she's with you."

"She's twenty-two, she doesn't need me for that."

"Jesus, I thought she was a kid."

"That's just her club thing. She works at it. Actually, she's a registered nurse and

261

more mature than I am. That's for sure."

"Same with me," Sweetness said. "Jenna is my cousin, and she's only sixteen." He went all glum, knocked off a *kossu*.

I had the girls' ages backwards. "What's with the sad face?"

"I like her a lot. You know, not like a cousin."

"Bummer," I said.

He nodded. "Yeah. And what's worse, I think she likes me, too. We just can't do anything about it. Plus, she's so young."

The girls were on their way back. The Russians lucked out and got a table two down from ours. I changed the topic. "When they get halfway through the bottle, let's make the snatch."

"I can do it alone," Milo said. "It won't look obvious that way."

"You sure?" I asked.

He rolled his eyes. "It's going to take, like, two minutes."

"Is Kate mad at me?" Sweetness asked.

"For what?"

"What I said. It's the truth. I ain't got nothin' against niggers."

"No, she's not mad. Just don't say 'nigger' in English or she'll get furious. And in Finnish, call them 'black people.' How did you get to be such a good dancer?"

"I took lessons when I was a kid. Mom made me."

The girls sat down. "I'm kind of afraid to go back home today," Jenna said. She looked like a child with huge breasts.

"Why?" I asked.

"I live in East Helsinki, and it ain't safe there." Her eyes met Sweetness's and I saw affection there. He was right about that.

The Russians drank fast. Their bottle stood half empty. Milo excused himself. When he came back, he brought more drinks.

I watched the news earlier. Anger over the bank robbery murder, in addition to Vappu boozing, equaled vandalism and violence. Drunken whites had beaten blacks, knocked out storefront windows, burned a couple cars. A black girl was even raped. Blacks had retaliated.

"We'll get you home safe," I said.

The Russians finished the vodka bottle, turned it upside down in the ice bucket and left.

Mirjami kicked off her flip-flops and propped her feet up in my lap. I was too embarrassed to move and my dick went stiff again. She felt it and giggled. She wiggled her toes against it to tease me. I liked it, stroked her brown feet. She liked it. She was chewing bubble gum. She blew a bubble until it got so big that it exploded in her face. Pow! She laughed and picked it off her cheeks.

Only one word came to mind to describe her. Yummy. She captivated me. Prior to the removal of my tumor I would have paid her scant or little attention, barely noticed her at all. A ninny half my age. I desperately wanted to fuck the daylights out of her. Other than Aino, I hadn't wanted another woman since I met Kate. Surgery had changed me.

Milo monitored the Russians' cell phones. "Hey, Kari," he said, "it's your round. Come on, I'll go to the bar with you." We stopped halfway between our table and the bar. He whispered in my ear. "One of the Russians just called his boss to say he got ripped off and killed the guy from the other gang. When they saw the empty trunk, he stabbed the guy fast, pushed him into the trunk, and shut it. We're going to have to get rid of another body."

"Fuck," I said.

"Yep, fuck."

We stood there for a minute and thought about it.

Milo said, "This is an easy one because we have a half-empty barrel. We don't even need the forklift, we just have to stuff the body into the barrel. We have a half a million in dope and half a million in cash. Sweetness and I will dump the body. You take the swag, buy the girls another drink to make them happy and take them home. We'll do the rest."

It was a kind gesture. "You trying to keep me out of the doghouse with Kate?"

He sniggered. "Yeah."

"Thanks." I put the stuff in my car, the guys left, and I bought a last round. The girls were tanked anyway.

I stayed quiet, listened to them talk. Jenna spoke East Helsinki Finnish, and Mirjami spoke *stadin slangi* — city slang. I didn't understand half of what she said. The kids have developed a slang dialect so rich that a dictionary of it was recently published. It's about three inches thick. Mirjami started talking to me, telling me a story, and I finally admitted, "I don't have a clue what you're talking about. Can you speak something resembling standard Finnish?"

This made her laugh. "Sure," she said, and made the transition for me. "It's like my outfit," she said. "When I go out, I play 'let's pretend.' Normally, I speak like somebody with an education."

I took them home, first Jenna, then Mirjami. As she got out, she said, "You like me, don't you."

"Yeah," I answered.

"I thought so," she said. "See ya," and bounded up the sidewalk to her door.

When I got home, Aino and Kate sat drinking a bottle of sparkling wine together. I checked the fridge, there was plenty of breast milk. It was still early. I was close to sober. I suggested they get out of the house, celebrate Vappu, have a few drinks. They leapt at the opportunity.

25

The post-Vappu blues. Kate woke, scurried to the bathroom, retched and vomited. I was asleep when Kate got home, but she and Aino must have really tied one on. Kate isn't much of a drinker. She was becoming more and more Finnish every day. She made it back to bed by way of serpentine tacking, too dizzy to walk straight.

Anu heard the heaving and woke up crying. I changed her diaper and used breast pump milk to feed her. I had coffee and a cigarette, got comfortable in my man chair, and Anu laid in my lap while I browsed the Sunday paper. Katt perched on my shoulder, as if reading along with me.

The violence, turmoil and rioting was downplayed, described as "displays of discontent and anger, as demonstrated by friction between blacks and whites and a lack of order in those areas in which immigrant populations were concentrated."

Cover-up.

Editorials discussed "the justified fear of whites, confronted by armed and violent malcontent foreigners."

Because our experience with people of color is relatively new, the Finnish language has yet to develop the wide range of hate vocabulary compared to, say, the United States, but write-in commentators did their best. Little nigger children should be vaporized, or at least sterilized, before they reached breeding age. Quotes by "Martin Lucifer King" were mimicked. "We shall overcome . . . all over your nigger faces." "I have a dream . . . to see your faces burnt off with blowtorches." And so on.

Hate congealed. Amoebas of hate divided and subdivided and renewed themselves in abhorrent mitosis. Almost all the countries in the European Union were faced with immigration problems. An interesting response to an editorial. "If we can't kill them outright, could we re-institute slavery and sell them as chattel, and thus receive compensation, recoup the monies spent on their maintenance?" The most reasonable suggestion was to simply revoke the EU membership of those countries with low per capita incomes, and send their former inhabitants back where they came from. A thoughtful comment by a good hater.

I expected a call from Saska Lindgren, and my premonition proved correct. He asked if I could meet him at the same address as before. The entire black family there was now dead. I told him I'd like to bring the rest of my team, and a consultant I was working with. He said no problem. I called Milo, Sweetness and Moreau, and told them where to meet me. I didn't need them, but Milo would want to take part, I had promised Moreau, and because of Sweetness's unusual reaction at the murder scene of the soldier in the forest, I thought he needed to get accustomed to death investigations.

I put Anu in her crib and told Kate I was sorry to leave her in such a condition, but I had to go to a murder scene. She was ghastly pale and nodded acknowledgment without opening her eyes.

On the way over, I called Jyri and arranged to meet him later. He was less than pleased that I called at such an early hour the day after Vappu, but I assured him it was worth the pain of having his hangover disturbed. I promised he would be glad to see me, because I had a hundred fifty thousand euros for him. I usually skimmed ten percent off the top, but there was so much money, and the amount had such a nice ring to it, that I didn't bother.

I arrived about ten a.m. The street was lined with vehicles. The press, cops, forensics people, curious citizens, all milled about. Police tape lined the whole of the property, meaning the house and its small front and back yards. Spring was here. The snow was all gone now, and likely wouldn't be back for the next few months. The temperature was about the same as yesterday, but a wet breeze made it feel colder. Milo was already there, sitting on the front stoop, talking to Saska. Sweetness and Moreau hadn't arrived yet.

"So they killed the rest of the family," I said.

Saska nodded.

"How?"

"It's too much to describe. Go out back and have a look if you want."

"I'm in no rush. I'll wait on the others."

"I don't like looking at it," he said. "It's just another murder in a sense, but this one is just so fucking disillusioning."

Milo got up and motioned for me to follow him out of hearing distance of the crowd. "We took the body and dumped it like we planned," he said.

"Good."

"Well . . . it was weird. We opened the trunk and the guy wasn't dead. Almost, but not quite. He didn't move or say anything, but he looked at us and blinked. I wasn't sure what to do. We could have dumped him in front of a hospital."

"But," I said.

"But Sweetness didn't even want to talk about it. He took a pull off that flask of his, felt around the guy's chest and found a spot between his ribs near his heart. Then he took that knife I gave him and just slid it into the guy's chest. Killed him dead as a hammer. 'Problem solved,' he said. Then we suited up, dropped the guy in acid, sealed up the barrel and left."

"What did you do with the car?"

"Took it to East Helsinki and torched it with a Molotov cocktail. I figured it would go unnoticed, since other cars were burned in the area."

"Good plan."

"That's all you have to say? 'Good plan'?"

I shrugged. "What should I say? What's done is done." I felt a little silly for thinking Sweetness needed to get used to murder scenes. Other than that, I had no other feelings about it, one way or another.

"Sweetness is a fucking psycho."

"I watched you kill a man. Are you a fucking psycho?"

"The circumstances were different."

"Semantics."

He stared at me for a minute. "That surgery changed you," he said.

"Listen," I said, "I hired Sweetness in part because I recognized in him the ability to commit acts of violence without angst or upset. You enjoy violence because it makes you feel like a tough guy and reinforces your self-image. But your self-image is a lie you tell yourself. If you hurt someone, you feel guilty about it, suffer, have to unburden yourself and cry on my shoulder. You probably feel bad about wrecking that SUPO agent's face. Sweetness couldn't give a shit less if he hurts someone, just doesn't care one way or the other, and I don't have to listen to his sob sister boo hoo hoo remorse."

I pounded Milo's ego to dust. I didn't mean to. He stared down at his muddy boots. "You can be really mean sometimes."

I fake smiled and held up my cane. "I can also be nice. You be nice, or I'll tell my lion to bite you."

He just shook his head and wandered off.

Sweetness and Moreau showed up, I introduced them to Saska, and we all went back to view the murder scene. The racists who promised retaliation proved as good as their word. First, the young men were gassed to death, and now this.

Their mother and sister were laundry-line lynched, then set ablaze. The laundry poles stood opposite each other, and cords to hang up wet laundry were stretched between them. The poles weren't high enough for a proper lynching, so the killers had tied their ankles and wrists, cinched them tight behind their backs so they only needed about three feet of clearance, and hoisted them up the laundry poles. One body lay on the ground. The other, miraculously, still hung. The rope hadn't quite burned through.

The bodies were mostly burned down to the bone, the flesh reduced to soot hanging on it. And in the grass near them, the words *neekeri huora* were burned into the lawn.

Milo shook his head in disbelief. "For God's sake, why them?"

"It was likely the most repulsive thing the murderers could think of," Moreau said.

Saska said, "I don't know what they used, but it was a really powerful accelerant."

Moreau did an impression. "I love the smell of napalm in the morning. Smells like . . . victory."

"Who's that supposed to be?" Saska asked.

"Robert Duvall from *Apocalypse Now*. These women were soaked in homemade napalm. I know it by the smell. It's basically just gasoline and soap. It causes the most terrible pain you can imagine. Even this homemade stuff burns at about fifteen hundred degrees Fahrenheit. And it's obvious to me, by looking at the burn pattern on their mouths, chests, and in the lawn in front of them, that they were forced to drink napalm and it was lit while they vomited. They died spewing fire like dragons."

Everyone went silent. Except for Moreau and myself, I believe they resisted the urges to both cry and puke.

"But why the words burnt into the yard?" Moreau asked. " 'Whore' is singular. There are two bodies."

"That's directed at me, as a taunt," I said. "I worked a case in which a black woman was murdered. Those words were carved in her torso."

Moreau chuckled and faked a different voice. "So this time it's personal."

I didn't ask which movie he quoted. "But what's the point?"

"It's obvious," he said. "To up the ante. To keep you enchanted and your enthusiasm high. The horror of the violence keeps the pressure up and the case top-priority. For some reason, the killers desire this. Probably for maximum media exposure."

Milo, Saska and I lit cigarettes.

"Why are you here?" Saska asked him.

Sweetness had been staring at the hanging girl, mesmerized. Finally, he reached out and touched her with his index finger. The rope snapped and she fell. An arm broke off. Only ash was left on the bone and it swirled away in the breeze. Sweetness watched as if in a dream state. Death fascinated him. A forensics tech started to yell at him. I poked the tech in the chest with my cane and told him to fuck off. He fucked off.

"I'm a French policeman," Moreau said, "and I'm here at the behest of Veikko Saukko, who has some influence with the French government. It's been almost a year since his daughter was shot and killed. His confidence in the Finnish police has waned. And so here I am."

"It's my case," Saska said, "and a major reason I haven't made any progress is that he refuses to cooperate with me in any way."

"He's an eccentric racist. You are half Gypsy. He calls you 'that thieving Gypsy.' He believes you steal when you come to his home. However, he likes me, because as a former soldier, I have killed many non-white people. He considers this the most admirable of attributes. I believe all these murders, beginning with the kidnap-murder of his family, are connected to this series of murders, and to the murder of Lisbet Söderlund."

"Have at it," Saska said. "I need help. I would appreciate it, though, if you share your findings with me."

"Consider it done. If I solve the case, I will ensure that you receive the credit." Moreau turned to me. "I think you should meet Veikko Saukko. It might lend perspective."

"I was hoping to," I said. "I've decided that the way to solve this case is through the interviews of a few key individuals. Some might call them interrogations, and the application of pressure may be somewhat more aggressive than is considered standard. Let's say, with extreme prejudice. We'll begin soon. You're welcome to accompany us if you like."

"You intend to go on a rampage?"

"Call it what you will."

Saska frowned, disapproving.

"I have little choice," I said, and pointed at the victims. "Look at these women. This can't go on. People are being murdered almost daily. It must be stopped."

To Milo and Sweetness, I said, "You have girlfriends, of a kind. You drink with them. That breeds loosened tongues. Don't tell them our business."

Milo smirked. "You mean like the way you don't tell Kate our business."

His point was valid. I ignored it. "Just keep your fucking mouths shut."

I thanked Saska, told the others I would call them later, then went home to check on Kate.

I took a circuitous route, gave myself time to think.

As a young beat cop, I spent a lot of nights cruising these streets, watching Helsinki in the wee hours. The drunks drifting home after the bars closed. I watched a city awash in pain. I saw people run without direction, scream, beat their heads with their fists. Their pain and frustration shone and sparkled, beacons of anguish and insanity.

I played surrogate father to a young man so broken inside that he drank vodka upon waking and could drive a knife into a man's heart without a thought. I spent my time examining women tortured and burned. I was lucky that I felt almost nothing. I remembered what it once was like to have emotions. Those poor tortured souls that felt were the ones who suffered.

Kate ordered a pizza and a bottle of orange Jaffa, her favorite Finnish soft drink. The salt and sugar in the pizza and pop did her a world of good. She was embarrassed and felt guilty, but for no tangible reason. She remembered little and wasn't certain if she should be mortified at her behavior last night or not. She had discovered *morkkis,* an integral part of the Finnish hangover. A state of usually irrational moral guilt inherent to the Finnish consciousness. I told her it was OK, I was sure she did nothing embarrassing, just got loaded. This usually helps people recover from *morkkis.* I chilled out with her for a while, then went to meet Jyri.

26

I cross the street, go back the way I came, toward the clock over the entrance at Stockmann. "Gimme Shelter" is still stuck in my head. The pretty girls have finished their ice cream, but they continue to bop, bebop and rebop, and once again, the syncopation of their jam box techno and the Stones annoys me. The Gypsy beggar remains prostrate.

So, between January twenty-sixth, the day I asked Kate if I could become a more effective cop, a man empowered to truly help people by bending the rules of engagement in the war against crime, and today, May second, I've gone from, if not a paragon of virtue, a cop who mostly observed the rules governing my profession, to a man who has no qualms about breaking any law, committing almost any act, to achieve my own ends. I had become a changeling.

I don't care. My transformation has brought me only success and wealth. Jyri's invitation to hang out with his pals means it has also brought me acclaim. I'm sure he doesn't brag about me as a thief. He doubtless describes me as his protégé, but as a tough guy who bends the rules and who has single-handedly done what an entire metropolitan police department had failed to do, and turned Helsinki into the only narcotics-free big city in the world since Las Vegas during its golden years, when the punishment for dealing dope was a bullet in the head and a sandy burial in the desert.

And also, doubtless, he invented a fiction about the source of the monies accrued — he would have admitted only to a fraction of the fortune accumulated — and claimed it had all gone to campaign funds and worthy causes.

I make calls, check crime reports. Helsinki continues to go to hell. White and black youth gangs attack each other with knives, lead pipes, sticks, whatever crude weapons are at hand. Women, both black and white, are raped. Especially Finnish white women converted to Islam, referred to as nigger-fucking traitors. Helsinki suffers a barrage of race-related incidents. At public transportation stops, name calling and spitting is the norm. Little kids get no exemption. The emergency room at Meilahti Hospital is overrun with casualties requiring set bones and stitches.

The media covers up the incidents. They're unreported or downplayed, maintaining a façade of racial harmony. Helsinki? A race problem? Nope, not us. Here in the Nordic Mecca, we live in brotherly paradise. Welcome to the City of Love.

I call Milo and Sweetness, tell them we're to be on parade for the powers that be. Bring the girls. Wear your .45s in shoulder holsters. Wear jackets over them as if to hide them. Make an impression.

The babysitter shows up at eight thirty sharp. She's a pleasant older woman in a floral dress and her gray hair done up in a bun, as if she's been typecast for the role.

Kate and I arrive at Juttutupa a few minutes after nine. The restaurant is the perfect place for such a party. The building is known as "the granite castle" and looks out over a bay, Eläintarhanlahti. Juttutupa began selling booze in 1898 and has performed a number of functions over the years, including a time as a gymnasium, but most of them political. Various factions had possession of it during its early years. The Red Guard used it during the Civil War. Now the restaurant is next door to the Social Democratic Party. Come to think of it, even the gym was political. It belonged to the Helsinki Workers' Association.

We take a taxi, since we'll be drinking, pick up Aino and so are late arrivals. After Anu was fed, I pumped Kate's breast milk dry while she was sober. The politicos obviously started boozing a couple hours ago, or maybe haven't stopped since Friday evening. They have that look about them. Milo and Mirjami, Sweetness and Jenna, excited as kids at Christmas, showed up at nine sharp. Tables have been pushed together. Jyri comes over and welcomes us all, tells us he has a tab open for the group and not to pay for anything, he won't allow it. He introduces himself to each of the women, and I see his charm for the first time. Without showing even a hint of the wolfish slut that he is, and without effort, he makes each of the girls feel like the only woman on earth. The man has a true gift.

We men go to the bar and get *kossu* and beer. Sweetness orders four *kossu*s, downs three of them at the bar, and brings one back to the table, for sipping purposes. We get *caipiroska*s for the girls. I don't know if the drink is a Finnish invention or not. Kate had never had one before coming here. It's half a lime and a couple teaspoons of sugar in a short glass, muddled, packed over the brim with crushed ice, snow-cone style, filled with vodka and mixed. The sugar makes the vodka go to the head quick, and they taste good as well, hence their popularity.

On the way back to the table, Milo stops me. "You're a lucky man," he says.

"How so?"

"Having two beautiful women."

And a child was born in Bethlehem. He's about to do what he enjoys most, and stretch a simple statement into a story of epic proportion. "As far as I know, I'm married to Kate and monogamous. Did brain surgery make me forget I'm a Mormon?"

"On the way over here, Mirjami told me she's in love with you."

"That's just silly. She doesn't even know me."

He shrugs. "She wasn't joking."

I ignore this foolishness, take Kate's drink to her, and sit beside her.

None of us had ever been in such company before. Prime Minister Paavo Jokitalo. Minister of Finance Risto Kouva. Minister of Foreign Affairs Daniel Solstrand. Minister of Foreign Trade and Development Sauli Sivola. The head of the Social Democratic Party, Hannu Nykyri. Member of European Parliament and the head of Real Finns, Topi

Ruutio, and Minister of the Interior Osmo Ahtiainen. Most of them are accompanied by husbands or wives, girlfriends, mistresses. It's a big do, decided upon last night, on Vappu, when they were drunk. They decided to continue today. Their country and their hangovers can wait.

The band is great. I eavesdrop on conversations held in loud voices that carry over the music.

I don't know what I was expecting. Maybe great people discussing weighty matters of state. It was the gossip of the smashed. So-and-so had a bad scrape job and now she's sterile. So-and-so gave so-and-so snout. She's a tampon — a stuck-up cunt.

Given my recent problem with teen-type hard-ons and sexual preoccupation, I thought having Kate, Aino, Mirjami and Jenna surrounding me might cause slavering and maybe even auto-ejaculation. The effect is the opposite. It's a bit like eating at a gourmet buffet. All that sumptuous quiff in one place adjusts my perspective and has a calming effect. The others are young beauties, but I still think Kate the most gorgeous.

At a certain point, the prime minister stands and taps his glass with a spoon for quiet. When he has the attention of all, he says, "We have special guests with us tonight." He asks Milo and me to stand. "These men are national heroes."

He talks about me being shot twice in the line of duty, and recounts the story of how Milo and I, without backup, entered a school for dysfunctional children under attack by a maniac and ended the siege. Who knows how many young lives we saved?

I imagine the school shooter's head slump after Milo put a bullet in the back of it. And then the prime minister both pisses me off and makes me cringe.

"And now," he says, "along with this young man . . ." He gestures for Sweetness to stand. Sweetness plays the role, lazily stretches his arms in a way that seems natural, and shows the twin monster .45s in their holsters under his jacket. The crowd is drunk and over-impressed. Sweetness gets up. ". . . they'll soon bring to justice the murderer of Lisbet Söderlund, an event of such horror that it will be remembered as a dark nadir in the annals of Finnish history. These men are our Untouchables." He slurs the word. "Untushables."

Milo shoots me a "Told ya so" smirk. "Inspector Vaara," the prime minister asks, "would you tell us how the case progresses?"

Rounds of shots start hitting the table at regular intervals. The true boozing begins.

Jenna gazes at Sweetness with an adoration that extends far beyond familial love. A Jerry Lee Lewis scenario is in the making.

I put on my practiced in the mirror smile, the extra-wide version. "With strong-arm tactics, shakedowns, extortion, threats, intimidation and beatings, we intend to terrorize Finland's racist community until they give up the killer of their own volition, to save themselves more pain."

The crowd doesn't know if I'm joking or not. Either way, they like it. They laugh and clap. I notice Kate does neither. The crowd gets drunker and mills around. All the men make it to our end of the table at some point. Whether they're interested in us crime fighters or not, we've got the young primo tail and they want a closer look. Of course, the nation's leading politicians combined with said primo tail makes our group the focus of attention of all the other patrons in the restaurant.

Kate makes friends with Mirjami and Jenna. Kate wears an evening dress and her Manolo pumps. Mirjami has forsaken Hello Kitty garb and *stadin slangi* for a white and pretty, rather conservative summer dress that accents her tan, and she speaks standard Finnish. Jenna wears nice jeans and top that shows her magnificent cleavage to good advantage. Casual dress is fine in Jut-tutupa — I'm wearing jeans myself — and I don't think Jenna has a big wardrobe budget. She doesn't drop her East Helsinki dialect. I doubt she can. She doesn't try to be anything but herself, and with her looks, she doesn't have to. Mirjami asks Kate questions about me. "What's it like to be married to a famous cop?"

Kate gives a smirk and drunken snort. "Like being married to Tony Soprano."

Mirjami asks more personal things, what I'm like as a person. Sneaky. Kate doesn't catch on. I don't care for it.

The male politicos all introduce themselves at some point. They're at that state of drunkenness where they've forgotten their own escorts and that our girls are taken and hope our lookers will shoot them some trim.

The prime minister isn't so drunk, just polite. He strikes up a conversation with Kate, finds out she manages Kämp, and suggests the possibility of making a deal for all foreign dignitaries to stay there at a fixed rate. She gives him a business card. He promises to call. She beams excitement. Everyone drinks too much, except me. A little after midnight, the interior minister suggests a continuation of affairs of state aboard his yacht tomorrow. All present are invited and should meet at the Nyland Yacht Club Blekholmen clubhouse at noon. He asks who's in. All shout approval.

The interior minister and Jyri approach me. "Allow me to introduce Inspector Vaara, my hatchet man," Jyri says.

I say, "I prefer the term 'enforcer.' "

The minister says he'd like for me to be at the yacht club, and hopes I'll bring Kate. He would like to speak with her as well. This piques my curiosity. I thanked Jyri for arranging the babysitter, she seemed perfect, but said I would need another tomorrow.

"She's my aunt," he said, "and she loves kids. She'd probably pay you to let her babysit again, just ask her. Come to the bar with me," he says, "and I'll show you something."

We walk over, lean against it, and Jyri keeps his voice hushed. "Did you know," he says, "that there are now more spies in Finland than at any time since the Cold War?"

"No, I didn't," I answer.

"Russia has by far the most here, around thirty trained operatives, followed by the U.S. and China, and then there are small representations by other countries as well. They're seeking information about our defense policy and intentions toward

NATO, and countries economically and technologically behind us are looking for shortcuts through espionage."

"And the point is?"

"I know who they are, and some of them are quite upset about heroin revenues lost by theft. Your campaign against the drug trade ends now until the Söderlund murder is solved, for the obvious reason that you're under scrutiny. You were upset because we've taken no steps to interdict the human slave trade. You made an attempt and it ended badly."

I start to speak, but he raises a hand to silence me. "Yes, I know all about it. I had you move money and drugs from one criminal's house to another. I then spoke to a Russian spy, told him I knew about his problem, gave him names and the address where you left the money and dope, and said I prefer they take care of it in-house. The men who raped and murdered the women you tried to help were among them. I asked him for proof when the matter was resolved."

He takes out his iPhone and shows me an image. Five men are in a warehouse, naked. Chains hanging from a crossbeam have hooks on the end. These hooks are driven into the soft flesh behind the chins of five men. Their toes are inches from the floor. They're in various states of being tortured to death. Electrodes are attached to tongues and genitals. A couple lack genitals and or other body parts. A couple have most of their skin flayed off.

"One would assume that they were told they wouldn't be allowed to die until they revealed the location of the rest of the drugs and money they've stolen," Jyri said. "Of course, they couldn't. I've seen the dossiers of these men. They've trafficked in hundreds of women and subjected many to unthinkable abuse. Now they've paid, and gangsters will no longer be searching for the real thieves, meaning you and yours. You have indeed done something to, as you put it, 'help people.' That was my gift to you."

He deletes the image. I thank him. Now I can believe that, in some small way, justice has been served by my activities. I go back to my seat beside Kate.

Real Finn boss Topi Ruutio stops by and one of his redneck nationalist supporters comes to worship. We're speaking English and the devotee, loud, drunk and rude, tells Kate to learn to speak fucking Finnish. He must think it will score points with Ruutio, who seems like a nice guy. Ruutio calls him an ill-mannered cunt-head and tells him to fuck off.

On the way out, Milo hands Kate a set of car keys. He points down the street at a brand-new Audi S4. "That belongs to you," he says.

"Why?"

Milo looks at the ground, hands in pockets. "I upset you the other day when I slipped and you found out about the body dump and I wanted to make it up to you."

Kate is second-day drunk and weaving a bit. She kisses his cheek. "You think you can buy my affection," she says, "but you can't."

He reddens, turns away. She giggles. "You don't have to, I already like you. But if you want to keep showering me with expensive gifts, I'll let you."

The guy that yelled at Kate is smoking in the corner of the patio as we come out. No one is looking. Sweetness ambles over and slaps him. Even openhanded, the blow lifts the guy off his feet, onto his back. He rolls over and pushes himself up onto all fours, tries to get up. Sweetness rests his foot on his back, puts his weight into it and slams him hard onto the ground. "Be rude to her again," he said, "and I'll kill you."

Sweetness walks away. The guy stands up. In the streetlight, I see the slap left about a thousand millimeter–sized little blood blisters on his cheek and jaw. He reaches in his mouth and pulls out a molar, then another tooth, and another tooth, and he cries.

I drive Kate home in her new Audi.

27

I get up early the next morning. I have a post-op checkup with my brother Jari. In his office, we do the usual stuff. He tests my reflexes and blood pressure and so on, but mostly we talk.

"Do you have any physical problems at all? Coordination. Weakness. Headaches. Any more seizures?"

"No, I'm fine."

"What about going flat? Have you had any improvement there, felt any emotions?"

"Of a kind," I say. "I don't feel anything, but sometimes I like or want things."

I pick up my cane. "Like this. I love this thing, would sleep with it if I could."

"What about people?"

"Women. I see a beautiful girl, it drives me crazy. Picture the wants of a six-year-old combined with the libido of a sixteen-year-old."

"Have you acted on those feelings?"

"No, but I could. I don't seem to care about what I do, either. My existence is binary. Want/don't want. Like/don't like. Will/won't. I have no shades of gray."

"What about your family. Anything there?"

"Not a damned thing. I practice smiling in the mirror. I remember what my feelings were, and act according to what I think I should do based on memories. It seems to work. I know what my duties are, and I fulfill them."

"I advised you to talk to your wife about this. Have you done it, or even considered it?"

"No, and I won't. I don't think Kate could accept it."

He leans forward in his chair, rests his elbows on his desk and his head on his hands. "It's been three months. No progress at all doesn't bode well. You *need* your wife and her support."

I say nothing.

"Do you really think you've hidden the change in yourself from her? How do you think this is affecting her?"

I think of the gifts she now accepts, knowing the source of the money that bought them. She never would have even contemplated accepting them a short time ago. She's trying to find a way of coming to terms with what I do now, and she refuses to complain because I asked her, openly and honestly, before all that has come to pass began. I realize, although she isn't coming to terms with it, that it isn't fair to hold her to the agreement, because she didn't understand what it might entail. Nor did I.

I was naïve and used. Arvid once told me that my naïveté would be the death of me. For the hundredth time, I think: this black-op was never for the forces of good. I was misled. I'm a rogue cop and a criminal. Sooner or later, I'll outlive my usefulness and they'll find a way to get rid of me. Probably set me up, discredit me, and see that I get a long prison sentence. The public will applaud such excellent skank. The mighty brought low. Even a savior of children. I can't quit because first I need to find a way to not only get free of the corrupt politicos that control me, but to destroy them in order to do it.

It occurs to me that her acceptance of the Audi last night symbolizes Kate's acceptance of the situation, that she's so fed up that she doesn't care anymore, and maybe my marriage is in trouble.

"Doctor-patient privilege," I say. "I do things that are illegal, with the blessing — no, under the mandate — of the establishment. Some of them are ugly. I don't hide them from her — or many of them, anyway. They bother her. I don't know if it bothers her because I do them, or because I'm untroubled by them." I don't mention her two-day drunk. It was Vappu, might mean nothing.

"Do you take the tranquilizers I prescribed for you?"

"No. Nothing makes me nervous."

He sighed, leaned back in his chair and folded his arms.

"As your doctor, brother and friend, I'm advising you to have an open discussion with your wife, go on sick leave, stop whatever it is you're doing, and seek psychotherapy. I'll find you a good therapist. You're not getting better on your own, and you need rest and assistance until your brain repairs itself."

I stood up and thanked him. "I'll give everything you said consideration." I left, having no intention of doing any such thing.

28

Noon. The Nyland Yacht Club. The whole gang from last night reappears, except for Aino. She had to go to work. Breakfast libations. Mimosas. Bloody Marys. Beer. The legal blood alcohol content for piloting a boat is twice that for driving a car. You can get pretty smashed and stay law compliant. Everyone dresses warm, coats with sweaters underneath. It's forty-two degrees Fahrenheit, and cold on the Baltic, especially with the boat in motion.

Living with a foreigner causes unusual habits. Kate can conceptualize minus temperatures in Celsius, but not the plus side of the thermometer, so I've gotten in the habit of automatically converting in my head for her benefit. Now I often think in Fahrenheit too, but only on the plus side.

The prime minister has a thirty-one-foot motorized cruiser, a sharp-looking newer vessel. Below deck, it has three double-berth cabins, a big saloon and galley, a head, and seating for navigational equipment.

I text messaged Milo before we left the house, told him I wanted heroin and a throw-down gun hidden in the vessel, along with a GPS tracker, so we always know where it is, and keys to the boat, in case we wanted to use it. I had in mind that it would make for a more convenient way to dump bodies.

We set sail, make our way out to deeper waters, and the blender starts churning. It's got a motor strong enough to power a car. Down in the saloon, mojitos and frozen drinks made of dark rum and fresh fruit start flowing for the women. I stay away from the hard stuff, crack a beer, find the fishing gear. I pull in perch, pike and sea trout. Milo and Sweetness felt ill at ease around the politicians, without me alongside them for the purpose of social lubrication. They looked for me, saw my catch, now seven decent-sized fish, and took the other two deck chairs on either side of me.

Sweetness had never fished before. I taught him the basics: casting and reeling, how to avoid tangling a line, how to bring a fish in and get it off the hook. He caught his first fish, a good-sized pike, and got little-kid excited. Milo is a good fisherman.

The other men come up on deck and sip scotch, to fight the chill, they say. They watch us reel in more fish, want a turn at it themselves. We give up our seats. The interior minister says he'd like a word with me.

We lean against the rail. The wind covers our voices. I hand him an envelope. I decided to deliver his cut personally today. This is one of the things he would like to discuss with me. At present, he takes a fifteen percent cut, which goes to necessities, such as the Kokoomus party's campaign funds. And yachts. I don't say it. He doesn't know I'm out of the drug-dealer-destruction business for the moment.

He needs another five percent bump out of the slush fund. Not retroactive, just from future earnings. He knows I don't like it and offers an explanation. The money is to go to the Real Finns.

I ask why he would ensure that his competitors have adequate campaign funds.

The interior minister asks me about my political views. I say I envision some kind of democratic fascism. I believe in democracy, but media manipulation and information control has rendered voters incapable of making informed decisions. He agrees, cites the Finnish plan to join NATO that has been crammed down the throat of the public. The minister calls my views simplistic but astute, and shares his own views. The minister waxes wistful.

Finland, not so long ago, he explains, was a paradise for the worker, the common man. Politics, like every other aspect of life, has been globalized. Finland once took care of its citizens. Education. Medical care. The poor. But in fact, all the way back to the post–Second World War days of Kekkonen, it was always a scam, just what it took to keep voters happy, not altruistic concern for the public welfare. The higher powers in government never really gave a damn. Now, the ideals are gone. The USSR fell and Socialist ideals died with them. Finland's far left and Communists got old, tired, apathetic and greedy, and the pretense of a caring government evaporated. Now, like almost everywhere, it's every man for himself.

He sighs, miffed. "The ranks of Real Finns," he says, "are growing by leaps and bounds. They're scaring the shit out of the other center and left parties with talk of leaving the EU, going back from the euro to the Finnish markka, their politics of hate, blaming the country's social ills on foreigners. Those parties are suffering mass defections. Kokoomus is the party of the rich, and those who wish to be rich. The fear factor is the key to winning the election. Liberals, knowing they don't stand a chance, will vote for Kokoomus, because it's the best way to keep Real Finns out of office. There are seventeen parties. The more momentum Real Finns gain, the more it will pressure members of the other fifteen parties to vote for Kokoomus, out of simple terror. Any show of weakness by Real Finns might give voters hope and encourage them to vote for their party of choice.

"Real Finns, being the party of the common man, receive common donations, and not enough. Veikko Saukko had promised a million euros in campaign funds for Real Finns in early 2009, almost a year and a half ago, then reneged because the party's anti-foreigner stance wasn't strong enough. Saukko is a man given to temperamental mood swings, and in fact, he likes me," the minister said. "I still hope to get him to come up with the promised cash."

I take the envelope back out of his hand. "You want something from me. After we discuss it, we can discuss money."

He wrapped his arms around himself, bunched himself up against the cold and laughed. "Most people fear me," he said.

"You couldn't give a fuck less. Why is that?"

I shrug. "It's not my nature."

"I've found a truism in life," he said. "People good at one thing tend to be good at others. You've proven yourself adroit in the assignments given you."

I say nothing.

"Veikko Saukko began in the scandal-sheet business and has a great fondness for dirt."

I laugh. "You want me to be minister of propaganda and start a hate rag?"

"Yes. And call it *Be Happy.*"

"What level of dirt?"

"Deep and evil left-wing gossip filth. An attack on Lisbet Söderlund's character should dominate the first issue. A 'Thank God that scourge of the nation is dead' type of thing. Discredit leftists as Commies, fags, dopers, reprobates, nigger lovers. Fear-mongering — armed blacks are organized, preparing to kill good, innocent, white God-fearing Finns — should be a major theme. Scatter it in with celeb skank to hide the purpose of the rag. It will impress the hell out of Saukko. Can you do that?"

I know just the guy, my old pal Jaakko Pahkala. "I can. I have to decide if I will. Tell me a couple things. Your guests, and I think they're your cronies, are from various political parties. Why is that?"

"Mutual interest."

"Such as?"

"For instance, to use the previous example, NATO. It makes little practical sense for Finland to join it, yet we're making it happen." He laughed. "I mean, can you really picture NATO defending little Finland if Russia sends tank divisions rolling across our border? We have no oil. There's nothing to be gained by NATO in coming to Finland's defense. However, joining NATO means the creation of positions of power with great prestige. It means contracts for weapons systems with companies that people on this boat own stock in. Energy to power the systems. It means more wealth for the wealthy."

"At the expense of the Finnish taxpayer."

"Inspector, this is the way the world has always been. I can't apologize for that."

"And another question. What happened to my predecessor?"

"Your predecessor?"

"Yes. I did have one, didn't I?"

He pauses, rubs his chin, deciding whether to tell me the truth. "He and his team are all dead. Their approach was low-tech compared to yours. They went to St. Petersburg to assassinate a human trafficking ring.

They failed. They were military, by the way, not cops."

I give him back the envelope. "Yes, I can start your skank rag and up the tithe. In return, from time to time, I'd like information, and military-grade equipment."

"Information such as?"

"Wait a second."

I don't know where Milo is and if he should be seen doing whatever he's doing. I call him and put it on speakerphone. "Tell the interior minister what it was you wanted to monitor cell phones."

"A GSM A5. 1 Real Time Cell Phone Interceptor. It's undetectable. Handles up to four base stations, up to quad band, and up to twenty phones," Milo says.

The minister says, "I'll get you two of them."

I ring off.

"You know the whereabouts of all the Real Finns leaders at all times?" I ask.

"Well, my people do."

"This race war must be stopped, and I intend to solve the murder of Lisbet Söderlund. Tomorrow, I want to interrogate Roope Malinen."

"I don't want him hurt."

"That's up to him," I say, "and it's part of the deal. Most leaders of racist organizations are criminals and to a certain degree hucksters, using hate in order to unify supporters and profit from it in one way or another, not because of true ideology. I think that's his profile, and I suspect he knows something about the murders. I'm going to get it out of him."

A cold wind gusts and rocks us. "All right. He's yours if you don't kill him. May I speak to your wife?"

"It depends on why."

"It's about Hotel Kämp."

I nod. She's downstairs in a circle of gossiping hens, drunk and talking overtop one another. I call her aside. The three of us go to an empty cabin. She's weaving, and it's not just the rocking of the yacht. She giggles. "The prime minister is an excellent host. My glass always seemed to be full. I think I drank more than I thought I did."

The minister says to her, "I want to bug your hotel. When foreign dignitaries come — say, Vladimir Putin — their private conversations could be used as an edge in negotiations. It's for the good of your adopted nation."

Solemn, Kate nods agreement. "That," she says, "is an excellent idea, and I would be proud to serve the nation. I'm on maternity leave, though, and not in charge. You need to ask Aino, whom you met last night."

"I'm sure encouragement from you would go a long way," he says. "Or if Aino doesn't agree, we can simply wait until your maternity leave is over."

I don't tell her what a giant mistake she made, or that she made a promise that goes against everything she stands for. The hotel will be used for honey traps. Diplomats and certain businessmen will be recorded engaging in illicit sexual liaisons. Failure to succumb to blackmail will result in the destruction of their careers and personal lives.

I decide I won't tell her. She goes back to drinking fruity frozen rum drinks with Mirjami and Jenna and her new political pals.

29

It's a little after six p.m. when we start the drive home from the yacht club. Kate is drunker than I thought. She's got that female drunk thing going on, by turns giggly and weepy. She's been drinking three days running. I'm not sure if this is just her first exposure to hanging out with a hard-drinking female crowd, keeping up with them drink for drink without paying attention and realizing how much she's consuming, or if something is troubling her and causing this uncharacteristic behavior. For me, it was a workday that entailed socializing. I had only two beers.

I stop and pick up some baby formula. Her breast milk is alcohol toxic. It unsettles me that she didn't take that into consideration before getting smashed. Again. Kate waits in the car while I shop. I get a text message. "Tomorrow, Roope Malinen will be at his summer cottage on the island of

Nauvo, near Turku." The message includes the GPS coordinates for the cottage.

Kate has never been to Turku. I get back in the car. "Kate, how would you like to go on a road trip tomorrow, to Turku? It's about two hours east of Helsinki."

"Just us?" She sounds hopeful.

"No, I have to do some cop stuff, but Milo and Sweetness will come with me, so I thought maybe Mirjami and Jenna could go with you. You can give your new Audi a good breaking-in. My brother Timo has a farm near there. After we do our business and you do your sightseeing, if he's available, we could pay him a visit."

She's in happy-drunk mode at the moment. "Sounds fun," she says.

We go home. I thank Jyri's aunt, give her a fifty, pre-pay a taxi for her, send her home and get on the horn. Kate passes out on the couch.

I promised Moreau he could accompany me while I conduct interviews. He promised to teach Milo how to use the advanced weaponry he bought, doesn't need, and doesn't know how to use. Sweetness has never fired a gun. We're searching for, I believe, military trained killers, perhaps mercenaries. He needs to learn to shoot. I'd like to kill all these birds with one stone.

"I have business in Turku anyway," Moreau says. "It suits me."

I tell him to meet me here at eight a.m.

Step two. Call my brother. This is harder. "Jesus, Kari," he says, "I haven't heard from you in two years, seen you in four. To what do I owe the honor?"

"I have some business in Turku and thought I'd drop by, if that's OK with you."

"It's more than OK. It would be great. I hear you have a baby now. You gonna bring her?"

"Actually, I may bring a few people. Cops and their women. And we'd like to do a little weapons training while we're there. Is that all right with you?"

Anger creeps into his voice. "For a minute there, I thought you wanted to see me. In fact, you want something from me. That's it. Right?"

The truth is, I don't give damn if I see him or anyone else, because of my lack of emotions. But I'm trying to do what I view as my duty toward my family, and I neglected my duty toward him when I felt emotions because of those emotions. It's easier now. "No, I want to see you. I can shoot guns anywhere. I'm a fucking cop, if you recall. We have practice ranges. I can come see you and *not* shoot, if you prefer.

Or I can go to a practice range and *not* see you, if you prefer that."

He goes quiet for a minute. "Just tell me why you haven't come to see me."

I tell the truth. "I don't know. Why haven't *you* come to see *me?*"

He's quiet again. "It's complicated. Just fucking come visit. Take target practice with a panzer if you want. And you're all welcome to stay the night. We have lots of room."

"It's good to hear your voice, big brother," I say.

"Yours too." He rings off.

Next, Milo. "We're going on a road trip tomorrow. Bring that nuclear arsenal or whatever it is you bought. Moreau is going to teach you to use it."

"Cool! Where are we going?"

"Different places around the Turku area. We'll probably stay the night, maybe at my brother's place. And Mirjami is invited."

"I don't know if she can come. She might have to work."

I recall that Mirjami told Milo she loves me. She pays me no undue attention. I find this strange. "Tell her if her love for me is true, to trade out shifts or something. Kate is coming in a separate car, and it will suck for her if she's alone. In fact, she probably wouldn't come and be disappointed."

Milo says he'll try. I tell him to be here at eight.

I make a similar call to Sweetness, and invite Jenna. It's no problem for her, she doesn't go to school and she's unemployed. The girls are too young and immature to become close friends with Kate, but she seems to enjoy their company, at least on a superficial level.

I save the worst for last and call Jaakko Pahkala. I have a love-hate relationship with him. I love hating him. His little rat face, his squeaky voice, his attitude — everything about him annoys me. Pre–brain op, I would have gotten an adrenaline hate surge just by picking up the phone to call him. He refers to himself as a journalist, and is employed as such on a freelance basis by our most yellow skank rags. He loves skank. Lives and breathes skank. The uglier and more loathsome, the more he reveres it. Also, he's petty and malicious. He once tried to have me fired because I refused him an interview.

Jaakko is like vile medicine. Sometimes it's required, and in the same vein, at times he has his uses. This is one of them.

He answers his phone. "Inspector Vaara, this is an unexpected pleasure. How may I be of service to you?"

"I'm starting a new publication," I say, "and I'd like you to be editor."

"I'm intrigued."

" 'Editor' is euphemistic. You're the sole employee, the publication date is uncertain, and you're not to let anyone know the publication exists until I authorize you to do so."

"And the nature of this publication?"

"We're going to revamp the classic *Be Happy.*"

"The best magazine ever made in Finland," he says. "I'm honored."

I describe it as the minister defined it to me, but with my own spin on it. "It's to be a hate rag under the guise of a scandal sheet. For instance, Lisbet Söderlund. You'll paint her black, invent vicious details concerning her private life, and leave the reader feeling she was a traitorous slut who deserved to die."

"My, my, Inspector. That is the skankiest skank that ever skanked a skank."

"You'll go after blacks, Jews and Muslims. Blame all our social ills on them. Picture 1920s American KKK hate materials, or prewar German and French hate propaganda. I assume you're familiar with those styles. As with the old *Be Happy,* do some career destruction. It's OK if we get sued, but stay just on the side of the line where we don't have criminal charges pressed against us for incitement of racial violence."

"My familiarity with those styles would be better termed expertise," he says. "I have a large personal collection of the literature."

"In your first mock-up issue, go after the leading center and left political figures, as well as celebs. A lot of drug-and-alcohol-problem material, nympho and fag accusations, with the requisite images."

"I have the latest version of Photoshop," Jaakko says.

"At the same time, however, you'll be collecting an equal amount of dirt on the right wing, Kokoomus, and Real Finns. You'll keep these files secret for now. And of course you'll have copies of everything for me. *Everything.*"

"Inspector, are you our new minister of propaganda?"

"You may consider me so."

"And my compensation?"

"Two thousand euros a month."

"Make it three."

"Two and half, and don't try to bargain."

"Very well. May I ask your sudden interest in the collection of blackmail material?"

"No. You have a duplicitous nature. You receive no unnecessary information."

He snickers. "We all have our flaws."

"In this instance, you'll suppress them, or you'll pay a high price."

He snickers again. "Will you have me shot?"

"No, but given the choice, you might prefer it. You'll be fired by all of your employers. You'll find your bank account emptied. You'll lose your home. You'll receive bills for loans you never took out. You'll be convicted for crimes you didn't commit, and I'm pretty sure they would make you the jailhouse sissy."

"Inspector, you seem to have become a man of importance. I'm impressed."

"I'm so pleased. It's important to me that you hold me in high regard."

"I'll do a good job. And I'll be your lap-dog. No duplicity."

"I'm glad we understand one another," I say, and ring off.

The skank dreck sheet will never be published. It will, however, be written and prepared, and the mock-up will be in the possession of the minister of the interior in the event that I need to entrap and extort him. My own version of the slander skank rag, featuring such gems as a round-heeled slattern giving him skull in the alley behind a bar, might just possibly make it to print.

I received messages while I talked to Jaakko. Mirjami and Jenna will be coming with us tomorrow. Kate is coming to on the sofa. I tell her all the arrangements have been made for the trip to Turku.

"What trip?" she asks.

30

Kate pretends that she's just sleepy, acts as if she hadn't blacked out. With a little assistance from me, she remembers everything and exhibits enthusiasm for the trip. Whether real or feigned, I don't know. I see that she has that kind of nerve-jangled hangover that comes from days of drinking, but puts on a perky face rather than admit how bad she feels. She doesn't comment when I feed Anu with formula from a bottle rather than hand her over for a suck on a tit. She doesn't want to discuss her behavior. I don't want to make her. She sits with her laptop and researches Turku, plans her day as a tourist. I go to the grocery and load up on snacks, beer and soft drinks for the trip.

Everyone shows up at eight a.m. sharp. The men will take the Jeep Wrangler, since we have Milo's guns to transport, and the girls will ride in the Audi. Kate is nervous but excited and looking forward to her first long-distance Finnish driving experience. Mirjami, once again in Hello Kitty attire, has a license, and says she'll give Kate driving pointers.

However, they have differing ideas about how to spend the day. Turku was Finland's original capital — its cathedral was consecrated in 1300, and it still has remnants of the Middle Ages, or re-creations of it along cobblestoned streets. Established by Sweden, it still feels more Swedish than Finnish, and Swedish is spoken at least as much, if not more, by its residents. The Aurajoki divides the city.

Kate would like to see handicrafts and go to the tourist area, where people in authentic clothing, blacksmiths and weavers and such, make things the old-fashioned way. Also, Turku Castle is, if not the biggest in Finland and the Scandinavian region, close to it. She suggests that exploring it could also be a fascinating way to spend the day.

Mirjami and Jenna want to go to Muumimaailma — Muumin World. Kate doesn't know what it is. We're all surprised. The Muumit — Muumi plural — are one of those things you just take for granted everyone knows about.

Jenna laughs. "You'll know about it soon.

All little kids love the Muumit." She explains that the Muumit are characters from a series of books by Tove Jansson. They're round white trolls with big hippopotamus noses who live in Muumin valley, and they and their friends have adventures in the forest.

I think it finally sinks in that she's twice Jenna's age. "And of all the things to do in Turku," Kate asks, "you would most like to spend your day with the trolls?"

Jenna grins wide and gives a vigorous nod of her head. "Uh-huh."

They compromise. Muumin World is on the island of Kailo beside the old town of Naantali. The town grew around an old convent, and is composed mostly of wooden houses along narrow cobbled streets that house handicraft shops. They can all have their fun.

Sweetness wants to drive. I say sure, but no *kossu.* He hands me the keys. I toss them to Milo. He likes to drive, I want to think. I notice Moreau has stubble blurring his wings of Icarus. I ask why. He says he believes we'll wrap this up soon. He's growing hair for changing identities.

We load up the vehicles and agree to meet in the market square for lunch. I put Anu's car seat in the back of the Audi, strap her in, and we get on the road.

In my mind, I replay my conversation with the minister of the interior. He said that in early 2009, Veikko Saukko promised to donate a million euros to Real Finns. A short time later, his son and daughter were kidnapped. Welshing on a million-dollar promise causes hard feelings. This provides motive.

Veikko's son, Antti, was himself affiliated with the racists. This provides potential accomplices. He disappeared, although the ten-million-euro ransom had been paid. The kidnappers had made good on their bargain to release the daughter. Why show good faith in her instance, and then dispose of the son? Unless Antti took part in the kidnapping, rather than being a victim of it. And if he then fucked his racist buddies somehow, it could have sparked the shooting of his sister as payback. Antti had recently been stripped of his position as chairman of the board of Ilmarinen Sisu Corporation. Fucked in the ass by his father without provocation. Well, there was that fucking-Daddy's-wife thing, but still, this provides additional motive.

Jussi Kosonen supposedly perpetrated the kidnapping. He's dead. His three children are missing. It stinks of a setup. Kosonen was a patsy. If they kidnapped his kids while his wife was away and forced him to keep Kaarina Saukko in his basement and later deliver her, he would be useless after retrieving the ransom money for them. Hence, a bullet in the back of his head. It would be the most practical thing to do with him. His children likely got the same treatment.

And I was right, our black-ops unit had predecessors, and they were military. My guess would be sheep-dipped Erikoisjääkärit, Special Forces, and they had gone to Russia on a mission concerning the human slave trade. So, like me, they had higher motives than ripping off dope dealers. And they were pros. And they died. And we're bunglers. We'd better goddamned well improve our paramilitary skills.

The quiet has gone on for too long. Nervous puppy Milo has to break it. "Want to hear a joke?" he asks no one in particular.

No one answers. This doesn't stop him.

"A priest checks into a hotel and says to the clerk, 'I assume your porn is disabled.' The clerk answers, 'No, Father, it's normal porn, you sick fuck.' "

Moreau chuckles. Sweetness guffaws. I smile. I never thought to practice laughing.

"Somebody tell a story," Milo says.

Sweetness asks, "What kind of story?"

Milo thinks about it. "A fuck story. And it has to be true."

No one volunteers.

"Kari, you taciturn bastard. Tell us a story."

I've never told a sex story, although I have a number of them. I spent years as chief of police in an area with a major ski resort. A perk of being a single cop in a tourist area is the availability of women looking for short-term affairs — vacation entertainment. I never went overboard with it, but if I felt the need, women were almost always there for me. I've seldom listened to sex stories, either. The kind of people I've mostly spent my life around don't brag about intimacies, don't need that kind of self-esteem reinforcement. I decide I'll try it, just this once, to see what it's like, even though I know this is some kind of brain surgery post-op quirk manifesting itself.

"OK. This one time. Some years ago, back when I lived in Kittilä, it was the night before Christmas Eve. I was making rounds, stopped in Hullu Poro, a big bar there. I was in civilian clothes but had my Glock in a belt holster. This girl comes up to me. She's a half-Arab and half-German aerobics instructor, about five foot five, had on a tight T-shirt and jeans, and I could tell she had a six pack and an ass so high and firm you could sit a beer can on it. Skin the color of milk chocolate. Black hair down to her ass. Perky breasts. Around twenty-five years old. A beautiful girl. She took a plane to Levi by herself for Christmas on a whim.

"She walked up to me, I didn't even see her coming. 'Can I see your gun?' she asked.

"I said 'No.' She asked if I was a cop, and I said 'Yeah.' 'Will you show it to me later?' she asked. I said 'Maybe.'

"She asked me what time I got off and I said midnight. She wanted to go techno dancing and asked if I would take her. I said I would be honored. She said it was too bad I was a cop, she'd like to do some X.

"As it happened, I busted some Austrian Eurotrash rich kid that night for speeding, going about a hundred and thirty miles an hour. Baron von Dogfucker or something like that, who had brought about a hundred of his closest friends to celebrate Christmas with him in Levi. He had enough Ecstasy with him for all of them to celebrate in high style for days. He had a baggie full of the shit and I had never tried it, so I thought, *What the fuck,* and stuck four hits of it into my pocket before I entered it into evidence.

"After work I went up to her room and brought a bottle of wine. We had a glass, I said 'Surprise,' and took a couple of tabs out of my pocket. We ate one each. I didn't like it at first, it felt like my mind was shaking apart, but it didn't last long and then it was a really enjoyable high.

"I took her to a place where they were spinning techno. She kept falling over, laughing, had no sense of up, down or sideways. I kept scooping her up and setting her back on her feet. She swept all the drinks off the bar with her arm. I bought us more.

"She wanted me to take her home. She wanted to hear Finnish language and asked me to read to her, so I pulled a Bible off the shelf and opened it at random to the book of John. Just when I got to 'and the Word was made flesh' — I'll always remember the citation. It's 1:14 — she made her move and we started fucking. The floor, the bed. The sauna. The snow. You can do it in the snow after the sauna for a few minutes when your body temperature is high enough, just don't get your genitals in it. I tacked a sleeping bag to the roof and we climbed up and fucked under the moon.

"And she was an expert at sucking cock. Every time I came, she sucked me again and made me hard, over and over. At some point, we took the other hit of X. She loved

69, had almost no bodyweight. I was three times her size and turning and lifting her was no more difficult than rolling myself over in bed.

"The date lasted thirty hours. After maybe the tenth time, my orgasms were dry, just powerful contractions. We did it nearly twenty times. Afterward, my dick was so tender it was hard to touch it without discomfort for days. I took her back to her hotel. She called me to say good-bye and I gave her a ride to the airport. We never spoke again. I never wanted to do it again. The experience was unrepeatable. At Baron von Dogfucker's hearing, I learned that the Ecstasy was in four-way hits. We were supposed to break them into pieces, so we were *really* high. When I drove her to the airport, she told me that her father had just died, and she came to Levi after his funeral with nothing but the clothes on her back. She was just escaping. She was a nice girl."

"Damn," Milo said, "that was a good story. I didn't know you can fuck in the snow."

"Milo," I said, "you can fuck in the burning sands of the Sahara. People always fuck. Always find a way."

"Got any more stories?"

A failed experiment. I took no pleasure

324

whatsoever in relating a sexual adventure. "Yeah, but you only get the one. Now it's your turn."

He grips the wheel with his knees to steer while he cracks his window and lights a smoke. "I would if I had any. I don't have that much experience. I've had two semi-long-term relationships, three or four short-term, and no one-night stands. I have the feeling I'm a lousy fuck, just don't know what I'm doing."

Moreau says, "It's hard to be a lousy fuck, unless you have a problem with premature ejaculation or are impotent. Let's face the facts. Sex consists of heat, lubrication and friction. If those things are all in order, your sexual performance is probably at least adequate."

"You're a man of the world," Milo says to him. "You must have some good stories."

"I haven't had a girlfriend for more than twenty years. I have sex exclusively with prostitutes. And never the same woman twice."

This intrigues both Milo and Sweetness. Their heads turn toward him. "Why?" Milo asks.

"Relationships and the emotions they entail are time-consuming and a distraction from weightier matters. However, like most men, I enjoy sex. A business transaction has no complications, and I have no concerns such as yours. The experience is solely about my pleasure. And why never the same woman twice? It guards against ennui. I never sleep with African women, because the AIDS rate is so high. I most prefer Southeast Asian woman. They tend to be beautiful, accommodating, and I find their vaginas interesting, reminiscent of elephant skin. There's something both exotic and erotic about it. I seldom engage prostitutes there anymore, either, though, for the same reason. AIDS is a danger."

There's something exotic about Moreau himself. He's a strange man. I've never met anyone quite like him.

"Sweetness, that leaves you," Milo says.

Sweetness reddens and takes a long pull from his flask. "I don't have any stories."

We're all quiet for a moment. We take his meaning and don't want to embarrass him further. Not even Milo.

"I'm between a rock and a hard spot," Sweetness says. "I'm in love with Jenna. I don't want to be with anyone but her, but I can't do anything about it. She's my third cousin once removed."

Milo and Moreau burst with laughter. I bury my face in my hands in disbelief. Milo loses control of himself, has to pull the car over to the side of the road.

Sweetness drinks more, fights back tears. His face is the color of strawberry jam.

I reach over the seat and put a hand on his shoulder. "If she's that distant a cousin, it's not incest. There's no danger of a genetic-related birth defect."

He looks back at me, blinks, unbelieving, afraid I'm teasing him. "Really?"

"If I fucked Mirjami," Milo says, "my aunt's daughter, our child might have eight arms and three heads. But you have no worries."

He takes this in for a while. "Still, she's only sixteen."

"She's of legal age," I say, "and you're only twenty-two. That's between you and her, and you and your conscience."

"For what it's worth," Milo says, "cousin or not, I would fuck the daylights out of Mirjami if she let me. That's why God made birth control."

"I wonder if Jenna has feelings for me too," Sweetness asks.

"I've seen the way she looks at you," I say. "I think it's safe to say that she does."

He looks at me, imploring, looking to me for truth, wisdom and certainty. "Are you sure?"

I nod. "Pretty sure. I think you can count on it."

His laughter diminishes to a chuckle, and Milo pulls out onto the highway again. I get a mental image of tiny Jenna and huge Sweetness. They take off their clothes. He must have a dick that would put Moby Penis to shame. She flees naked into the night, terrified.

The oddity strikes me. My killer, my Luca Brasi, and I have just had our first father-and-son talk.

"May I see your cane?" Moreau asks.

I hand it to him. He turns it over in his hands, examines it, admires it. "It is quite unique. At least, I have never seen such a thing. It must have been made for a very rich man, most likely royalty. The lion's-head handle must be close to a half pound of gold, plus the jewels are large and high-quality, and it is the work of a master crafts-man. How does it function?"

He hands it back to me. I smack the bottom tip of the cane hard against the car floor. The lion's mouth snaps open to near a hundred-and-eighty-degree angle. Some-times I carry it with the mouth open because it offers more surface area to hold on to, and also because I like the feel of the razors against the skin of my fingers. Of course, I can't shift my grip without drawing blood.

"The teeth are daggers and the edges razors on both sides. The two canine fangs aren't for cutting. They're spring releases. When pushed backward and depressed, the springs engage and the mouth clamps shut. So when swung like a baseball bat, the canines hit the target and the lion bites."

"Ingenious," Moreau says.

I'm curious about him, and suspicious of his motives. He's a spook for another government. He likely has an agenda that I haven't even guessed at. "Tell me about Mexico," I say.

"It is a miserable shithole."

I feign the practiced smile. "I meant about what you did there."

"As I said, as with all commodities, narcotics distribution is a global enterprise and delicately balanced. Many nations depend on drugs for the economic stability of their countries. The U.S. and Mexico among them. The balance was disturbed in Mexico and many thousands died in a war for control of the trade between the Sinaloa cartel and the Juárez gang.

"It reached a crisis level so acute that the U.S. would soon have to invade Mexico, the drug trade truly would be halted, or at least severely damaged, and the economies of the two countries along with it. What made the situation unique is that the vast majority of the drugs pass through a tiny area, the border crossing of the twin cities of Ciudad Juárez and El Paso, Texas. Through this funnel — which, ironically, the U.S. supposedly created as part of its War Against Drugs — dope passes into the States. Money and weapons pass into Mexico. To control this crossing is to control the drug trade.

"The answer, of course, was for one side to win the war and halt the killing. Some colleagues and I analyzed the situation and decided Joaquín Guzmán Loera's Sinaloa cartel was the best candidate, having exported more than two hundred tons of cocaine and a vast amount of heroin into the United States over the past decade. Their army was killing many people, but the wrong ones. We assisted them in killing the appropriate rivals, and trained their best soldiers, bringing them up to Special Forces standards. Sinaloa won the war, the death toll dropped significantly, and the economies of both countries remain intact. Mission accomplished."

"So you were an assassin," I say.

"In Spanish, an assassin is an *asesino*. Not a person of importance. I held the title of *sicario,* an executioner."

"What's the difference?"

He scoffed. I was a babe in the woods. "The number of zeros in my monthly pay."

"As a French advisor, Guzmán paid you as well?"

He grimaced, losing patience with me. "Of course I double-dipped. He also gave me the heroin I gave to you. A parting gesture of thanks. He was most grateful. He made last year's list of the world's top billionaires."

We entered Turku. I changed the subject. "Can you acquire false passports for me?"

"Of course, but does 'false' mean fake or registered in the country of identity?"

Kate, Anu, myself, Milo, Sweetness, and then I think: Jenna. Sweetness might refuse to leave without her in a romantic hissy fit. "Six, registered, and preferably diplomatic."

He laughed. "My friend, you may be overestimating my capabilities."

"I doubt it."

"That you realize you may need them increases my estimation of you. Let us make an agreement. As regards the passports, when our business is concluded, if I am satisfied, I will see to it that you are also satisfied. They will not be diplomatic, but from a country with a predominantly white population, so that you do not stand out."

Good enough. The passports will bring us one step closer to safety.

31

We enter Turku. I call Kate. They just arrived in the town square. We park and walk down a long row of stalls, flowers on the right side, fresh vegetables on the left, the cathedral looming in front of us. The temperature is brisk, but the sun warming. All of the big cities in the countries east of Russia in this part of the world seem the same to me. Helsinki, Turku, Tallinn, Stockholm, are almost interchangeable. There's always an old town, a market square, and malls and shopping centers with exactly the same chain stores in them. Tourists *über alles.*

I take Anu and put her in the carryall in front of me. We get lunch straightaway. More like brunch. It's not even ten thirty yet. The girls have plenty of time to wander around while we go about our business. From a stall specializing in grease, Mirjami, Jenna, Milo and Sweetness get *lihapiirakka.* Bread dough filled with a pork paste, I suspect oinks and assholes, and deep-fried. Sweetness eats three. Kate, Moreau and I get smoked fish on rye bread. We all have soft vanilla ice cream in cones for dessert. Even Moreau. I've wondered if he wears a permanent façade, or if what I see is his true self. Ice cream helps answer the question. His "too cool for school" demeanor is his natural deportment.

It's an hour and half to Nauvo. No one speaks. Moreau and I aren't talkers. Milo and Sweetness, I think, feel in their bones that something will happen. I can, too. Malinen will come on haughty. The lion will bite. Sweetness puts on Miles Davis's *Sketches of Spain.* It soothes. We listen to it twice. We wait twenty minutes on the ferry, and then, once on the island, it takes another half hour to find Roope Malinen's summer cottage.

We park a few minutes' walk from his cottage and approach from the forest instead of direct on the dirt path. I check my belt and pockets. Knife. Sap. Taser. I screw the silencer onto the threaded barrel of my .45. The silencer is too fat to holster the pistol. I slip it into my jacket pocket. The others do the same. Malinen is out back, behind the cottage, about twenty yards from a little jetty that extends out over the sea.

He has family money, owns this cottage and a big, costly apartment in an upscale building in the district of Töölö, in Helsinki. Topi Ruutio may be the head of the Real Finns party, but Malinen is its unofficial spokesman and minister of propaganda. His blog is the most popular in Finland because he's gifted in vocalizing hate while masking it as an academic voice of reason. Much like Nazi propaganda from its early years.

He's a professor of anthropology at the university, and a self-professed genius who claims his unique understanding of our species is too far ahead of its time to be fully comprehended by lesser mortals. He's a little man with apple red cheeks and thick glasses in black frames that calls to mind Jerry Lewis comic sketches. He squirts lighter fluid on the coals in his grill. He lights them with a long match and I see the flames leap and hear it go WHOOF. A massive dog sits beside him, implacable.

I step out of the tree line. "Hello, Roope," I say.

My voice startles him. I walk up to within a couple meters of him, the grill between us.

"Have we met?" he asks.

"No."

The others come out of the trees and stand in a line behind me. He sees a massive man with twin .45s visible, another with the wings of Icarus under stubble, the circles under Milo's eyes like ink stains. My cudgel of a cane. Something has gone terribly awry. He doesn't know what it is or why, and it visibly unnerves him.

He has a curt and run-on, rather absurd manner of speaking. Rat-a-tat-tat. Rat-a-tat-tat. "I don't know what you want but you're not welcome here and if you don't leave right now and I mean right now I'm going to call the police."

I show him my police card. "They're already here, and they'd like you to answer some questions."

"I have nothing to say to you and I want you off my property and I mean right now."

I speak slow and calm. "I'm afraid that's not going to happen. Where is your family at the moment?"

He picks up a spatula and points it at me like he's holding me at bay with a Sten gun. "You have no right to be here or to ask me about my family and it's none of your business where my family is get off of my property this instant or I'll call people and they'll make you sorry."

"It would be better if you tell me where

your family is. If your answers to my questions aren't satisfactory, the situation could become a little . . . humiliating . . . and I would spare your wife and children having to witness it."

I move closer and lean against a birch tree near the grill. It's a nice grill, made by hand with stones that he probably gathered from the shoreline and cemented together. The others move in closer too, in formation. The dog eyes me. I'm too close to his master. I give my cane's tip a bang on the ground and the lion's mouth flips open.

"They're out for a ride on the boat and I want you gone when they're back and I have company coming and they will be witnesses to this. Witnesses."

Moreau ambles into the cottage to look around. He comes back and nods. It's empty.

I say, "I'd like to discuss the murders of Kaarina Saukko and Lisbet Söderlund with you. And I'd like to talk about a website called I Would Give Two Years of My Life to Kill Lisbet Söderlund. She's dead. That same group had a member whose user name was Heinrich Himmler. This member discussed sending Finland's blacks to the gas chamber. Two young black men were murdered in a makeshift gas chamber. I want

Himmler's identity."

"I know nothing about any of those things why would I know anything about murders and threatening websites and their contributors."

"Veikko Saukko promised to donate a million euros to Real Finns. He reneged. Shortly thereafter, his son and daughter were kidnapped and the daughter murdered. On your blog, you've slandered Lisbet Söderlund countless times, blamed her personally for Finland's immigration policies and, after her death, implied that it was the best thing that has happened to our country in years. You see, I read all your blogs. I'm a big fan. And, as you're so active in racial social networking on the Internet, I'm willing to bet that you were a member of that Facebook group, and that, beloved as you are by so many racists, and as a representative of the Real Finns party, you're privy to a great deal of information, even if it's just gossip and hearsay."

He put his hand on his dog's back, as if for comfort, or perhaps as if the dog was a kind of talisman for him. "As I have stated many times I am not a racist. I am *maahanmuuttokriitikko* — a critic of immigrants. In the words of 'Martin Lucifer King,' 'In the end we will remember not the words of our enemies but the silence of our friends,' and so I write my thoughts because I love my country and other thinking people read those thoughts because they see the truth in them and the lies behind stinking ruiners of our race and nation like Lisbet Söderlund."

"I've noticed that racists seem well-versed in the thoughts of Dr. King."

"Know thy enemy. We'll have a Muslim niggertown surrounding Helsinki and then they'll burn their own homes down like the niggers in LA and like the niggers in Paris. And just the same when they start looting instead of stealing from their so-called oppressors downtown that own valuable merchandise they'll knock out the front windows of stores in their own neighborhoods and steal flashy sneakers and flat-screen TVs and designer jeans and toaster ovens. That's how much brains they have and that's how much thanks they give us for bringing them here and saving their lives and letting them live on our dime. Fuck them. Send them home to face genocide by machete-wielding niggers just like themselves. And if it came to a national referendum, every nigger in Finland would be executed. They should never have been let out of their self-created hellholes in the first place. And fuck you and fuck Lisbet Söderlund that nigger-dick-sucker traitor. I'm glad she's dead and get off of my property now."

"I can't. You still haven't answered my questions."

Malinen pets his dog. "Meet my dog Sparky. Sparky is special. He's a Fila Brasileiro. A breed so aggressive that they're outlawed in certain places, a hundred-twenty-pound monster and a trained attack dog and doesn't like people who threaten me and I'll turn Sparky loose and order him to kill you."

"Go ahead," I say.

Malinen shouts the command and the dog leaps. I swing my cane and the lion bites it in the loose skin on the side of its neck. I hold it at arm's length and hit it on the snout full blast with my Taser. The dog falls to the ground and quivers. I zap it again.

"Milo," I say, "amputate a leg off that thing," and I drag it over to him with my cane.

I choose Milo because, with his fertile mind, he would get the point I was making, and would also know how to do it. He uses a zip-lock handcuff for a tourniquet and pulls it tight around the dog's left hind leg at the hip.

Malinen shakes, starts to cry. "Why would you do that to poor Sparky?" he asks, apparently forgetting that he had ordered it to attack me.

"You mean amputate a leg instead of kill it?" Milo asks. "You said it was a special dog. You shouldn't eat a special dog like that all at once, and believe me, you're going to fucking eat it."

I say, "The threat was to amputate Kaarina Saukko's limbs when she was kidnapped. If it was good enough for her, it's good enough for your pooch." Then: "Somebody get this asshole on his knees."

Sweetness whips out his steel sap, flicks his wrist and telescopes it to full length, and hits Malinen hard in the back of his thigh with it. He screams, falls down on all fours. "You may think you're an important man," I say, "but we're all subservient to the laws of pain."

He grovels something incomprehensible.

"Do I need to repeat my questions, or do you eat Sparky?" I ask.

Malinen breaks, starts rambling. He sits up, but is afraid to stand. He gives me five names of members of the Facebook group. Heinrich Himmler, who rambled about gas chambers for Somalis, was none other than Veikko Saukko. Malinen was himself a member. His user name was the same as commandant at Auschwitz. Rudolf Höss.

Malinen rambles defenses. Neo-Nazis would like to firebomb mosques, but Real Finns keep them in check. With their numbers growing so rapidly, they'll win a majority of seats in the 2011 parliamentary elections and maybe take the presidency in 2012. The right wing will take the country back through legitimate means and through the will of the people.

"Tell me everything," I say, "so I don't have to come back. Lisbet Söderlund. Who killed her?"

"I don't know. A rumor started that whoever killed her would get enough support to guarantee winning a seat in Parliament and would take her place as minister of immigration. That wasn't true. I'm going to be minister of immigration."

"To take her place, the killer has to be known. *Who is her murderer?*"

"I swear I don't know."

"Who started the rumor?"

He doesn't answer. I take this to mean he started it himself. That makes him accessory to murder.

"Kaarina and Antti Saukko. Who killed her? Where is he?"

His fear is passing. He grasped that answering my questions would truly stop the cruelty and beating. He looks up at me. "I don't know those things. It's true that Saukko lied to us but to my knowledge no one in our party had anything to do with it. I knew Antti. Topi Ruutio knows Saukko and introduced us. Saukko wanted to meet me because he likes my blog and I met Antti and I introduced him to other Real Finns and I know that through those other Real Finns he met neo-Nazis but that's all I know except he hated his father."

I hear a boat engine. His family is on their way home.

"More," I say.

The sound of the engine instills panic. "The neo-Nazis sell drugs and they donate part of the profits to Real Finns. Please go now."

We walk back out through the forest to the SUV. I take a last look back. He's still on his knees, unable to move. He's a piece of shit.

He finds his courage and calls after me. "I'll get you for this!"

I answer. "If you do, I'll burn down the cottage while your family is sleeping inside it."

He has no recourse to "get me." And I wouldn't hurt his family. But it's something for him to think about, to give him some nightmares, as he has done to so many immigrants with his hate tracts.

We get back in the SUV. "I'd like to conduct the business I told you I had to take care of now," Moreau says. "You're welcome to come along. In fact, that's part of the point. I would appreciate it though, if you don't arrest anyone you meet."

"That's fine. When we get back to Helsinki, I think I should meet Veikko Saukko. Could you arrange it? I get the impression he likes you."

"I'd be happy to. I've killed many persons of color. I'm one of his favorite people."

32

Moreau directs us to a shop, La Cuisine, in downtown Turku. It specializes in French food: Chaource and Époisses de Bourgogne cheeses, pâtés, fine fruit preserves, game and ham, beef from Charolais cattle, Géline fowl. Moreau claimed he hadn't been to Finland for many years, but his explicit directions indicate either that he has the proverbial memory of an elephant, or lied.

The store has no customers at the moment. Two men recognize him, and their pleasure at seeing him is evident. They greet him with smiles and kisses on both cheeks, and the three of them converse in French for a bit.

Moreau introduces them to us as Marcel Blanc and Thierry Girard. They greet us in Finnish with accents much like Moreau's. The three of them entered the French Foreign Legion together. Blanc and Girard gave up military life after ten years, and after their careers as Legionnaires came here and opened this shop together.

The store's interior is attractive, obviously designed by a talented interior decorator. Soft new-age music plays. Sounds of chimes and rippling water. The proprietors are middle-aged, dress preppy. Marcel wears Nantucket Reds and a Lacoste shirt. Thierry, a button-down oxford cloth shirt and an argyle sweater. I picture the business model. They pretend to be French and a touch effete. Customers think maybe they're a couple. Gays and bored, rich housewives come in for the tony eats and to chat with the high-brow owners. They sell foie gras, reveal their heterosexuality, act surprised that the women thought otherwise, and bang the boredom out of the hausfraus. Not a bad racket.

"Ten years," I say. "Why didn't you re-up, stick it out and draw your pensions."

Marcel has black muzzle scorch scars on the left side of his face. Got a little too close to the barrel of a blazing machine gun. I wonder how he explains them to said fraus. "The Legion," he says, "is all about marching. I must have marched enough to circle the planet. I just didn't want to do it anymore."

Thierry takes a couple steps to show me.

"The marching wore out the cartilage in my knees. I just couldn't take it anymore. So we came back here and retired. It's not a bad life."

Moreau unzips his backpack, takes out two plastic bags of white powder identical to the one he gave to me at my party. "It's already cut to fifty percent pure. Don't step on it. That's all you get for a while. I won't be back to Mexico. I suspect the next will come from Afghanistan."

Marcel and Thierry eye me with fear and suspicion.

"Don't worry," Moreau says, "he won't arrest you. But I promised him that in return, you would answer some questions he has for you."

Moreau turns to me. "As former Legionnaires, they live pleasant lives here, but the boredom hurts them, so sometimes they play at crime. I supply them with heroin, out of friendship."

The two young black men, known drug dealers, on the day they were executed by carbon monoxide poisoning, came to Turku. Jussi Kosonen, kidnapper of Kaarina and Antti Saukko, was executed with a bullet in the back of his head, on the riverbank here in Turku. And now here I stand, in a shop with a kilo of heroin lying on the counter, in Turku. Hmm.

I snap open the lion's mouth on my cane, let the razor teeth press into the flesh of my fingers. "And what questions am I supposed to ask them?"

"Ask them who they sell heroin to and who they know."

I don't bother to repeat it.

Marcel says, "By far our biggest clients are neo-Nazis. We wholesale to them. We also sell Ecstasy from a source in Amsterdam, but have a different customer base for it."

"Are you racists, selling to neo-Nazis for political reasons, or is it simply an economic issue?"

"I admit we are racists," Thierry says, "and we are active in the racist community, but we are not rabid racists who commit our lives to the cause of hate." He chuckles. "We are excellent haters, but we are smart haters. Hate is like a drug. It will consume a person if excessive. I wasn't a racist until I served in Africa and lived amongst niggers, by the way, and discovered what vile creatures they are." He gives a disgusted shiver.

"Because we have killed many people of color, we are well liked by the racist community — hero figures, if you will. And so we have been shown off and introduced to many people."

"I'm investigating the murder of Lisbet Söderlund. Who do you know that might have been involved?"

"Well, the Nazis, of course, and possibly Real Finns or members of Finnish Pride, or a person acting alone."

"Do you know Antti Saukko?"

"Oh yes, and his father. It went like this. We already knew Antti. We were talking to Roope Malinen and he discussed the failure of the Finnish authorities to bring the persons who kidnapped and murdered his children to justice. We told him we knew one of the best policemen in the world, Adrien. Malinen told Real Finn party leader Topi Ruutio about Adrien, thinking that if Adrien found the criminals who violated the Saukko family, Veikko Saukko would show his appreciation in the form of a generous campaign contribution. Veikko asked to meet us, and our recommendation led to Adrien's presence here today."

He clasps Moreau's shoulder. "It's so good to see you, old friend."

"I have a theory," I say, "that the knowledge of who killed Lisbet Söderlund is an open secret. A sign of prestige. Tell the truth. Do you know who murdered her?"

"No, I do not. And neither does Marcel."

"I have no interest in your drug dealing at present, and will give you a permanent free pass to sell limited quantities of dope if you tell me who killed her. If I find out that you lied to me and you know the identity of her murderer, I will heap suffering on you far beyond your legal punishment. Do we understand one another?"

"Yes, Inspector, we do. But we do not know and cannot help you."

The prim racist dope dealers make delicacy samplers to take with us, give us the address of neo-Nazi HQ in Turku, and send us on our way.

33

An excellent basic rule of thumb for a policeman, or anyone for that matter, is never to anticipate. The reality of what we imagine seldom meets our expectations. I expect the neo-Nazi headquarters of Turku to be a run-down house with an unkempt yard with a couple of junk vehicles resting on concrete blocks rusting away in it. I anticipate a dwelling littered with empty beer cans and the air thick with marijuana smoke. Thugs passed out. Love pulp magazines with the pages stuck together.

The address Marcel gave us is an upscale and expensive apartment building. I was given no name, but don't need one because on the resident list alongside the door buzzers, instead of a name, is a swastika on a red field. I ring it, and when asked my name, say "Hans Frank." The front door opens. In the elevator, we all attach silencers to our Colts and pocket them.

I ring and the door opens. A young, well-dressed man with round wire-rim glasses answers. "May I help you?" he asks.

I show my police card. "I hope so."

"Do you have a warrant, Officer?"

"No."

"Please return when you have one."

He tries to shut the door. I jam it open with my foot. "Warrant or not, you and I are going to have a conversation. What's your name?"

"I don't intend to give you my name," he says, but relents, having little choice, and opens the door. We all step in and look around. Seven young men are in a well-furnished and spotless home. A bay window looks out on the river and beyond. There is no television. Only well-stocked bookcases.

He sits down. The other young men are equally well-groomed. Only one stands out, because of his size. He's bigger than Sweetness. The only clues that these men are neo-Nazis are their skinhead haircuts. They're all seated around a coffee table covered with cups and saucers and a plate of cookies. A large Waffen SS flag dominates one wall. I walk over and look at it.

"That's a family heirloom," the young man says. "My great-grandfather served in SS Viking and brought it home from the war. In case you don't know, SS 'Viking' was the 5th Heavy Panzer Division, recruited from foreign troops. A number of Finns served in it with distinction."

"We're off to a bad start," I say. "I only want to ask you a few questions and we'll be on our way."

"First, it's extremely discourteous for you to walk around my home with your shoes on. I would request that you remove them, except you won't be staying. Come back when you have a warrant."

I sigh. "There are a number of things we could discuss, such as trafficking in heroin, but I'm investigating a murder and I'm not interested in your criminal activities at the moment. But I could become interested."

"Warrant," he says.

I cross the room and examine his bookshelves. No pop fiction to be seen. He reads philosophers with related beliefs: Heidegger, Descartes, Hobbes, Spinoza, Leibniz, Locke, Berkeley, Hume, Kant, Hegel, John Stuart Mill, Nietzsche, Schopenhauer, Ayn Rand, Plato, Aristotle. He's educated in philosophy, but the education isn't well-rounded.

I say, "It's up to the judgment of an investigating officer to proceed without a warrant if a crime is imminent or in progress or causes peril of some sort. The officer must have reasonable cause. I'm told you have narcotics and suspect you have illegal firearms on these premises, and I view this as reasonable cause. We're going to search this apartment."

"I have no narcotics and my firearms are registered. I'm in full compliance with the law."

"What's your name?" I ask again.

He remains defiant. "Fuck you."

"What is your name?"

"None of your fucking business."

I didn't want it to come to this, but Lisbet Söderlund was murdered, and it pleased people like him. Come mud, shit or blood, he will cooperate. I light a cigarette.

"I don't allow people to smoke in my home," he says. "Extinguish your cigarette."

"OK." I take a deep drag to heat it up, then grind it out in the dead center of great-grandpa's flag. It leaves a nasty hole with scorched edges.

He shoots out of his seat, but then freezes, uncertain what to do.

The big man stands. "Jesper," he says, "I will deal with this."

He's about six foot six, upwards of three hundred pounds. His build says he's a power lifter. "You've gone too far," he says to me. "Your position doesn't give you the right to disrespect the homes of others and destroy their most precious belongings. I'll sit my time for assaulting an officer before I'll stand by and watch this."

He's about four yards away from me. I take the silenced Colt out of my pocket and aim it at his chest. In my peripheral vision, I see Sweetness take a swig from his flask.

"Shoot me, then," he says, and takes a step toward me.

"Fight me first," Sweetness says, and gets in between us. It's Godzilla versus Rodan.

Big Man laughs. "Did you need some liquid courage, little girl?"

"Naw, it just relaxes me," Sweetness says, and takes a fighter's stance. He shuffles his feet, fakes, draws a punch from Big Man so his weight is too far forward for him to escape the countershot, then Sweetness splits his left eyebrow open with a jab. There's a lot of blood. They circle.

A neo-Nazi starts to record the fight with his cell phone video camera. Moreau puts his Beretta to the man's head.

Big Man is dumb, falls for the same fake and jab. Sweetness is *fast.* Now both eyebrows are split bad and his eyes are full of blood and flesh hangs down into them.

Moreau removes the memory card from

the guy's cell phone and hands it back to him.

Big Man is blind now. I count punches. One two three. Sweetness hits a little harder each time, to make sure Big Man can't fight back, before throwing the big hard punches that will take Sweetness a little off balance and put him at risk. Four: nose breaks. Five: teeth come out and patter on the carpet. A glop of blood sprays the bay window. Six: jaw breaks and more blood and teeth fly. Seven: a right roundhouse crumples Big Man's eye socket. He falls. His head bangs the coffee table. Cups turn over and spill. Big Man is on the floor, semiconscious. The eye bulges because there's not enough solid bone left to hold it tight in the socket.

I pick up a cookie, take a bite and turn to Jesper. "These are really good. Did you bake them yourself?"

The room is corpse silent except for Milo. The looks on the neo-Nazis' faces have given him the giggles. He takes a cookie. "You're right. These are really good." He asks Jesper, "Have you got any coffee left? Don't make a fresh pot on my account."

Jesper, in a daze, doesn't understand that Milo is teasing him and goes to the kitchen. "Do you take milk and sugar?" he asks.

"No, black is fine."

Jesper returns with a cup and saucer and Milo thanks him.

I say to Jesper, "Now, either we have a conversation, or you become that." I point at Big Man.

I take a seat on the couch and pat the cushion beside me, gesture for Jesper to sit beside me.

"My friend needs medical attention," Jesper says.

"And he can have it as soon as we're through here. So please cooperate. None of this was ever necessary in the first place. Where's your gun safe?"

"There are three. In my bedroom. The keys are on top of the middle one."

Milo goes to check them out. He's looking for the sniper rifle that killed Kaarina Saukko.

I say to Jesper, "My question to you is: Who killed Lisbet Söderlund?"

"I don't know."

"You sell heroin. Correct? This conversation is off the record."

"We're performing a public service. We wholesale to people who only sell to blacks, in an effort to sedate the nigger — well, actually, the entire immigrant population. And the proceeds don't line our pockets, they go to political causes."

"Such as donations to Real Finns?"

He doesn't answer.

"I'm curious," I say. "You don't want immigrants in Finland, but why Nazism?"

"Because it offers societal protection. Is it too much to *not* want cultural diversity, to want to preserve everything I hold dear? To live in a country with others who share the same race, values and beliefs that I do? Jews, Slavs, blacks, Arabs — they're genetically and culturally inferior. They hold beliefs antithetical to our own and would destroy the fabric of this nation. In fact, I'm glad we've had our little experiment with immigrants, so that our citizens can see the havoc it carries with it on even such a small scale. Look at Belgium. Immigrants overran it and their culture and way of life is destroyed beyond repair. Given the relatively few immigrants we've taken in, we can still get rid of them and correct our error."

"You want another Holocaust?"

"There was no Holocaust. It's a myth. Tell the truth, Officer. Don't you want our race and culture preserved?"

Given the ordeal I've put him through, he at least deserves an answer. "I think your beliefs and everything you hold dear are a myth." I stop our political discussion here. My curiosity about his hatred is satisfied.

Milo comes back, grinning. "He's got seven Sako AK-47-style rifles, but they're not full auto and so legal. A dozen Smith & Wesson 9mm automatic pistols. Four riot shotguns, but no .308 sniper-type rifle. Check these out." He holds a target up in each hand. One is a man in profile with a huge nose. A supposed Jew. The other has huge lips and an afro. A supposed black man. Nice.

"Two young black men," I say, "known to deal drugs, came to Turku and later that evening were murdered in Helsinki, in a garage that had a running car in it, turning the place into a gas chamber. This has Nazi overtones. Did you or anyone you know have contact with those men on the evening they were murdered?"

"We have no truck with niggers under any circumstances," Jesper says. "We don't sell drugs directly to niggers — we let others taint themselves — and we're not murderers. We seek to accomplish our goals through political means. And it's working."

"Then why are you stockpiling such a large quantity of firearms?"

"As an insurance policy."

I address the group. "I believe that quite a few people know who killed Lisbet Söderlund and that, most likely, some of the people in this room are among them. You're all guilty of various crimes that carry heavy jail terms. If one of you tells me who murdered her, I ignore the crimes. If not, I see to it that every neo-Nazi in Turku goes to prison."

I walk around the room, hand out business cards, and make each and every one of them put them in their wallets. "I wouldn't expect you to rat out your comrades here and now, but you can call me. If you took no part in the killings, you've nothing to fear and everything to gain."

Doubtless, some of them have been recording this conversation or managed to make a video clip. We take the memory cards from all their phones.

"I don't care about your politics," I say to the group. "I just have a murder to solve." I point at Big Man. "I'm sorry it had to come to this."

And we leave.

34

I call Kate and tell her our business is done for the day. She says they're in a bar called The Cow, not too far from where we are right now. My first thought is if she's drinking again. I'm not sure why her drinking over the past days concerns me. She's never been a heavy drinker and she started on Vappu, when drinking is almost enforced by law. She's been spending time with people who drink a lot, like Mirjami and Jenna, and so it's natural that she would drink a little more, too.

I suppose my concerns are twofold. One: it's interfering with her responsibility as a mother. It prevents her from breast-feeding. Two: I'm concerned it's the result of something deeper, caused by me or my job. I know this is going to be a drunken evening, so I brought baby formula in case she gets three sheets to the wind again.

We meet up with them at The Cow. Mirjami and Jenna are drinking Lumumbas. Kate is having hot chocolate. One might say, a virgin Lumumba. I observe Mirjami's reaction to me. There is none. She still turns me on, but I suppose her love for me has waned, thank God. The girls are half in the bag. The day didn't go as planned.

They went to Naantali, but it's early in the season. Muumimaailma isn't open for a couple weeks yet, so they couldn't play with the trolls. Kate got her fill of handicrafts and the old town. It's on the chilly side, so the girls thought the wise thing to do would be to start drinking early. Kate is a little bored, sitting in the bar watching the girls drink, but she says they have good senses of humor and keep her entertained. Also, she can't quite get accustomed to the idea that it's acceptable to bring a baby into a bar. But it's different here than in the States, she's come to realize. People come to bars to meet, drink coffee, read newspapers. It isn't all about boozing. Bars are also social centers.

We've had quite a day and sit down for a beer — Sweetness lines three shots of *kossu* up at the bar and downs them one after the other — and after relaxing for a few minutes, we head out to my brother Timo's place. Sweetness shows no sign of inebriation. It's mostly because of his size, but I've never met anyone with a head for alcohol like his. It's often considered a manly attribute, but also often leads to liver failure and early death. It concerns me.

Timo is five years older than me and the black sheep of the family. Dad always told him what a worthless piece of shit he was. Timo took it to heart and set out to prove him right. As a teenager, he was always in trouble, committed petty crimes, skipped school more than he attended it and dropped out at sixteen. At age twenty-five, Timo did a seven-month stint in prison for bootlegging. Because of this, Mom has spent years singing his praises as an angel and proclaimed him her favorite child. It's obvious she does this because his criminal past is an embarrassment and disappointment to her, and it humiliates him when she goes on about him.

He was too much older than me for us to spend much time together or get to know each other well while we were growing up, but we've always gotten along. There are four of us brothers. He and I are big men. Jari and my other brother, Juha, are little guys. Juha, the oldest of us, settled in Norway years ago and I don't even remember the last time we were in contact.

Timo is bright and foresaw the future. He drifted for a while before eventually settling in Pietarsaari, in western Finland. He got a job in a paper factory and worked there for seventeen years. It was a union job, he made a lot of money and he saved. When the plant got outsourced to India or China or somewhere, he bought this farm outright. Timo's got the full-fledged redneck thing going on. Overalls, beer belly, full beard and baseball cap.

The place has a lot of charm. He and his common-law wife, Anni, give us a tour. They live in a rambling old farmhouse next to a lake. They've been together for more than twenty years, raised two kids, a boy and girl. They've grown up and moved out. Timo and Anni have a big barn, a sauna building with room for guests to sleep over in it, just a few steps from the lake, and a tiny house, like a dollhouse, just big enough to walk into. It's just got a bed in it, another place for overnight guests. Jenna gets all excited. It's like a home for Muumit and she wants to sleep in it. I read Sweetness's face. He's hoping he'll spend the night in there with her.

They take us on a tour. Timo has a still in the barn. He makes *pontikka* — moonshine. He has a tin cup beside it and offers tastes.

"What exactly is it?" Kate asks.

"Alcohol made from malted grain," Timo says. "I've infused this batch with mixed berries that we grew or picked ourselves, and I put some chocolate bars into the mash." He turns the tap, puts a healthy measure in the cup. "Have a sip."

"What's the alcohol percentage?" I ask.

"A little over eighty."

"Careful Kate," I say. "It can burn your lungs. Put it in your mouth and sip it without inhaling."

She tries it, her face lights up, and she declares it delicious. The girls sip too and agree it's yummy.

Timo offers the cup to others. Milo says, "We have some shooting practice to do. I think I'll wait until after."

I check my watch. It's eight. The long days are upon us. We still have plenty of time to shoot.

"Actually," Moreau says, "a small amount of alcohol will steady your hands. If you have problems with shaking hands, I suggest you get a prescription for a beta blocker. It will steady you considerably."

Milo sips the *pontikka* and also pronounces it top-notch. I skip the booze for now, as does Moreau. Sweetness takes a big mouthful, swallows, and sighs from satisfaction.

He takes his flask out of his pocket. "Do you mind?"

"Help yourself," Timo says.

Sweetness sucks the flask dry of *kossu* and fills it with *pontikka*.

"Not to seem inhospitable," Timo says, "but my home is your home, except for the loft of this barn. It's off-limits to law enforcement."

So he supplements his income with stolen goods or some kind of contraband. It's not always about money. Some people need to commit criminal acts to feel alive. I guess Timo is one of them. "No problem," I say.

"Where do you want to shoot, and can I shoot with you?" Timo asks.

"Of course," Milo says. "We want to shoot some pistols, a shotgun, a sniper rifle, and try out some flash-bang stun grenades."

"For the rifle," Moreau says, "we need at least five hundred meters."

Timo points across the road at a hillock. "My neighbor is away. We can set the targets down here by the lake, shoot down from up there, and the bullets will just land in the water. The others we can just shoot here by the barn."

"I'll put the grill and sauna on," Anni says, "so after you boys have your fun, we can eat, drink and relax."

"Sounds perfect," I say.

Milo and Sweetness bring the arsenal from the SUV. We start with the lockbuster shotgun, which is self-explanatory. Use eye and ear protection. Special ammo made from compressed zinc powder or dental ceramic expends all its energy and disintegrates the lock. Angle yourself away from flying shrapnel when you shoot, and that's it. We don't have any locks to break, so we just fire it once each so we know what it's like.

We set up pistol targets at twenty-five feet, which Moreau says is a longer shot than you think, since most gunfights with pistols take place within seven feet of the combatants.

Milo considers himself an excellent shot and he is, but Moreau tells him that he's doing it wrong if he wants to be a true pro. Milo uses both front and rear sights. He should ignore the rear sight, pay attention to only the front sight, and use the pistol as if he's pointing his finger at the target, in a sense, without aiming the pistol. Milo didn't come for a lesson, just to try out his Colt. I see that he resents the lecture.

Moreau demonstrates. His Beretta is cocked, locked and holstered, meaning he draws, flicks off the safety, a round slams into the chamber and the pistol is ready to fire. He warns that many shooters lose their toes by shooting them off while learning this most efficient manner. I throw seven empty beer cans into the air. He hits each one while it's at the top of its arc.

Milo can't hit anything without using the rear sight. He takes great pride in his shooting skills. His frustration level is high but he tries to hide it, just purses his lips and says nothing.

"Not to worry," Moreau says. "Burn up a few thousand rounds on the practice range and you'll shoot as well as me. Anyone can."

I try. "I'm right-handed but left-eyed. Shooting is difficult for me because of it. I can keep the bullets on the target, but can't shoot a tight pattern."

"I retract my previous statement," Moreau says. "You will never be an expert marksman."

I don't mind. "I'd better just keep my gunfights within those seven feet you talked about."

"You've already killed a man, though," he says. "After the first time, people usually stay calm and are able to perform. That counts for as much as practice."

This is Sweetness's first time firing a gun. Ambidextrous, he's wearing the two Colts

Milo gave him in shoulder rigs on each side. He makes a couple of tentative first attempts, just trying to aim and pull the trigger. Both were close to bull's-eyes. "I think I got the idea," he says. He re-holsters, cocked and locked. I cringe, certain he's going to shoot himself. He draws smooth and proceeds to blast the center rings out of two side-by-side targets. "Like that?" he asks.

Moreau's grin is wry. "Yes, like that."

Milo's hands are bunched into white-knuckled fists. Sweetness stole his thunder and left him seething.

Timo tries all our pistols, blasts off about a hundred rounds fast. He's a pretty good shot. He practices, he says.

We set the targets up by the lake, careful to make sure the rounds will hit the water, and at a steep enough angle so they don't ricochet off the surface and land in someone's living room miles away. Moreau drives a stick in the ground, blows up some balloons he brought along, and attaches them loosely to the stick with string. We drive across the road and up the hill, about six hundred yards from the lake.

Milo takes out the .50 caliber Barrett sniper rifle, a cannon that can kill at two miles in the right hands, wants to show off his knowledge, starts reciting the user's manual. This makes Moreau impatient. "Yes, yes, yes, an integrated electronic ballistic computer that mounts directly on the riflescope and couples with the elevation knob. Three internal sensors automatically calculate the ballistic solution."

Milo shuts up. The shadows surrounding his eyes are dark and cloudy. The corners of his mouth turn down. He thought this would be his day to shine and he's outclassed.

Moreau lectures on how to set the weapon up, and it's complicated. He talks quickly and much of it is lost on me. He explains body posture, how to lie down and take pressure off the chest so breathing and heartbeat don't interfere. He loads four rounds in it. He says it should take only three rounds to sight it in. He shoots three times, making adjustments. His fourth shot is a bull's-eye. Each shot sounds like the crack of doom, and the recoil looks punishing.

He loads the clip full. "Now let me show you what is possible."

He lies down and shoots. He cuts the stick and frees the balloons. They drift and bounce. He pops them all, never misses.

He turns the gun over to Milo. Much of

the skill in using the Barrett depends on understanding the science behind it, and so it falls into Milo's sphere of excellence. He sights it in with three shots and fires a few more rounds in a pattern as tight as driving a nail. I can see he's had enough. He's a small man. I'm guessing the recoil will leave him black-and-blue.

It's Milo's baby, and must be sighted in for an individual shooter. Sweetness declines to shoot it, so Milo won't have to sight it in again. Also, he says he's getting hungry. Sipping *pontikka* is building his appetite. I decline because that kind of shock doesn't seem therapeutic for a post-brain-op patient. Timo blasts it a few times because it looks fun. He shoots a tight pattern lower and to the left of Milo's because the gun isn't sighted in for him, and he wears a big grin when he's done, so I take it he enjoyed himself.

It's getting late and the sun is setting, so we set off a couple flash-bangs. The noise and intense light are intended to incapacitate. Instructions: Pull pin, throw, turn away. Plug ears and close eyes. They blow in three seconds. They're still bright and loud enough to slightly disorient, even out here in the open. In a closed room, they must be devastating.

We drive back over to Timo's house. I'm starved and good smells emanate from the grill and sauna. We go around back and find Anni, Mirjami and Jenna relaxing in lounge chairs on the patio. I hear the sounds of retching. Anni has Anu in her lap. "Bad news," Anni says and points. I walk over and find Kate on all fours, hiding in some bushes, puking her guts out. She manages to look up at me. She says it slow. "I sorry."

I sit down beside her for a minute and put an arm around her.

She slurs, *"Pontikka."*

I'm afraid she's going to get puke in her long red hair, and so I pull it back and tie it in a loose knot to keep it away from her mouth.

"Please go away," she says.

I've been there, know the feeling. "OK. I'll come back in a little while and check on you."

I go back to the patio. "What happened?"

"Mirjami and Jenna wanted some more *pontikka,*" Anni said, "and Kate took some, too. I gave them all doubles, and Kate didn't drink any more after that. It just hit her bad."

Drinking is like anything else, it takes practice. Kate doesn't practice. Mirjami and Jenna do. They have small glasses of *pon-*

372

tikka on the brick floor of the patio beside their chairs, alongside bottles of pear cider. They're hammered.

It's chilly out. The girls have their jackets on and blankets wrapped around them, but this is early Finnish summer, and the attitude is *Goddamn it, we* will *enjoy ourselves outside, no matter how much it sucks.*

I take Moreau aside. "I want to talk to Veikko Saukko tomorrow."

He doesn't answer, just starts typing a message into his cell phone.

It's almost eleven p.m. "Isn't it a little late for that?" I ask.

"He never sleeps. It interferes with his drinking."

The answer is immediate. "Ten tomorrow morning."

Boozing, puking people preparing to drink rotgut all night. It's going to be an ugly morning.

Milo, Sweetness and Timo plow into the *pontikka,* chase it with beer. I get a plate of grilled sausages and vegetables and sit next to Timo. He says, "You know what we discussed, about talking things out, about why we haven't seen each other."

"Yeah."

"I got an idea. In general, it's because we come from a fucked-up family. Why don't we just leave it at that, not talk about it, and enjoy the evening."

"Deal."

And we do. I go back in a little while to check on Kate. She's done puking and near to passing out. I carry her to a spare bedroom. Moreau and I don't drink. He because he doesn't, and me because I have to care for Anu. I'm not in the mood anyway. Moreau, Timo and I had a good sauna and dip in the freezing lake. Anu had her first sauna and seemed to enjoy it.

We come out of our second round in the sauna to find Milo and Sweetness in a drunken fistfight. Moreau moves to stop them, but I say no, it's been a long time coming. I think Sweetness will stomp a mud puddle in Milo's chest, but he holds his own. Sweetness is fast, but Milo is small and even faster. He gets in close and works inside Sweetness's reach, slips his punches. Sober, Sweetness would have killed him, but the *pontikka* evened the odds. Milo lands some good ones, but they don't pack enough power to put Sweetness down, and in the end, they're rolling around in the grass, drunk and laughing. They go to the sauna bleeding together.

Afterward, Sweetness and Jenna disappear, and I hear love grunts come from the Muumin house. Anni wakes Timo up from a lounge chair and takes him to bed. Milo and Mirjami must have passed out in the sauna. I set an alarm for seven, and join Kate in the spare bed.

35

The alarm goes off. Kate doesn't stir and I shake her awake. "I can't move," she says, "I'm sick."

"I'm sorry, but you have to. I have an appointment that has to do with the Söderlund murder and we have to leave."

She has trouble sitting up but manages it. "I'm woozy. I can't drive."

"That's OK, someone else will drive. Can you eat?"

She shakes her head no.

I'm a little tired myself. We stayed up late, and I was up twice in the night with Anu. "You weren't the only one drunk. I doubt the others are in much better shape. Can you pull yourself together while I get them up and moving?"

She nods yes. "Kari," she says, "I'm sorry. I fucked up. I've fucked up a lot lately. I —"

She has a king hell case of *morkkis*. I cut her off. "Everything is fine. Anu is fine. You didn't do anything embarrassing. You just got sick, passed out, and I put you to bed. You didn't even drink half as much as the others. It just hit you wrong because you're not used to it. We can talk about it later if you want."

I go downstairs. Anni is up and in good spirits. "Should I make everyone breakfast? Help kill their hangovers?"

I have a feeling their hangovers are beyond redemption. "Thanks, but we don't have time. I have to meet someone in Helsinki."

I make the rounds. Moreau made a pillow out of his coat and slept on the floor. He's already waking. I go outside and hear laughter in the Muumin house. Jenna speaking in a soft voice. Sweetness whistling. Kissing slurps. He got his cherry busted with his true love. Nice. Maybe the life affirmation will give him some perspective, he'll come to terms with the death of his brother and stop staying drunk morning, noon and night.

Milo and Mirjami are sleeping head to foot, clothed, on a cot in the washing room in the sauna. I wake them. They're not sick yet because they're still drunk. The hangover will come soon enough. I get everyone roused and in the vehicles. I don't get a chance to say good-bye to Timo. He's still passed out. I have a feeling we'll talk again soon, though.

I drive the Audi, and Moreau drives the SUV. The others snooze along the way. We drop them at their homes and take the Audi to Veikko Saukko's mansion.

His foundation museum is near the road. His mansion sits near the rear of the sprawling grounds of his property, the sea not far behind it.

A man resembling a two-hundred-eighty-pound bullfrog, in a tight black turtleneck with a thick gold chain hung around his neck, opens the door. Bodyguard chic. He checks his visitor's list on an iPod and asks us to wait.

Veikko Saukko comes to the door to greet us. He pumps my hand and tells me it's an honor to meet a law enforcement officer of my caliber. He hugs Moreau, pats his back and calls him "old friend."

He ushers us into his study. It calls to mind a Victorian gentlemen's club. Dark wood paneling and deep leather chairs. A Parnian desk with only an Aurora Diamante pen on it. The diamonds, platinum and gold sparkle. He insists, despite the hour, that we join him in a Richard Hennessy cognac and a La Gloria Cubana Reserva figurado. He sits with us in a circle of three chairs around a small table rather than behind his desk, to create an air of intimacy. He asks how he can help me.

"I'm investigating the murder of Lisbet Söderlund," I say, "and I believe it may be related to the kidnap-murder your family suffered last year, for which I offer my condolences."

He takes a deep draught of cognac, just poured a couple hundred euros down his throat. "I'm glad the bitch is dead, but if you convince me of some connection to my family . . . well, let's just say I'll hear you out."

"You've created some enmity with Finland's extreme right. I'm told you promised them a million-euro campaign contribution but reneged. It created antipathy, and may have led to the crimes perpetrated against your family. These same factions also despised Lisbet Söderlund and openly discussed killing her. Only a limited number of people in our little country are capable of such crimes, both in psychological profile and technical skill, and so the natural train of thought is that the murderer or group of killers is one and the same."

"You killed a nigger, didn't you, Inspector?"

I assume he refers to the Sufia Elmi case, in which her father died ablaze, doused in gasoline.

"It would be more accurate to say that I sat and watched him burn to death." I was unable to reach him in time because of my bad knee. I test Saukko's limits to see how crazy he is. "I shot the head off an Estonian, odds are good he had Slavic blood. Does that earn me points?"

He laughs haw haw and slaps his knee. "Adrien here has killed many niggers. That's why I like him. How many niggers do you think you've killed, Adrien?"

Moreau exhales a long plume of smoke. He knows how to play this game and manipulate Saukko. I think Moreau kills many but hates no one. "Do you want to count Africans only, or Hispanics such as Mexicans? Beaners are just little brown niggers. And Arabs such as Afghans, sand niggers. And do you want to count killing by including the calling in of artillery fire and air strikes, or long-range killings, or only killings committed while close enough to look in the men's faces?"

"Wow," Saukko says, "so many options. Let's include all the minorities, but count two ways, faceless and face-to-face."

"Faceless, some thousands. I wouldn't

hazard to guess. Face-to-face, some hundreds." Moreau's smile spoke of indulgence. "Veikko, you've heard all of this before. Do you enjoy it so much?"

"Can niggers dance?"

"I thought that the French Foreign Legion has been primarily involved in peacekeeping missions over the past couple decades," I said.

"Many people require a demonstration that it is to their benefit to be peaceful," Moreau said, "and I haven't been in the Legion for some time. My missions have had a wide variety of objectives since then."

I say to Saukko, "May I ask you some questions?"

"Fire away."

"Why did you change your mind about your donation to Real Finns?"

"All the patriots are connected. Real Finns. Neo-Nazis. Others. There are several groups populated by many of the same members. I wanted a demonstration of intent from them, not just talk. And I didn't ask them to kill anyone, just be more up front about the contagion of non-white immigration."

"What form of demonstration?"

He hesitates, considers the ramifications of his answer. "Are you a real white man? Is our conversation off the record?"

"Yes."

"Finland was a white man's paradise. Now good Finnish blood is soiled by poisonous nigger bacterial infection. We're overrun by mud people. Zionist vampires. Jewish cancer. It's time to take our country back. Sacrifices must be made. Blood spilled."

He starts to ramble. I put on my practiced smile that shows agreement. At the moment, it's good that I feel no emotion. If so, I might have given him the beating of a lifetime. I listen.

"Mud babies. Filthy white girls with no self-esteem desecrate themselves with filthier septic black men — tar people — and make mud babies. Certain parties sell the niggers heroin to sedate them. They should contaminate the heroin with strychnine to reduce the numbers of tar people and slow the contamination of pure Finnish blood. The whites that use it are flawed, of no use to society. Good riddance to bad rubbish. But these men who supposedly are ready to lay down their lives for the cause refuse to poison tar people because they're afraid of prison, as if they would be common criminals rather than patriots and political prisoners. Cowardice. Pure cowardice. Yet, they come to me with their grubby hands out."

I neglect to point out that his own daughter was a heroin addict, and now a methadone addict, or that, although I don't know the statistics, Muslims aren't inclined toward the use of narcotics. On the other hand, I've noticed that quite a few Muslims here have taken up drinking. Maybe a significant number use narcotics as well.

"Have you considered that the murder of Lisbet Söderlund may have been just the sort of demonstration you sought?" I say.

"I have considered it, and would reward it, if I knew who did it."

I sip cognac I don't want and force a sound of satisfaction. "Excellent."

"Indeed." He tosses his off, gets up, pours a triple, sits down again.

"I understand that you and your son Antti had a falling-out before his kidnapping."

He smirks. "We had many falling-outs. He always came groveling back, and I rewarded his cringing monetarily."

"What if this time he didn't come groveling back? What if this time he teamed up with the extremists who felt betrayed by you — I understand they were all well acquainted — and together, they faked the kidnapping? It does appear, after all, that Jussi Kosonen was a patsy. Upon examining the man, it even seems ridiculous that he could have pulled off such a crime."

"Then why," Saukko asks, and pours another couple hundred euros down his throat in a gulp, "was Kaarina murdered? Antti wouldn't have shot her."

"But Kosonen was shot. Maybe Antti fucked his buddies, killed Kosonen, and disappeared with the money. They might have shot Kaarina as payback."

"Antti," Saukko says, "is a fucking pussy. He hasn't got the balls to shoot anyone."

I smoke, try not to choke on the cigar and damage my manly image that he seems to value so highly. I hate cigars. "On the contrary, I'm told he's crazy for water sports — surfing, yachting — and also extreme sports like skydiving and bungee jumping. The impression is that he has plenty of balls and is reckless."

"A façade, and far different from physical confrontation."

"True. However, people will surprise you. I understand that the three paintings stolen from you were as yet uninsured. That would be difficult information to ascertain and to cull out from your vast holdings."

He takes this in. "Somewhat difficult."

"Who, may I ask, saw to the installation of the security system, which I understand is relatively new?"

He's coming around and takes time to think before answering. "Antti."

"How much of this information have you shared with the detective now in charge of your case, Saska Lindgren?"

He scoffs. "As little as fucking possible. That goddamned Gypsy comes here to the house and he steals, and I have to have the place sterilized after he leaves. That's why Adrien is here. To sort this out, get my money back and kill my daughter's killer."

I never really believed all that crazy shit they said about Howard Hughes before now. His soul mate is sitting in front of me.

"Sir, would you have any objection to me exploring the possibility that Antti was involved in a bogus kidnapping, set up and killed Kosonen, and escaped with your ten million euros?"

"No. You may explore it."

"I'll have to call Saska Lindgren and ask for his go-ahead."

"I'll make the fucking call." He disappears to another room. He comes back and hands me his cell phone. The prime minister is on the line. "I know you can't talk in front of Saukko," he says. "Yes, you can take the case, at least for now, and I'll square it with Detective Sergeant Lindgren. And I'll see

385

that he gets credit if you solve it. He's got a year invested in it after all. It's only fair, because Saukko impeded his investigation."

"OK," I say. The PM rings off.

I sit down again. "You have your own dry dock here, correct?"

"Yes, I have a number of craft of different sizes and varieties, including my smallest yacht. I also collect vehicles and have a large garage for them. And I employ a full-time skipper, crew and mechanics to maintain them all."

"Would you notice if a small craft was missing?"

"Not necessarily. As the whole family has access to the vehicles and watercraft, only the skipper would know by checking the manifest. The kids sign them out when they take them."

I finish the cognac, stub out the cigar. "Kosonen was killed on the riverbank. Antti would have needed a small craft to get away. Could we go now and check the manifest to see if a suitable craft has been missing since the kidnapping?"

"Sure."

The three of us ride across the estate in a golf cart and pull up at the dry dock. We go inside. It's massive for a personal dock, has about fifteen vessels in it. Most are small, but one is a thirty-one-foot yacht. But, I reflect, he is the richest man in Finland. I suppose this is to be expected. The skipper, who must have the easiest job in the world when Saukko isn't about, compares the vessels to the paperwork. Two vessels are missing and haven't been recorded as taken out for over a year. One is a normal boat meant for fishing, but with powerful twin engines. The other is an underwater Jet Ski.

I ask him to check the specs on the Jet Ski, its possible speed and range. It can travel seven and a half miles an hour underwater, faster on the surface, and the battery holds a charge that lasts about an hour.

This is perfect for following the Aurajoki undetected out to sea. But he had to pull not only himself but two heavy bags of money.

The skipper says they own three batteries. All are gone. So, Antti had the ability to bear a load and an extended range.

Saukko fires the skipper on the spot. The skipper stammers, shocked, "I've . . . I've worked for you for eighteen years."

"You have ten minutes to gather your things, and then security will escort you off the property."

I meet some of the nicest people in my profession. I ignore all this and say to

Saukko, "Let's picture this scenario. Kosonen was to meet Antti, who had come to pick him up in the boat that Kosonen purchased a few days earlier. But Antti kills Kosonen, ditches the boat, and leaves with the Jet Ski. Where would he go?"

I copy the makes and serial numbers of the Jet Ski and missing boat down in my notepad. Like Sweetness, the alcohol seems to leave Saukko unaffected. Practice makes perfect. "To Åland," he says.

I suspect the same. Åland, an archipelago in the Baltic, between Finland and Sweden, comprises over six thousand five hundred islands and skerries, sixty-five of which are populated. Many of them are little more than flyspecks that stand only a few inches over the waterline. In the summer, Åland is bustling, infested with boats and tourists. However, most congregate on Fasta Åland, the main island, and the islands in the surrounding area.

Some of the islands are flat as planks. The most popular ones have well-kept bicycle paths, and the area is a favorite of cycling enthusiasts. The residents own far more bikes than motorized vehicles for this reason. In some places, they're rendered almost unnecessary. Many of the islands have old cottages, most just shacks, the most basic of structures — that were once used by commercial fishermen. Now they serve as crash pads for whoever wants to spend the night.

"Can you think of anywhere in particular he might be drawn to as a place to hide? Do you own a private island Antti could be hiding on?"

Saukko laughs. "You know, I almost forgot about it. I own so much shit. I have a private island called Saukkosaari — Saukko Island — and it has an excellent summer cottage on it. In fact, it's a bit sumptuous to be called a cottage. I bought the island and it had an old, run-down house on it, which I had refurbished. This was fifteen or twenty years ago. I went there a couple times and got bored with it. Just never went back. And none of the rest of the family uses it, either. I hired a gamekeeper who lived in a cottage there. I have no idea if he's still there or not. For all I know, he might have dropped dead and is still on the payroll. With three batteries, Antti could have made it there."

This heartens me. However, there's also the other missing boat. He could have used it to flee considerably farther away.

Saukko says, "I also owned over a hundred islands up north in the archipelago. I created a foundation out of them but kept the hunting and fishing rights. Not even tourists go up there much. And it's a barren area. No amenities. Nothing. I doubt he's there. If he is, he'll be damned hard to find. But I still don't put much stock in this Antti-is-a-murderer-theory shit."

I seriously doubt he's there, either. But still. "Doesn't cost anything to look."

"True," he says. "What the fuck. Take my yacht."

"Thanks, but we can take a police boat."

"Do police boats have fully stocked bars and come loaded with fishing gear?"

I admit that they don't.

"Then I insist you take the yacht." Then it dawns on him. "Fuck. I just fired the skipper."

This boat is motorized. No sails. Doesn't take the same level of professional skill. "First, I want to check out Saukkosaari. My partner Milo knows how to sail, he can pilot. I'll call him now."

Moreau says he can also handle a yacht. Moreau. Master of All. It's starting to get on my nerves. I call Milo and Sweetness and tell them to be here in an hour.

36

Milo's father is dead but apparently was something of a character — Milo's mother once stabbed him for philandering — but Milo seldom mentions him. However, he taught Milo to sail. He fires up the engines, gives instructions, and we're out on the open sea in just a few minutes. Milo can be an aggravating fuck, but his confidence with all things technical can be reassuring at times, and this is one.

He's dog sick from *pontikka* overdose, pukes over the rail a few times. Sweetness is no better, even by his standards he got shit-faced and looks like death. In addition to being sick from drinking, they're covered with cuts and bruises from fighting. Milo has a butterfly Band-Aid holding his eyebrow together. Both of them have black eyes. Milo limps. Sweetness has a fat lip, split open but short of needing stitches. Neither holds a grudge, though. Instead, they laugh about it. It was just what they needed. Men are like that sometimes. Sweetness finds the bar and hair of the dog.

After a couple hours, we find the island, tie the boat off at the dock next to an older, smaller and somewhat dilapidated vessel. We walk up a winding path to the so-called summer cottage. I would guess it's about a hundred years old, and as Saukko said, "cottage" is a misnomer. It's bigger than a house, too small to qualify as a mansion.

We find no one here, but someone was here, a while ago. The garbage wasn't taken out. Dirty dishes left in the sink. And Saukko was right about the gamekeeper. His cottage is empty. His belongings are in the house proper. I guess at a certain point, maybe after some years went by, he realized that the place was forgotten, that he was employed but forgotten too, and moved into a lovely remodeled home in an idyllic setting. We take a walk around the grounds, both forest and meadows are behind the home, the ocean view in front of it.

The gamekeeper must have lived in peace and comfort, until one day a bad man or men came and ruined it all. We find four shallow graves behind the house. A little scooping and kicking away dirt with our hands and feet reveal four bodies in late decomp, consistent with about a year since death. A grown man and three children. The gamekeeper and Kosonen's three kids. So they were kept here as blackmail to force their father to carry out the kidnapping. There's still no solid proof that Antti was behind it, but I'd give good odds on it.

A hypothesis forms of its own accord, just hits me all at once. Killing three children wouldn't come easy to an inexperienced killer. I think he had an accomplice or accomplices. In this investigation, I've come across three men I believe capable of the crimes that have occurred. One of them is here with us now. The other two sell heroin and pâté.

My guess: The gamekeeper was murdered straightaway. Antti hid out here on this island while he was supposedly kidnapped. His job was to kill Kosonen, come back here with the money, wait for his accomplice or accomplices, divide up their ten million euros, and then they would go their separate ways and he would disappear, begin life anew under a different identity.

But he didn't wait. He had another boat he had stolen from his father, an Ocean Master 310 Sport Cabin, according to the manifest. He abandoned the children to his partner or partners in crime to deal with them and left. Realizing they had gotten fucked, they killed the kids — they were witnesses, after all — and set about finding Antti and their money. They're still looking, most likely why Moreau is here, because they enlisted him, offering him Antti's share. They killed Kaarina to punish Antti and, if my guess is right, are now just making foie gras and waiting for this to all play itself out.

Lisbet Söderlund. How does she fit into this and why was she murdered?

Her death wasn't what Saukko asked for, but was the kind of symbol he sought in order to relinquish his million euros. He and Jesper talked about selling heroin to sedate the black masses. I'm in charge of cleaning up drugs in Helsinki. I proved myself more than capable. Moreau told me the lesson learned is that narcotics are needed but must be controlled. The interior minister told me that he believes men adroit at one task are nearly always adroit at others and gave me an additional task, the skank sheet, hinting at additional responsibilities. He and others believe I'll find the money. It will disappear. Saukko will never get it back.

I think they all know the pâté peddlers murdered her, and that Antti has the ten million euros. Plus the other promised million in exchange for "a display of dedication to racist policies" makes eleven. This money is to be pooled and divided among various interests. Am I reading too much into this, or are the Legionnaires to have the heroin importation concession, the neo-Nazis the wholesale concession, our immigrant population to be the target consumer market, this money also to be shared? As I've learned, the amounts involved in dope are huge, and even small pieces of the pie could make many men rich. And I'm to be Finland's drug czar, discouraging other narcotics entrepreneurs around the country, as I have in Helsinki? I'm to be a cop in name, but Finland's narcotics power broker in truth, much as the former Legionnaires are foie gras dabblers in name but heroin kingpins in reality.

It's so insidious that it's difficult to conceive, but I believe it entirely possible.

Saukko won't like it, but the discovery of the children's bodies rightly goes to Saska. I call him, suggest he come here in a police helicopter, chopper them home and concoct a tale to explain the breakthrough in the case.

The question remains: Where is Antti? I think he's hiding somewhere, just waiting to be forgotten. We leave so we can be out of the way when Saska makes his fake break in the case, and go back to Saukko's mansion.

Saukko is so thrilled that the hunt is on again after a year that he doesn't even gripe about Saska's involvement. Saukko insists I hunt to the north. I give in and ask him for a map of his foundation properties. After some searching, he produces one.

I also call the interior minister and explain the situation. I ask him if he can make arrangements to use the radio-controlled pilotless planes as during the original search for Antti, to avoid his suspicion should he be in northern Åland. I tell him the type of craft we're looking for.

Some of the islands have rock shelves or caves on their coasts. Small craft could be hidden there, invisible from above. I suggest the Border Guard send vessels to circle all the islands and ensure Antti hasn't hidden his boat in such a place.

"No, Inspector," the interior minister says, "these are not good ideas. They limit our options. The Border Guard would have to arrest Antti. If you were to take him into custody, our options would remain open."

"Such as?"

"Such as his father is a powerful man and might prefer if his son doesn't rot in prison, no matter what he's done. He would be in great debt to us if we made that happen. If you find Antti, call me, and I'll instruct you as to what's to be done."

I hear myself sigh. Corruption has no limits among the powerful, even when it involves murder. My previous self would have expressed outrage. I've hidden my emotional stunting through the remembrance of emotions. I notice that my memories of them are fading, growing more distant.

"I want you to go, Inspector, and circle each and every island yourself. If you fail to find him, I'll consider your suggestion."

"You understand," I say, "that this is a wild-goose chase. He would have had to winter there, and it would have taken a great deal of time and preparation for him to do that. The only reason I think it remotely possible is because his father has the means to search to the ends of the earth for him, and this desolate area fills the bill."

"I understand, and I agree with you. But after all, he also has resources. He could have made a home winter-worthy in secret."

"Very well," I say and ring off.

I ask Saukko if I can use his yacht again tomorrow to continue the search, say that it will likely be an overnight trip, and he's happy to oblige. He wants to come. I suggest that it might be best for all if this was kept strictly police business. If we were to find Antti, his emotions would run high and might lead to something that could impede prosecution. He grudgingly agrees. Finding Antti there truly is only a shot in the dark. He's abandoned his wife and children, so he wanted out bad. His father has pretty much every resource in the world at his disposal to find Antti. If he really wants to disappear, as I said to the minister, it has to be somewhere at the ends of the earth. It's a thousand-to-one shot, but northern Åland pretty much qualifies.

37

Moreau rides with me back to Helsinki. I tell him he can't come with us tomorrow. "It's a snipe hunt, but if we should find Antti and the money, I won't be able to explain your presence. Maybe you could be at Saukko's side in his moment of triumph. He'd like that."

Moreau agrees. I ask where I can drop him off.

"I'm staying at that little hostel your wife runs, Hotel Kämp." I drop him off, pick up more baby formula and go home. Kate looks ghastly. She's drinking a glass of water with two hands. Her hangover is so bad that she trembles.

I pick up Anu, bounce her on my knee, and tell Kate all I've learned. She couldn't give a fuck less.

"Is something the matter, besides your hangover?" I ask.

"Where should I begin? Maybe we should

talk about how I've ignored my child for days while I stayed drunk."

I've learned that in marriage there are times to console with hugs, and times when they aren't wanted. Right now, it's the latter.

"Kate, you tried to run with the big dogs. The people you've hung around with the past few days drink a lot. You don't and couldn't keep up. Maybe you should have learned from your mistake the first time. But last night, drinking *pontikka,* it happens to everybody. Anni told me you didn't even drink very much of it. You're not a bad mother, you just had a very Finnish learning experience."

By the look on her face, I think Kate would be yelling at me now if she wasn't too sick to manage it. "Have you considered the possibility that I've been drunk because I'm so fucked-up that I'm not in control of my actions, even at the expense of our child, and that maybe the reason I'm so fucked-up is you?"

I thought my work might be affecting her, but not to this extent.

"You met us at that bar yesterday and Sweetness had blood coming out of puncture wounds in his knuckles. Now, why do I think he got those by knocking out someone's front teeth?"

"I'm investigating a murder of historic proportion and dealing with evil people — the kind of people who cut an innocent woman's head off — trying to solve it. I'm doing whatever I deem necessary."

"Is it necessary for you to commit crimes that could put you in jail, and do you see that you're working with buffoons that don't have a fucking clue what they're doing? You came to me with this song and dance about a black-ops thing that was supposed to help people, and I couldn't bring myself to say no because I thought you might die. But these black-ops actions aren't to help people, they're to generate graft for corrupt politicians. I put up with all this because you gave me a choice and I agreed to it in the beginning and I kept my word. I was wrong. We should have left and gone back to the States. You and your team are dupes and pawns, and you're going to pay a high price for your stupidity."

I've never seen her like this, so bitter.

She says I've become like the people I swore to combat and have broken my oath to uphold the law. "You've gone astray," she says. "You'll end up dead or in jail. I'm disappointed, disillusioned, I've lost respect for you. You have to change, to be the good man I married."

"I'm trying to make things right," I say.

"Arvid is dead," she says. "Your surgery changed you. And everything that came after has changed all of us."

"Kate, this hasn't gone the way I planned, either. Yes, I've been duped and used as a pawn. I'm also disappointed and disillusioned. Had I known where this road would lead, I never would have taken us down it. I made a mistake. And yes, I know brain surgery has affected me. I can't help that. I'm doing the best I can. I'm going on a wild-goose chase tomorrow. We're going to spend a couple days cruising around Åland. Come with us. It will do you good. And if we should by some miracle happen to find Antti Saukko, the man we're looking for, you'll see that we're still policemen, not just murderous thugs. The sun and sea air will do us all good."

She smirks, skeptical. She considers it, her face almost a sneer. "OK," she says.

38

It's a warm today. The sky blue. A perfect day for sailing, and we have hours until we reach the islands of northern Åland. Saukko had his cook stock the boat with enough food for an army. Saukko thought of everything, from fresh fish bait to a box of the figurado cigars we had smoked. I guess I did a good job of convincing him I liked them. The sea is calm, and I hope the trip will smooth the waters between Kate and me as well.

After I solve this murder, and I'm near to it, I'm going to solve my work-related problems as well. I didn't become a cop to be a thug. Time will fix this. I'll accumulate dirt on powerful people so they can't hurt me without destroying themselves. I've collected much skank, I'm close to it now. Then I'll do my job on my own terms or just walk away. Resign. Do as Kate said. Take her back to the States with the money

I've stolen and collect stamps.

Kate and I slather on suntan lotion, make sure Baby Anu is sun-protected head to toe, and sit side by side in deck chairs that fold out so you can lie down in them. Her hangover fades and her mood improves, and after a while she hooks her little finger around mine. We snack, sun, drink soft drinks, let Milo do all the work. I notice Sweetness isn't boozing. I wonder if the change in his relationship with Jenna has sobered him up. The sea was crowded with all manner of craft when we left Helsinki, but the farther north we go, other vessels are fewer and farther between.

Life on a small island in Åland must be interesting. Waterworld. An alternate way of living. Inhabitants take boats to the grocery store, to bars in the evening if they want to socialize. Everywhere.

Milo has the map, and after several hours he tells us we're now in waters that contain the islands donated by Saukko's foundation, and it's time to start watching. Some are only specks of rock, some are large. Kate softens, her bitterness dissipates. At a certain point, we go downstairs to a cabin and make love. When we come back up, the yacht is moored near a largish island. A dock juts out into the ocean, but beside and behind the dock is a cave. Its roof is several yards high and it goes about twenty yards back under the island. We're on the south side of the island, and this end of it is lightly forested and around a hundred yards across.

Inside the cave are a twin-engine fishing boat and a Jet Ski. Whodda thunk? We've really found Antti.

"We saw no hurry and waited on you," Milo says. He edges the yacht up to the dock. Sweetness hops over to it and ties us off.

I doubt we'll need them, but we don bulletproof vests and the rest of our gear. After all, if my theory is correct, Antti did kill a man. We follow a narrow path and the smell of cooking meat. We walk about fifty meters and find a big ramshackle hut in a clearing with two people outside it in folding chairs, making dinner on a grill. One is Antti. He's wearing a tie-dyed shirt, shorts and flip-flops. The other is a pretty woman in her mid-twenties, about eight months pregnant.

Antti smiles. "Damn, it's been a year. I thought you'd have stopped looking by now. And we were going to leave next week and move to Fasta Åland where there's medical care, before Mari gives birth. What can I do for you?"

"I'm sorry to say this," I tell him, "but I

have to arrest you."

"For what?"

OK, we can play this out if he wants. "The faking of your kidnapping, your sister's actual kidnapping, the theft of ten million euros, and the murder of Jussi Kosonen."

He sits back, crosses his legs and sips at a beer. "I haven't got a clue what you're talking about. I was kidnapped and released. When they released me, I decided I didn't want to go back to my old life. I came here with Mari for the peace and quiet, waiting to be forgotten. There's no crime in any of that."

"I'm pretty sure that when we search, we'll find the ransom money. That's our proof."

"Search to your heart's content," he says.

Mari hasn't said a word, but she looks scared. "Are you OK?" I ask her. "Do you need anything?"

"Just for you to go away."

"Let's start inside," I say. "Antti, would you please accompany us?" I want to keep an eye on him.

What we find inside startles me. He's built a small but lovely modern home with all the amenities, and then camouflaged the exterior with boards from old fishing cabins.

"This is great," I say. "I'm impressed."

"Thanks," Antti says. "I did everything

myself in my spare time. Took me five years. I've been waiting to get away from my old life for a long time."

"Couldn't you have found an easier way?"

He shakes his head. "You don't know my father."

He's so relaxed and amiable that we ignore procedure. We don't cuff him. No nothing. Like idiots. I bend over to look under the bed. A gunshot scares me so bad I almost piss myself. The bullet whizzes past me and shatters a window on the other side of the bedroom. The next round hits me in the side. The bulletproof vest stops it, but the shot knocks the wind out of me. Milo was drawing his pistol as Antti took aim at his head. And then boom after boom after boom, all hell breaks loose and Antti jerks like a puppet until half his head flies off and he falls. Then Sweetness stands over him and dumps the remainder of his ammo in Antti's face until his .45s are empty.

After sixteen rounds in the chest, face and head, there isn't much of him left. It's a real fucking mess. His girlfriend tries to come in but Milo pushes her out so she won't see it.

For a couple minutes we all just stand there, uncertain what to do, then a familiar voice repeats the phrase I first heard it utter. "I hope I haven't interrupted you at an inopportune moment."

I turn, and Moreau stands in the doorway, Kate in front of him with Anu in her arms. The muzzle of his Beretta touches her head.

"Shall we step outside?" he says. "The stink of open intestines is a bit overwhelming in here."

We trail out and he tells everyone to make themselves comfortable. He takes his gun away from Kate's head and brings a chair for her. "Please, one at a time, place your weapons at your feet and kick them toward me." Milo, God bless him, tries to prove himself the pistoleer he always wanted to be and quick draws, tries to save us all. Adrien is like lightning and puts a bullet through Milo's wrist. His gun drops and he holds his arm up to look at it. He tries to wiggle his fingers but they don't move.

"I told you," Moreau says, "Deputy Dawg can never beat Yosemite Sam. I'm the rootinest tootinest here outlaw in the West. Your carpal tunnel and radial nerve are wrecked. I doubt you'll ever use that hand again. It's going to hurt like hell in a minute."

"Fuck you," Milo says. His repertoire of comebacks is limited at the moment. He slumps to the ground but sits up, holds his wrist with his other hand.

Moreau collects our Colts and piles them well out of our reach.

There are only two chairs. Kate has one, I take the other. "What do you want?" I ask.

"The ten million. Hand it over and I'll leave you in peace."

"Antti died before he told us where it is."

"I am sorry. I cannot believe that you would be so stupid as to kill him before he told you."

He'll never believe I was too stupid not to cuff and guard him, but I try. "He pulled a gun, Sweetness shot him."

"And with verve! Still, you are just not that stupid."

I consider pleading with him. Nothing I say or do will make any difference. He'll stick with whatever agenda he's planning. "Do you know everything?" I ask. "For instance, who killed Lisbet Söderlund?"

"Of course. I've known all along. This is the way it works," Moreau says. "I am going to torture the group of you until I have the money. We have all the time in the world, and I will cause you immense pain. I would spare you that. Please give me the money."

"I'm sorry," I say, "I would if I had it. But I don't."

"Then I'll fill you in on the details as you suffer," he says. "As leader, you must suffer first. As once you were, so again you shall be."

I try to blank my mind, to steel myself for what's to come. I don't ask him to spare Kate, because the sign of weakness might entice him to hurt her first.

"I will start at the beginning," Moreau says. "Over a year ago, my former Foreign Legion comrades engineered the kidnapping of Kaarina Saukko with Antti. They found Kosonen, the dupe. He frequented their shop, and they took his children. They planned the crime, robbed the home, did the technical work. Antti knew the user name and password at the security company because he had been there while they planned the system, watched the technician open his computer and memorized them. No magic there, but the B&E at the company made the robbery seem more sophisticated and less of an inside job."

I have shorts on. Moreau examines my knee, puts his pistol to the exact point of entry from when I was shot before, and fires. The bullet passes through the old exit scar. The pain is awful and I grunt, but won't allow him the satisfaction of a scream. Good-bye, reconstructed knee.

"The patsy collected the ransom money, Antti killed him, betrayed my colleagues and

410

disappeared. He left them the paintings, I suppose as recompense, without considering that they have provenance and are worthless without a pre-heist buyer for a private collection. Apparently, he came here, to this island, to meet his girlfriend."

She nods and confirms this.

"As punishment for betrayal, they shot Kaarina. They assassinated her with a .308 Winchester, which they, arrogantly enough, kept rather than disposed of. Find it. You'll have your murder weapon and no doubt solve the crime in short order. Then they set about looking for Antti, with no luck. They surveilled the police for a year, kept up with their progress. The police couldn't find him. If they could follow the police but jump one step ahead, as police act cautiously while they build cases, they could take their ten million. Too much time passed. Afraid police interest in the case would wane, they called me, offered me a split, and used their connections to convince Veikko Saukko to have me brought in. I contacted you to convince you that the Saukko kidnap-murder and the Söderlund assassination were likely related, to keep the Saukko case a police top priority while I remained informed of developments. Then I could kill Antti and take the money back.

411

To aid in this effort, Marcel and Thierry committed the robberies posing as Islamic fundamentalists — they wore charcoal camo stick to disguise themselves as blacks and spouted some rhetoric in ridiculous accents — and also committed the racial murders, simply to make it appear they were related to the Söderlund assassination, to keep your enthusiasm high."

He examines me with a speculative eye. "Open your mouth."

I refuse.

"Well," he says, "it's either my way or I shoot you through both jaws."

Wisdom dictates I open my mouth. He sticks the barrel in it, blows out the bridgework from where my own teeth were shot out, and creates a wound that will leave a scar just like the one I had removed. The pain is awful. I feel woozy. He reaches in his pocket and hands me something. "It's a bindle of heroin. Sniff only a tiny bit. You are what is called opiate naïve. If you use too much, you will overdose, or at least pass out. I want you aware."

He moves to Antti's girlfriend. "If you do not tell me where the money is, I will kill your baby."

She screams and covers her belly with her hands. "I don't know, he never told me."

"You have ten seconds," he says.

She cries, begs, pleads. He counts. I open the bindle, pour some heroin on my thumbnail and snort it. The pain melts away. Relief makes me sigh. I'm not opiate naïve. I used narcotics to combat my headaches. I remain coherent.

He counts to zero and fires at an angle through the side of her belly. The bullet exits the other side of her stomach. The baby, if not dead, soon will die. She only moans and weeps silent tears. Her man, her dream, her child. She's lost everything.

"We now have a time constraint," Moreau says. "If she does not receive medical attention, she will die of internal bleeding."

Kate makes not a sound, but on her face she wears a scream of terror and clutches Anu tight.

He kneels beside her. "You need not fear me. You remind me very much of someone so close to me that I would die myself rather than harm you. She is gone, but as long as you exist, in a way she does as well."

He walks back over to me. "Yes, there was a rumor that whoever killed Lisbet Söderlund would get her job, but it was just that, a rumor, started by Roope Malinen. In truth, my Foreign Legion colleagues murdered her by agreement with Malinen, who

413

promised them a permanent, lucrative, and competition-free concession in the Finnish heroin market. Malinen lied. He had no authority to promise anything in return for the assassination of Söderlund. He hated her and made a false promise concerning a heroin concession in the hopes that he could make good on it later, simply because he wanted her dead. You have gone a long way toward seeing that promise kept. They cut her head off with a meat saw in their food shop. I'm sure, if you live through today, you can find plenty of DNA from the saw and blood-spatter specks around their kitchen to prove it. Saukko demanded a spectacle of dedication to hate, which they gave him. Saukko said quit bullshitting around on the Internet and do something, hinting that it might change his mind about his campaign donation. Word went down the line via Malinen that Saukko wanted a display. Marcel and Thierry did it for political reasons, in the hopes that Saukko would then honor his million-euro campaign commitment. Saukko welshed anyway."

Kate finds her voice. "Why would you let us live? We know who you are."

"I assure you that you do not. I do indeed work for the French government, but I have a stack of various identifications two inches thick. They will tell you that I work for them one day, then deny it the next."

"Have you considered that we don't know where the money is and you're killing us all for nothing?" she asks.

"I recognize it as a possibility."

"You're an ugly human being," she says.

"As I once told your husband, I am a peacekeeper. Sometimes, keeping the peace requires extreme measures. Giving me the ten million euros will restore harmony to all our lives."

"For such an altruist, you seem quite concerned with wealth."

"In fact, I have no interests other than my work, and my tastes are frugal. My wealth is symbolic. In darker moments of doubt, I tally my accounts, and the sum figure serves as proof and reassures me that I have followed the career that was my destiny. There is little more to it than that."

"But still, you would kill us all to acquire it?"

"Oh yes, with the exception of you."

He walks over to Milo, flicks open his stiletto, and lops off Milo's right ear. Blood slops down his neck. "You are the weakest. I believe you will talk first. This is also a matter of time. If you wait too long, it cannot be sewn back on. The next time you get a turn, I'll sharpen a stick, pop out your eye and perform a makeshift lobotomy on you. Instead of calculating ineffable permutations with your big, big brain, you'll spend your life being pushed around in a wheelchair with a drool cup strapped to your chin. It's remarkably easy to do. The man who popularized the procedure sometimes performed hundreds in a single day, divided the brains of whole institutions full of mental patients."

Milo doesn't make a sound. Not even the look on his face changes. The ear looks like an odd mushroom lying on a rock in the sun.

Moreau continues his explanation. "Antti kept the children at the summer cottage — which the family had not used in years — while he disappeared during the kidnapping. When he left with the money, he abandoned them. With their father dead, there was little to be done. Marcel and Thierry overdosed them with heroin hot shots in their sleep."

"And you don't think they'll try to hunt you down and kill you after you've stolen their hard-earned fortune?"

"They were no longer required and a hindrance. I saw no reason to share the ten million with them after they bungled their

416

own mission and called upon me to fix it. My purpose here is manifold. One is to control the drug trade. Another is to squelch the racist movement that seems to be veering out of control in Finland. These upset the order of things. My mission for my employers is, succinctly put, to restore order when situations require it. The heroin you watched me give to my former comrades had some parts of it, near the bottom of the bag, poisoned, in order to confuse matters and hide the poisoning for a time. Notice that the heroin I gave you was pure, not cut. And so they sold strychnine-laced heroin to racist elements, who in turn sold it to dealers who primarily deal with blacks in the name of, as they put it, 'nigger sedation.' Unfortunately, this will lead to some deaths, but the trail will lead back to the white supremacists. It will, however, result in the incarceration of these racist drug dealers, while at the same time rousing sympathy for their immigrant victims. My comrades became liabilities. If you live through today, you'll discover that I've made it easy for you to solve your cases and, once again, shine as a hero. Albeit, a crippled one. It might make you feel better to know that, after all the unnecessary pain they caused — mostly out of enjoyment, I might add — they died badly indeed."

Kate says, "Milo is in agony. Would you let me give him some heroin and put his ear in the shade so maybe it can be saved? It's cooking on that rock."

"For you," he says, "anything."

He hands her a bindle and she walks to the other side of the clearing to tend to Milo. Kate picks his ear up and moves it to the shade, to keep it cooler and slow decomposition.

Moreau strides over to Sweetness. He's sitting cross-legged on the ground. His flask is in his hand. He sucks at it.

"Wise move," Moreau says. "Breaking you, big man, requires forethought. How to torture an elephant? I have a feeling you can endure a great deal, but you are a romantic and feel much affection for the others. That's why I hurt them first."

His back is to Kate. Milo wears his leather jacket with the specially made holster to make his sawed-off invisible. Apparently, Milo never showed it off to Moreau. Kate sets Anu on the ground, slides out the shotgun and points it at Moreau. It looks huge in her hands. It's hard for her, but she puts a thumb on each hammer, pulls with all her might, and slowly they ease back and click into place.

Moreau doesn't have to look, doesn't even turn to face her. He knows the sound.

"And after all the nice things I just said about you."

She says, "Don't move."

He doesn't.

She keeps the barrels straight although she's shaking hard and the gun is heavy. When she gets to within about four feet of him, she pulls both triggers. The gun roars, flames and smoke leap out of the barrels. Milo was supposed to have the gun loaded with rock salt. Instead, the ammo was razor-sharp fléchettes. The blast cuts Moreau near in half, along his midsection. Not much holds the two pieces of him together. His blood and guts, bone chips, gore, spray out and onto Sweetness. Moreau falls, yet he still lives. I see him blink. His jacket is on fire. The flames spread.

The gun kicked up and back and lacerated the side of Kate's head. Blood runs down her cheek. She wipes at it and smears it. It drips onto her shoulder. She drops the gun and slumps to the ground. I speak to her but she's withdrawn inside herself, in shock. She doesn't move or speak. Her mouth hangs open and spittle dribbles down her chin.

Now Moreau's shirt and pants are burning. Sweetness pours *kossu* on him. The flames leap. Moreau can't move but winks at Sweetness, as if this is a joke only the two of them can share. Sweetness pulls out his horse dick and pisses on him, says "Adieu."

I look over. Mari, the pregnant girl, is dead. She bled out. Only Sweetness is functional. I ask him to take Milo's ear to the boat and put it on ice.

The heroin kept me able to think. The pain is returning in spades. I sniff a little more and push myself up with my cane. I hobble over to Milo and shake a little more onto my thumbnail. It's hard to talk and I slur. "Sniff thith."

He inhales it and still doesn't speak, but I see his body relax.

I hobble to Kate and slump beside her. She stares straight ahead, won't speak to me. I look at her head. There's a lot of blood, but that doesn't mean anything. Head wounds always bleed a lot. I think it's just a simple cut, nothing more. I pick up her hand and let go. It drops back in her lap, limp. The lights are on but nobody's home. Traumatic shock.

Sweetness comes back. "I know where the money is," he says.

I want to beat him to death. "Then why didn't you tell him?"

"I just figured it out. Look at the graveyard behind the house."

Set back in the clearing are four cairns marked with wooden crosses. They mean that sometime way back when, fishermen got stranded here, probably waited too long into the winter season to leave and got frozen in and died. The ground was too hard to dig, so they covered their friends in rocks and marked their resting places.

"The weathering is the same, consistent, on all the piles except one," Sweetness says, "and the cross is a little different, too. The money is under the rocks."

I have to call for a helicopter to medevac us all out of here, but I will *not* leave that money to be returned to that racist motherfucker Saukko, or to be stolen, probably by Jyri, when they tear this island apart looking for it. After all the suffering that's been caused by it, I'll burn it first. I try to speak as little as possible. It hurts like hell. "Try to get it."

He brings Anu to me, then goes to work. He throws the rocks onto the other cairns as he digs. Breaks up the cross, leaves no evidence that the cairn was ever there. And people call him stupid. The two sports bags of cash are at the bottom. It took ten minutes.

Milo walks over. He's a bloody mess, but the heroin pulled him together. He says to Sweetness, "Can you drive a boat to Turku?" Milo points. "It's that way. The boat's GPS map will guide you."

Sweetness nods. "I think so."

Milo talks slow and pauses in the middle of sentences, but stays focused. "Antti's is the fastest boat, and it's long forgotten except by us and Saukko, and he won't think to start tracking it. The keys are on a nail over the kitchen sink. Make sure it's fueled and leave now. When you get to Turku, take a bus to Helsinki. While you're on your way, go for a swim and wash the blood off you the best you can. The wind will dry you before you get there. As soon as you get to Helsinki, before you go home, hide the money where no one would ever think to look."

Kate rolls over on her side, balls up in a fetal position. I ask Milo, "Can you call?"

He requests the helicopter, tells him there are dead civilians and officers down. Fucking Milo. He can't part with his toys. He collects the Colts and his sawed-off, puts them in our holsters and pockets, and lies down beside me.

I hold Anu on my chest with one hand. I put the other hand on his shoulder. I say,

"Just tell them the truth, except say that Moreau shot Antti."

"OK," he says, and passes out.

I think about Moreau. He flew too close to the sun, his wings of Icarus melted, and he fell burning to the earth, plummeted to his death.

39

I awaken in a hospital bed, doped up. My first thoughts are whether I still have a leg and a jawbone. I lift the sheet. My leg is still there. I feel my face. It's swathed in so much bandage that I can't tell.

I ring the bell, the nurse comes in, chipper and smiling, tells me it's wonderful to see me awake. I thank her and ask her if she could get a doctor to speak to me. I'd like to know not just about my own condition but the status of my wife, daughter and colleague as well.

An hour goes by, a doctor breezes in, also smiling, and asks, "How are we doing today?"

I wish I could hit him.

"Do I still have a jaw?" I ask.

He looks at my chart. "Your jaw is fine. All the bone is intact. In fact, you suffered little damage in that regard. The teeth that were shot away were prosthetics, weren't your own anyway. The bullet inflicted injury on a previously damaged area. You may have some additional nerve damage and some trouble with mobility on that side of your face. Only time will tell."

"And my knee?"

He sighs. "The original gunshot to your knee destroyed a great deal of cartilage, and more was worn away through normal use over the years because the damage made it fragile. During your recent partial knee replacement, some of that damaged cartilage was removed. The new gunshot destroyed the prosthesis. I doubt a new one is viable. Again, time will tell. But best guess, you'll have the same problems you had before the replacement, only worse. I doubt you'll be able to walk without aid, at least a cane. But you keep the leg. Be thankful for that."

"My wife and colleague were also injured. Can you check on them for me?"

"Of course."

"And I want some cigarettes. Can you help me out?"

"I'll go to the office and see what personal effects you have locked up there." He gives my shoulder a pat. "I'll buy you some and take you outside myself, if need be."

He comes back a little while later. He has

my wallet, cell phone, cane, cigarettes and lighter. My other things are in police custody. He wheels me outside to smoke and I find Milo there. "Your friend can relate his own condition. Your daughter is in our nursery, and your wife responds only to her. Your wife is suffering from acute stress disorder, as evidenced by her inability to comprehend stimuli, disorientation, and dissociative stupor. She's heavily sedated. Her condition will likely improve, it's just a question of when. Days, or weeks, at most."

"When can we all go home?"

"You need professional in-home care, since neither of you can take care of the other, and your conditions need close monitoring. The changing of your bandages, for instance, must be done precisely. I can bring you the contact information for in-home care firms. If you can't afford it, you can remain here until the situation improves."

The doctor takes me back to my room and Milo comes with us. I thank the doc and he leaves us alone. "The room is probably bugged," I say, "don't say anything private. How are you?"

His head is also wrapped in bandages. "They saved my ear. It may hang funny. My hand will never work right again, if at all.

Physical therapy may or may not help."

"I guess you have to learn to shoot left-handed."

He sighs. "I guess so. I can go home tomorrow, though. That's something, at least. I hate this fucking place."

"I don't want a stranger in my home. You said Mirjami is a registered nurse."

"If you recall, she's in love with you. I doubt she'll say no."

I also recall she turns me on so much, I almost came in my pants when I met her. But sex is very low on my list of wants at the moment. "She doesn't pay much attention to me. I think she got over it. Would you call her for me? Tell her I'll pay her anything she wants."

"Yeah. And I'll stop by again in a while and take you out to smoke."

That's all I have to look forward to at the moment. "See you later."

As he walks out, two SUPO detectives walk in to take my statement. I give it to them. They ask no interrogation-type questions, just tape-record it. Then they congratulate me on breaking the Saukko case, shake my hand, and wish me godspeed in my recovery. I find myself nodding off.

I wake up and Sweetness is sitting in a chair

beside the bed. "Here," he says, and hands me a bouquet of flowers and a box of candy. I don't know if it's a joke or not.

"It was supposed to make you laugh," he says.

I put on the fake smile. "Sorry, everything hurts. Watch what you say. I'm sure the room is bugged. Everything OK with you?"

"Everything went as planned, and yeah, things are good. I'm dating Jenna now."

"That's great, you must be a happy man."

"I had to bargain to get her. No more carrying the *kossu* flask."

"That's even better. Wise girl. The shit was going to kill you."

He shrugs. "Something kills everybody. Just ask my brother."

Milo wanders in. "Hey! The gang's all here."

"How are you guys?" Sweetness asks.

Milo says, "Fucked-up and permanently damaged, but alive. How is everything from your end?" meaning the money.

Sweetness gets the drift. "Under control."

"Mirjami took a leave of absence to care for you," Milo says to me. "They didn't like it until she told them she was going to take care of the great fallen hero. She'll be at your house as soon as you give her the word."

"Then we can leave. Sweetness, would you do me a favor and take us all home in the SUV?"

"Get your stuff together. It's parked outside."

I'm a shot cop, get VIP treatment. I ask a nurse if they can dress my wife, get my child, and meet us in the lobby. She says give her half an hour.

We get outside, have a moment without listening devices monitoring us, and in turn walk, gimp on crutches, and are pushed in a wheelchair to the SUV. "I have a plan," I say. "We'll wrap these murders up in a couple days, and make some people unhappy along the way."

40

The guys help us get our stuff into the apartment. Mirjami shows up, all business. She's wearing jeans, no makeup and a plain gray sweatshirt. Kate walks to the couch and sits down. She shows no signs of cognition, but this, evidently, is where she wants to be. She holds out her arms. I put Anu in them. Kate's eyes don't so much as waver, but she seems satisfied. I ask Sweetness to go with Milo and get the anti-surveillance gear. They go through the house. Every room is bugged. They de-bug the house and leave to let us get settled in.

I call my former psychoanalyst, Torsten Holmqvist, explain about Kate and her condition. I tell him I have an opinion from the hospital, but I'd like a second opinion and follow-up care, and I'd like all this done in my home. I can almost hear him scoff, and then I tell him cost is no object. He's the best money can buy and that's what I want for my wife. He agrees.

Mirjami tells me she would like to examine my wounds and takes me to the bedroom. She unwraps them, spends a long time examining them, tut-tuts concern, and applies new dressings.

Torsten arrives. I don't tell him the story, just that Kate's been through a terribly traumatic experience. He diagnoses her with acute stress disorder, and cites the same symptoms as the first doctor. So the original diagnosis was correct. She responds only to Anu, whom she will hold and allow to nurse. He deems this a good sign.

The condition will probably last from two days to four weeks. He prescribes eighty milligrams of the tranquilizer Diazepam per day, spread out over four doses, for a few days, during which she'll sleep most of the time, and then, depending on how things go, cut it back to sixty milligrams. He'll check on her in a few days and tells me to let him know if anything requires his attention.

Within the day, I expect everyone from Heinrich Himmler/Saukko to Jyri Ivalo are going to call or pound on my door and tell me to give them that ten million euros. Even if it were true, they wouldn't accept that I don't have it. They want it too badly to allow themselves to believe it's lost.

I think about calling Saukko myself. He would want to know about his son. Then I think, *Fuck him, he's a pig. And he never even bothered to call me to ask how his son died.*

I decide I want to proceed with the investigation now, whether I can directly participate or not. I call Sweetness and ask him to go to Turku, to B&E the houses and business of the two former Legionnaires and find their heroin and the rifles used in the murders. I call Milo and tell him what we're up to, and he wants to go too, shattered hand be damned. Unless they've been cleaned, the rifles used in the murders should be the only ones with gunpowder residue. They get to Turku and find both men in Marcel's home, both dead.

Sweetness calls me over our encrypted phones. They ODed. One had a needle in his arm, the other a needle in his dick. As Moreau said, they died badly. Vomit everywhere. Face and bodies twisted from convulsions. Strychnine. They weren't users. They bore other needle track marks, though, to give the impression that they were users, undoubtedly created by empty syringes, possibly after they were dead. Moreau murdered his old friends in one of the most painful ways imaginable. I say to leave them there for now to decomp. Mostly so I can rest for a couple of days before the denouement.

I tell Sweetness to find the rifles used in the race murders and leave them somewhere not too hard to find. To locate the .308 Winchester used to murder Kaarina Saukko, go to Malinen's summer cottage, use print transparencies from his possessions and transfer his fingerprints to the rifle, then plant it somewhere semi-hidden in the cottage, along with a quantity of heroin. He orchestrated murder, he can pay for it. Morally, I can see no difference if he pays for the murder of Lisbet Söderlund, which he caused, or that of Kaarina Saukko, for which the weapon was used. I ask Milo if he's capable of cleaning out Jyri's bank account. He says consider it done. I tell him to wait until I give the word.

Mirjami does a good job. She's attentive and, I discover, quite intelligent as well. Kate remains in a state resembling catatonia. Mirjami's attention doesn't waver from her, Anu and their needs. She also changes the bandages and cleans the wounds on my reconstructed knee, now deconstructed, and the wounds in my mouth and face. She sleeps in the spare bed in Anu's room.

That first night at home, I'm doped up and exhausted. I fall into a deep sleep. I have a sex dream about Kate. It's vivid, intense. It wakes me, but it's not a dream. Mirjami has my dick in her mouth. The beautiful girl. The rush of pleasure amidst pain. The dope. I close my eyes and sigh. Then I hear Kate stirring in her sleep in the living room. It's hard to remember what I would have done when I felt emotion, but I dig deep and try.

I twist Mirjami's hair in my hand and pull her away from me. "No. Please." My strength is sapped. I can muster only those two words.

She says nothing, makes her way up the bed. Her body is near mine, but not pressed against me. She puts an arm around me. It means nothing to me. I let it rest there and drift off to sleep again. When I wake, she's gone from the bed, spoon-feeding Kate. I ask myself if it really happened. We don't speak of it.

My wounds have taken a great toll on me. I'm in much pain. I use a lot of narcotics. I mostly sit with Kate and Anu or in my massive chair, read, watch TV. I sleep a lot. I don't read newspapers. I don't watch news. I don't answer calls unless I recognize a friendly name on my cell phone.

The next morning, Jyri comes to my home uninvited. He sees me and my condition, sees Kate and her condition. I tell him the story minus the ten million. It was never found. Antti Saukko is dead. Moreau is dead. Three children murdered. All over Helsinki, junkies are dying of strychnine poisoning. Twenty-nine at current count. Twenty-two are black.

He doesn't believe me, or thinks the money is there but I just couldn't find it. I tell him to let it be. This is over. Jyri threatens me, tries to intimidate me. I counter, "Watch and see what happens if you don't fuck off. Go home, take a look around your attic, on the rafters, and in the second snow tire from the bottom of the pile of four in your garage. Check your bank account." He storms out.

He calls a couple hours later. His voice is controlled. I think he's both shocked and awed, and finally developed respect for me. "A MAC-10 and an assortment of drugs," he says. "And I'm broke."

Jyri asks if I think I'm in charge now. I answer no, but I took this job and started this illegal operation after being promised that it was for the purpose of helping people. At the time, Jyri specified young women being forced into the slave trade and prostitution. That was a lie. This has been nothing but a corrupt scam to make the rich richer. A travesty that cost lives. No longer.

He hems, haws, agrees. I tell him he'll have his money returned today. But next time, if I'm ever duped again, more contraband and unaccounted-for money will come to light. After I fly a video on YouTube of him with a big green dildo stuck up his ass by a murder victim, I'm going to kill him in the process of arresting him. I ask him if he understands and force him to say yes.

I call Saska Lindgren and give him a tip, with the promise that it didn't come from me. The rifle used to kill Kaarina Saukko is in the back of a closet in Roope Malinen's summer cottage. The murder is solved, he just has to concoct a story to go with it. Also, I've solved the Lisbet Söderlund murder and will announce it today. Evidence I find should also prove that her killers murdered the black people who were gassed and napalmed, and committed the bank robbery. He starts to ask me how I know. Thinks better of it. Thanks me and hangs up.

The strychnine-laced heroin that has killed so many is traced back to the neo-Nazis. They claim innocence, try to pin it on the two ex-Legionnaires. Unfortunately, they're dead, unable to provide evidence or testimony. Forty-seven neo-Nazis in total are arrested.

I go to Turku with Milo. For some reason I want to appear strong, not crippled. I use my cane instead of crutches, despite additional pain. We find the meat saw that was used to decapitate Lisbet Söderlund. A forensics team goes over the room. They find her DNA on the saw, and in nearly invisible blood spatter surrounding it. A tough job, separating her DNA from the hundreds of animals the saw has dismembered.

I suppose we're once again heroes. I continue my media blackout and tell Milo and Sweetness I need a few days alone. I go home to rest, to take a sick leave and let my wounds heal.

I still have no emotions. Each night, after I'm asleep, Mirjami clambers into bed with me. I never realize it until I feel her hand stroking my hair or brushing my arm. I once told her to go away and she did, but I think she came back. I'm not sure. She never comes too close or attempts seduction. For myself, in terms of meaning, it could be a dog in the bed with me, so I let it be.

We never speak of it, it's not happening. Until one day, while eating lunch, while

Kate sleeps.

"You know I'm in love with you," she says.

"You don't even know me. You told Milo that about five seconds after you met me."

"You never heard of the lightning bolt?" she asks.

"I'm honored," I say. "You're a beautiful woman and a lovely person, but I'm married and my emotions are . . . not as they should be."

"You're damaged. I see your pain. I want to heal you."

I don't know what to say.

"It's OK," she says, "unrequited love is sad and beautiful. In a way, I'm at least able to borrow you for a little while. And you'll never forget me."

"No, I won't."

I feel as if I'm getting worse, not better. I'm sleeping even more. When awake, I'm zonked on painkillers and tranquilizers. And I need them. The pain is severe. I'm living on soup again, as I did the last time my teeth were shot out. My knee throbs and something like knife stabs shoot through it. I can feel it, don't have to be told they won't be able to put it back together again.

That afternoon, Kate reaches over and takes my hand. She's back.

She's not only back, but lucid. And I snap

back, too. Just like that. In the blink of an eye. Emotions start rushing, surging through me. It's overwhelming. So much so that my mind blanks, just swirls. It's both agonizing and joyful. The shock freezes me for a minute. I can't move and the room disappears first into blackness, then to blurry white light.

As Jari told me it might, an event brought my emotions back. I feel love for the first time since my surgery. I feel relief that Kate has come back to me. I make my way over to her. We hold each other for a long time without speaking.

"The last thing I remember," she says, "is shooting Adrien. Where have I been and what has happened since then?"

"Mostly, you've been right here. I'll tell you what's happened later." I remained faithful, but I won't tell her about Mirjami falling in love with me. I explain, though, that she's been caring for us.

Finally, Kate lets me go, picks up Anu so she can nurse. She's quiet for a long time, a couple hours. Then she says I've done terrible things. She doesn't know if they were the result of my surgery, or if she doesn't know the man she married. And now she's become a killer, too. She's become everything she despises.

Mirjami asks if her services are still required. I say I'm not sure, but Kate and I can get by for at least one night. We need the time together.

Mirjami gathers her things. "If you want me," she says, "just call."

Kate doesn't catch the double entendre.

Kate rarely speaks through the evening, and we sleep together, but the distance between us is great.

In the morning, she says, "I'm taking Anu and going to stay at Kämp for a while."

I lost her to brain surgery, finally got her back, and now she's leaving me. I say as much.

"I'm not leaving you, I just need time to think. Are you able to care for yourself?"

I nod. In fact, it will be difficult. I've realized that I'm in such bad shape that I'm in trouble. The pain is at times exquisite.

She offers me no sign of affection. The door clicks behind her.

41

Over the next twelve days, we have dinner twice. It was a mistake to try. She didn't want to be with me. The silence roared.

One day, I get a text message from Saska Lindgren. "They covered up the murder weapon I recovered from Roope Malinen's summer cottage. He got a free pass." No surprise.

June twenty-sixth is Midsummer Eve, the third anniversary of Kate and my first meeting. On the twenty-fourth, I text Kate, ask her if she would like to spend our anniversary together. She doesn't reply.

Except for our two disastrous dinners, I've seen no one since I went into self-imposed isolation. I call my brother Timo. He's having a party. He invited me a while ago, and I ask if I can still come. Sure.

I go, get whacked on Timo's *pontikka,* eat grilled sausages. They light the bonfire at midnight. I get a text from Kate. "I miss you." I don't think she wants a reply. I put the phone back in my pocket, have a long drink from my glass of *pontikka,* and watch the flames climb higher.

BEYOND THE STORY

In the first Inspector Vaara novel, *Snow Angels,* I wrote, "Finns hate in silence." At the time, I believed it was true, but it's true no more. The sounds of racial hatred resonate like the tattoo of a beating war drum that grows louder every day. This atmosphere inspired me to write *Helsinki White.*

The hatred became vocalized with the meteoric rise of the political party Perussuomalaiset, or True Finns. In the previous parliamentary election, they took five seats. In the election of 2011, they took thirty-nine, a close third, behind Kokoomus, or National Coalition Party, and SDP, or Social Democrats.

This gave True Finns the right to participate in government and push their agenda, which includes, among other radical ideas, by way of example, withdrawal from the European Union. Not all but many True Finns are anti-immigration and blame immigrants for Finland's social ills. One influential blogger describes his solution as "the D-word." Deportation. Shortly after the elections, upon finding that none of the critical items on their agenda had a chance in hell of being implemented, True Finns declared themselves an opposition party.

Finland is far from the only Nordic country to have large factions holding such anti-immigrant beliefs. Other nations have instituted immigration laws that can only be described as draconian. In fact, large numbers of people in all the wealthier European Union nations are angry about the influx of foreigners, in particular Muslims.

Last year, *Newsweek* magazine declared Finland the best country in which to live. This presented a skewed view of the nation at best. Inflation is rampant. Wages stagnant. Real estate prices in urban areas soaring. Unemployment high. The number of poor growing because so many jobs have been outsourced. Public health care is in crisis. Perhaps *Newsweek* should send a journalist here and document hundred-yard-long bread lines and the queues at the soup kitchens. That's how Finland takes care of its poor these days. Finns are very good at generating and manipulating statistics. *Newsweek* bought into it. It's not all a lie.

Industrialists and financiers are thriving.

It was all of these things that compelled me to make politics and social ills prominent themes in this novel.

Helsinki White is also in part a true-crime novel. The story of the Saukko kidnapping is closely based on the real kidnapping, in 2009, of Minna Nurminen, the daughter of Hanna Nurminen, who is the eldest of the late Pekka Herlin's five children. The Herlin family is perhaps the most well-known Finnish industrial dynasty. The family is among the principal owners of the elevator company Kone and the cargo-handling equipment manufacturer Cargotec. The true story ended well. The ransom was paid and Minna returned to her family unscathed. The kidnapper, Juha Turunen, was a forty-four-year-old corporate lawyer and well outside the profile of a person likely to commit such a crime. A kidnapping of such magnitude had never before occurred in Finland.

Shortly after I completed *Helsinki White,* an event occurred which threw the novel's theme of hatred into sharp relief.

On July 22, 2011, Anders Breivik bombed government buildings in Oslo, Norway, and then proceeded on to a Labor Party youth camp on the island of Utøya. Disguised as a policeman, he murdered sixty-nine people, mostly kids.

On the day of his attack, Breivik released his one-thousand-five-hundred-word manifesto, entitled *2083 — A European Declaration of Independence.* In nature, the work is xenophobic, ultranationalistic, Islamophobic, and calls for the destruction of "Eurabia" by violent means. He claims connections with far-right-wing political movements, both Norwegian and international. This has not been proven. Breivik envisions a latter-day Knights Templar that will drive the Infidel from Europe.

Breivik finds a kindred spirit in the premier True Finn blogger and Finnish parliamentarian Jussi Halla-aho. Breivik writes:

Jussi Halla-aho, running for parliament in Finland as an independent candidate, has come to some of the same conclusions as I have regarding the Leftist-Islamic cooperation in many Western nations: The Left milks the working natives to maintain a predominantly idle immigrant population, who thankfully vote for the Left. The welfare state society thus has to support two parasites, each living in a symbiotic relationship with the other. This will eventually cause the system to collapse. Why would anyone support a policy that leads to certain destruction? Well, because a career politician never sets his sights 20, 50 or 100 years to the future but instead focuses on the next election. The short-term focus of our democratic system can thus, combined with Muslim immigration, turn into a fatal flaw.

But Halla-aho asks an even more important question: "Why do the voters let all this happen? It is because Westerners like to be 'good' people and believe that their fellow men are equally good people. It is because they have humane values." "It is because the moral and ethical values of Western man have made him helpless in the face of wickedness and immorality."

It's surprising how much support Breivik's manifesto has received, even from some European politicians. The usual patter goes something like: "Yeah, he did a really terrible thing . . . but a lot of what he wrote needed to be said."

The story *Helsinki White* is over, but the issue of hate it addresses, in reality, is just in the offing. A new era of racial hatred in

Europe seems imminent, and the terror such eras have carried with them in the past may come with it.

JAMES THOMPSON
Helsinki, Finland
August 6, 2011

ABOUT THE AUTHOR

James Thompson, eastern Kentucky-born and -raised, has lived in Finland for more than a dozen years; he now resides in Helsinki with his wife. His debut novel, *Snow Angels,* was selected as a *Booklist* Best Crime Novel Debut of the Year and was nominated for Edgar, Anthony, and *Strand Magazine* Critics awards. Before becoming a full-time writer, Thompson studied Finnish — in which he is fluent — and Swedish, and worked as a bartender, bouncer, construction worker, and soldier.